MW00413895

GROUNDED IN *January*

Savannah Hendricks

BROTHER MOCKINGBIRD • DIAMONDHEAD, MISSISSIPPI

For Mom & Bayouzzzii, my angels.
For David, my rock.

Cover Design by: www.beapurplepenguin.com

For information please contact:
Brother Mockingbird, LLC
www.brothermockingbird.org
ISBN: 978-1-7322155-6-6
First Edition

GROUNDED IN January

SAVANNAH HENDRICKS

Chapter One

The chill of outside air seeping through the jetway caused Kate Wilson's already petrified body to tense up more. She did not want to get on the plane.

A sunny but cold morning, as cold as Phoenix could be in January, only reminded her that going home was a necessity. She wanted, and needed, an honest winter. As an added bonus, winter was the best time to fly since turbulence spiked more so in the spring and summer months. Kate had learned this during her extensive research on the ramifications of flying for those with anxiety.

Kate paused and took a deep breath before stepping from the jetway onto the plane. The gap resembled a drawbridge, except below she didn't see pavement, but a possible way out. Her mind raced. *Does anyone else ever try to shove their foot into the gap and push it apart in order to squirm down onto the tarmac below? Or maybe they try to open the side door leading to the portable stairs which only employees use.*

Caught up in her thoughts, Kate's ebony boot, the right one, clipped the lip of the plane's threshold throwing her midair.

A pilot and nearby flight attendant reached out in horror as Kate went down, face first. Her eyes just inches from their polished dress shoes. Her *InStyle* magazine went right, her *US Weekly* went left. Her unzipped faux leather purse landed in first class while its contents rolled into coach. The mauve scarf now attached Kate to her carry-on bag.

"Oh, my dear!" a female flight attendant exclaimed. An arm locked around Kate, hoisting her to a standing position once again. Shaken from the mishap, she pushed her copper curls off her face.

"Good thing you aren't flying this winged beast today, ma'am," the pilot said, trying to make light of the situation.

Kate smiled, grateful that she was now perpendicular with the plane and once again on her feet. Yet her scarf remained caught on the carry-on bag. She wrestled the scarf free, as her carry-on thumped onto the plane's floor. Kate's face went as red as the anti-collision lights on the plane's wingtips.

Behind her, there was complete silence. She stood, convinced that outside the gate the entire airport stood still, waiting to see what would happen next.

The pilot handed Kate one of her magazines. An attendant had fetched her purse and its contents.

"Are you okay, dear? Would you like someone to check you out?" The attendant held Kate's purse as though it were her own.

Glancing down, she saw that her jeans were not ripped, but her knees burned. She wiggled her toes in her boots, and they felt fine. Her long-sleeve, charcoal-gray sweater protected her elbows from anything worse than being sore.

"I think I'm okay," Kate murmured as she reached for her purse. She picked up her carry-on, smiled, and said, "Embarrassed, but okay, thank you." She turned around to the line behind her. "However, I'm afraid I don't know what happened to my ticket. I had it in my hand."

The pilot, the two flight attendants, and Kate searched the floor, making sure they weren't stepping on it. A little white piece of paper peeked out from behind where the pilot stood in front of the lavatory door.

"I think my ticket is there." Kate pointed.

The pilot popped open the lavatory door to confirm Kate's suspicion. Her face scrunched. *Why am I even getting on this flying gasoline-filled death trap in the first place?* Kate bent down to pick up her ticket at the same time as the pilot. Their heads smacked.

The ticket remained on the lavatory floor as they rubbed the pain from their foreheads.

"Here." The pilot handed Kate her ticket.

"Thank you." Kate took the ticket, her bag, and her diminished pride and headed down the aisle to locate her seat.

"Just make it to your seat and sit down," Kate mumbled to herself. *This day cannot get any worse.*

Locating seat 13A, she stood on her tiptoes and reached up to place her carry-on into the overhead compartment. However, Kate could not get the bag over the compartment lip. In addition, the pain from the fall started to creep into her toes and knees.

"Let me help you," a lanky, travel-chic woman said from behind her.

Kate spun around, allowing the bag to nearly fall onto her head.

"I saw what happened when you got on the plane," the woman whispered. "You need all the support you can get."

The travel-chic woman winked, snatched Kate's bag from her hands, and placed it without any effort into the compartment.

Kate produced a half smile and said, "Thank you."

In a meek attempt to hide as quickly as possible, Kate squeezed past the seats' edges and sat. Even without anyone else sitting in the seats, it remained a challenge to move in such a cramped space.

Kate rubbed the spot on her forehead, which felt as though it sprouted a small bump. The sunlight bounced off the airport's windows as she gazed out. She prayed the actual flight would be far less of a mess than trying to get on the plane. Closing her eyes, Kate ran through her checklist. *Dramamine, check. Motion sickness wristbands, check. Lavender oil, check. Puke bag in the seat pocket.* Kate leaned forward and searched the seatback. *Check. Safety instruction manual, check. Deep breath and counting, check. Plus, I hope I don't have a seatmate who (a) got sick, (b) gets sick, and/or (c) skipped a shower in the last day.*

As the plane filled up, Kate lucked out. Her seatmates consisted of a businessman who was more worried about when he could use his laptop and headphones than flying, and a woman focused on when she could get a glass of wine and read on her tablet.

The air pressure fluctuated and hummed in the cabin as they taxied out onto the runway. Kate took deep breaths and went over her mantra in her head. Remember, a real winter. Maybe she could even dig her skis out of her parents' garage. This would be a time to clear her head and figure out her unhappiness. She checked to make sure her wristbands were in the correct spots and held her scarf to her nose, breathing in the lavender.

"You can do this," she muttered as the plane shook with the roar of the engines gaining power. Kate closed her eyes. The plane lurched forward, pushing her firmly into the seat. She tightened the seat belt strap as the front wheel lifted off the ground. The back two were still on the runway. The plane's nose pointed toward the sky. This was one of Kate's favorite moments of flight. In that moment Kate was reminded of how amazing a plane can be, and how light her body could feel. She felt as though her body took a breath of freedom in that moment of weightlessness.

But then, the back two wheels came off the ground, and Kate's stomach dropped. Her favorite moment was over. *Put the wheels back down!* Kate wanted to scream at the pilot. Noticing the choppiness of her breathing, she returned to her mantra. The last thing she needed was to have a panic attack at thirty-five-thousand feet.

The plane continued to climb, putting pressure on her ears. Kate attempted to fake yawn, encouraging them to pop, but without any success.

"Here," the businessman seatmate said, and he held out

a stick of gum. "I saw you trying to fake yawn. Try this, it works better." The businessman made eye contact for half a second, before returning his eyes to the seatback in front of him.

"Thank you," Kate said. She smiled and took the gum.

She folded the spearmint gum into her mouth and shoved the wrapper into the seat pocket. The plane began to level off, as Kate peered out the window at the brown landscape below. It had been an extra dry summer, without much monsoon rain, which set fall and winter up to fail. A few areas of green were scattered here and there. December had seen some rain, but Phoenix definitely needed the monsoon storms to bring enough moisture to make it through the dry spells. Seeing Arizona from above reminded Kate of why she still loved Washington. The state's lush green landscape and snow-capped mountains often remained throughout the summer months.

The flight attendant came by with the beverage cart as Kate flipped through her glossy magazine pages. She ordered a glass of red wine. Even with all her checklist items checked, she wanted to be anywhere but here.

"Cheers," Kate's other seatmate said, reaching over the businessman to tap their plastic glasses together. Despite their toast, he didn't lose focus on his electronic spreadsheet.

The wine and the Dramamine began making Kate drowsy. She dozed until the pilot's voice broke through the humming of the pressurized plane.

"We are beginning our final descent into Seattle. For those of you who are visiting, welcome. For those of you coming home, welcome back. Flight attendants, prepare for landing."

While most people find landing to be the worst part of a flight, Kate found it to be the only other thing she liked about flying. She listened for the snap of the landing gear like a child waiting to hear Santa on the roof.

The plane dipped to the left as they circled around the

Space Needle. Rain skimmed across the window. It was as though the sky were crying tears of joy along with Kate. The gray clouds were so thick that it was impossible to tell where one cloud ended and the next one began. Evergreens popped into view as though they were reaching up, trying to touch the plane's belly. The aircraft lined up with the runway as the houses below came into view. They appeared like a child's playset, miniature and without the flaws of life. Kate envisioned a tiny toddler's hand coming in and picking up the plane; spinning them around the room before dropping them onto the carpet.

The wheels touched down on the rain soaked runway and the brakes worked hard to slow them. Kate yanked her seat belt tighter for safety. Once, as a child, her seat belt had not been tight enough, and she went shooting forward. The seat belt caught under her arms as her legs flailed around, soon choking her.

The brakes finally took hold, grabbing the runway with force. Then the plane bounced softly forward as it taxied toward the gate. The dampness of the air crept down the aisle from the now open door. Passengers hurried to get their bags and disembark. Kate remained seated, staring out at the rain. She hated all the shoving and bumping just to get somewhere one minute faster.

When the last passenger exited the aisle, Kate stood and reached for her carry-on. Forgetting she didn't put it up there, she now realized she could not get it down.

The flight attendants were busy thanking and saying goodbye to the remaining passengers, so Kate placed her left boot on the armrest of the seat and her right boot on the seat. Hoisting herself up, she grabbed the compartment edge. Letting go with her left hand, she snatched the bag, yanking it toward the edge. In an attempt to climb down and take the carry-on with her, Kate's boots tangled around the seat arm. Trying to fall forward into the row, she braced herself as she slid awkwardly into the aisle seat.

Getting to her feet, she rubbed the side of her hip. At

least her carry-on was on the floor now where she could reach it. Taking a deep breath, Kate headed toward the front of the plane.

"Are you okay?" a flight attendant asked.

Of course, the attendants saw her latest mishap. Kate rubbed at the pain.

"I'm fine," Kate said. "Have a wonderful day."

"You too, dear," the flight attendant replied.

As Kate turned back to give her a smile, she tripped over the airplane door gap again. She stumbled forward, but was able to catch herself this time. Kate straightened her scarf and readjusted her sweater.

With a fake smile plastered across her face, she headed downstairs to baggage claim with her head held high, regardless of the giggles she heard from behind her.

Chapter Two

Oxnard Swanson arrived home from another neurology appointment and buried his face in the yellow fur of Bayou, an English Lab he rescued from Louisiana. Ox was ever grateful he had been there at the right time and place to save the puppy. Now fully-grown at about three years old, Bayou resembled a stick of butter with legs. While Ox loved the support Bayou gave him, he often missed receiving a return hug from a human.

One could not call Ox tall, nor could they label him short. His constant facial scruff let everyone know that he was not big on shaving. Nor did he care about fiddling with hair products enough to keep his ear-length brown hair under control. He thought tucking it behind his ears worked rather well.

The news remained the same every time Ox's neurologist lowered the chart of notes, there were no changes in the progression of his multiple sclerosis and no improvements with the latest medicine trial either.

Other than that, Ox was having a good day today. He didn't need to use his cane. This allowed him to ready his inn for his regular January guest, Maggie. She and her late husband, Stan, had been regulars since the inn first opened. Sadly, Stan had passed away unexpectedly in the summer. Ox did not expect Maggie to return at all this winter. The first solo visit could be a challenge; however, he hoped this visit would be good for her.

He checked his wristwatch. It was about one hour until her

flight landed, and it would be another thirty minutes before she would enter the inn with a much needed hug and smile.

Ox poured Bayou's rather late breakfast into his stainless steel bowl. "Brunch time, buddy."

He opened the refrigerator, undecided about what he would have for lunch. When Ox did not have guests, he stuck to simple meals, saving the more creative ones for visitors.

He removed a green bell pepper, a white onion, some brown rice, and a jar of tomato sauce from the cupboard for a throw-together lunch. A blue flyer on the counter caught his eye. It was a reminder of the upcoming pie contest at the Winter Wonder Day. This would be his third time entering, and he needed to make it count.

The pie contest was a great way to get free publicity for the Inn of the Woods. Not that January was peak tourist season in Washington, but there were some family and friends who lingered in town after the holidays. And there were those unable to get the holidays off that traveled through town this time of the year.

"What pie should I make?" Ox asked Bayou, who paid zero attention, his face still buried in his bowl. Bayou sucked up the kibble like a vacuum picking up pebbles. "I need to make it memorable, don't I? Can't do a basic fruit pie again." Ox turned on the stove's burner. Rolling up the sleeves of his royal blue shirt, he diced the onion and pepper on the cutting board, and then scraped them into the sauté pan.

Beyond the sound of simmering veggies and Bayou lapping up water, the inn sat quiet. Not a day passed when Ox did not appreciate his beautiful home. The wood beams, the pine trimmed windows and the ironwork staircase were all works of art. However, his thoughts sometimes drifted to what his home was missing, a family.

Two years ago, Ox sat in the neurologist's office after several episodes of dizziness and numbness in his fingers and toes and a prior trip to the emergency department at the local hospital. At first he thought it might be a deficiency in his diet, but to be safe he went to his primary care doctor. The doctor performed routine tests, but they all came back negative. Then, the doctor referred him to a neurologist who broke the news of his multiple sclerosis diagnosis. Until he started researching it, Ox knew nothing about multiple sclerosis.

Admittedly, he cried reading page after page of what MS does to a person's body. With a firm pat on the shoulder, the neurologist instructed him that there were several alternative medicines and continued advancements in research. He added that since the condition affects everyone differently, it meant a wide range of possible outcomes.

At the age of thirty-one, Ox knew he had a lot of life left to live, but with the diagnosis on his mind, he could no longer see that far in front of him. He had tried to isolate himself romantically after his diagnosis, but allowed himself a few remaining dates, albeit, unfruitful ones.

Not that he had found a woman who matched what he needed or wanted. In fact, most seemed glued to social media. When he finally found a woman he could take up in his Cessna, she was too worried about her outfit to admire the view. One adventurous woman he dated could have cared less about cell phones and outfits, but she made it known that she wanted independence over a relationship and children.

There had been one woman who seemed to fit his life like a puzzle piece, but she stopped returning his phone calls once he told her about his diagnosis. This made it easy for Ox to put a stop to his love life once and for all.

"Maybe we're better off anyway, Bayou." Ox knelt down and rubbed the lab's ears. "I can be the crazy dog man, if there is such a thing. With an inn full of dogs, we don't need a woman!"

Bayou tilted his head as though he were trying to figure out what Ox meant.

"We don't need a woman. Do we, buddy?" Bayou tilted his head the other way.

The thoughts of his future remained in question as Ox returned his focus to the veggies simmering on the stove. He would love nothing more than to chat with his dad about what he should do with regards to relationships.

Unfortunately, their early passing meant he could not go to them for the advice he desperately sought. As Bayou rested on the kitchen rug, something outside drew Ox's vision to the window. Snowflakes.

"It's snowing, Bayou." Ox moved toward the window. "The weatherman got it wrong, again."

Kate managed to make it to baggage claim without incident, which seemed like a true miracle after how boarding and disembarking had panned out. As the carousel started up, folks eagerly gathered around ready to snatch their suitcases. It was as though they were waiting for a child to come sliding down in need of catching. But because the carousel looped around for a good five minutes without anything appearing, everyone returned to their agitated stances.

The sliding doors constantly opening allowed for bursts of icy air to come in, causing Kate to shiver. She re-wrapped the scarf around her neck. If the weather report showed zero chance of snow, so there should be zero reasons to endure freezing temperatures, especially inside. She pulled her gloves out of her purse and slid them over her already frozen hands.

As a teenager, Kate would watch the weather reports with her dad. "If it's going to be below freezing, it might as well snow," he always instructed the television. Kate had picked up this motto, especially when it came to school days. Oh, the utter joy of a snow day!

The first piece of luggage slammed down the chute, sending people scurrying to claim their bags. Travelers stood shoulder to shoulder trying to get a glimpse of the next piece coming around the bend. Kate wiggled her way between two very tall men and joined in the hope that hers was next.

"Let me know if you see yours," one of the tall men said, eyeing Kate from above. "I'll grab it for you."

"Thank you," Kate said, "but I do have actual muscles under this bulky coat. I can get my own suitcase just fine."

"And they say men are not chivalrous anymore. Maybe this is why," the man sneered.

Kate peered up at him. "I said thank you, but I'm capable of getting it on my own."

"Okay then." He scooted over as though Kate had suddenly coughed on him.

She backed out of the line and found a new spot to stand. There was nothing wrong with refusing a man's help. Kate did not want to be labeled as needy, especially now that she had done so well in life as an independent woman. Sure there were times when she would scream, "I need a man to do this!" especially when it came to lugging eight loaded bags of groceries inside. All of her friends were either engaged or married, except for her best friend, Ali Yang, who only focused on her career. Kate yearned for a family, but she had yet to figure out how to get off the carousel of dating losers.

Kate sighed. Maybe she should not have been rude to the tall man. He was only trying to be nice. She rubbed her gloved hands together. *Does SeaTac Airport not have money to turn the heat up?*

A horrid tumbling sound, like a box of broken dishes, came crashing down the conveyor belt onto the carousel. Everyone's eyes darted to see which person would claim ownership of the suitcase.

"I told you to wrap them better," a woman snarled to another woman, who appeared to be her twin, followed by a dirty glare.

Another suitcase tumbled down with a slap. It was bright aqua blue with red zippers. Kate's luggage, a clearance item she had not thought all the way through. As it came around, she leaned over the reached for the handle. As she did, she felt a tug at her neck. She tried to pull the suitcase and herself up, but it was too late. Kate let out a low shriek as she fell on top of her luggage.

"Hit the stop button!" someone yelled.

Kate frantically attempted to undo the scarf from around her neck, as the carousel jerked to a stop. As Kate stumbled to stand, a hand grabbed her right arm and lifted her to the safety of the airport's linoleum.

"Thank you so much," Kate said, gathering herself.

It was the same tall man.

"Oh, crap," Kate mumbled, trying to yank her scarf free.

He lifted Kate's suitcase off the carousel and placed it next to her feet.

"Please." He raised his hands in defense. "Don't thank me." With that, he pivoted and walked out into the Seattle cold.

A tap on her shoulder startled Kate.

"This is yours," an airport security guard said as he handed her a two-piece mauve fabric mess. "Sorry we had to cut it free, but better it than you."

"Thanks." Kate took it and held the pieces up, observing the damage.

Extending the handle on her suitcase, Kate proceeded to make her way to the rental car area. She dropped the shredded two-piece scarf into the first trash can she walked past. After signing a few pages of paperwork, Kate made her way out to the shuttle van that would take her to the rental car.

A blast of frigid air smacked Kate's bare neck. While she had zipped her cherry-red coat as high up as possible, the wind still found its way in. She regretted throwing the scarf away.

Glancing at the time on her cell phone, she realized that without any traffic issues she could easily make it to her parents' house in about two hours.

As gracefully as possible, Kate lugged her suitcase up the shuttle steps. The sky had turned a light shade of pink that meant only one thing: snow. As the shuttle entered into the traffic lane, Kate checked the weather app on her phone. It now showed snow. Kate smiled and did a little jiggle in her seat. *Snow!* Yet, this being Washington, the luck of the convergent zone meant it might start snowing here, but not down the street, or vice versa.

"Lot B," the shuttle driver announced.

Kate clutched the handrail and unloaded herself and her luggage without mishap. Clicking the unlock button on the car key, she located the pearl colored sedan by its blinking lights.

Kate popped the trunk, loaded her bag and took one good long look at the pink tinted sky before sliding into the front seat.

She turned the key and started the sedan. The faint smell of another person's rose perfume came wafting through the vents as she cranked up the heat. Pulling out her cell phone, she sent a text to Ali back home in Phoenix.

KATE: landed safely, thank goodness!!!! minus a few snafus and looks like it's going to snow!!!!

ALI: Great! Now please turn back on autocorrect. Your improper sentences drive me crazy. Wait … snafus? What happened?

KATE: i think i bruised my hip, my elbows, and knees and my scarf is in the garbage. and no. i don't like my phone predicting everything, messing up my texts. do you know how many pool party invites i replied to with: i'd love to attend your poop party.

ALI: Sounds normal ;)

KATE: gee thanks ;P

Savannah Hendricks

Chapter Three

Ox threw open the inn's front door before Maggie even made it out of her rental car. Hurrying down the front patio steps, Bayou attached himself to Ox as though he were a sidecar.

"I made it just in time." Maggie stood at the trunk of the car. Her body nearly swallowed up beneath her cream colored parka. The snowflakes coated her gray bob.

Ox removed the suitcase for Maggie with one hand and used his other arm to hug her. The human contact warmed Ox's heart. He needed it after all the depressing future thoughts he had had today. "It's so nice to see you, Maggie."

Maggie pushed back from the hug, holding Ox at arm's length. "You look great, Ox." She glanced down at Bayou. "And you, young man, look the same." She stretched her gloved hand out and petted Bayou on the head.

"Let's get you inside and warmed up." Ox held out his arm for Maggie to take hold so she could safely walk through the snow.

"I don't remember the weather calling for snow," she said.

"You know Washington weather by now, Maggie." Ox laughed, stomping the snow from his boots at the entrance of the inn.

He set Maggie's suitcase at the bottom of the stairs. "Thank you for coming out here again. I'm always grateful for your visits. Especially now that ..." Ox trailed off and shook the thought of Maggie's late husband from his mind.

Maggie reached out, squeezed Ox's arm, and smiled. "Stan."

A forced smile appeared on Ox's face as he placed his hand on Maggie's shoulder. Maggie's face showed a few more life lines than last year.

"Your parents and Stan are having some grand conversations, I'm sure of it," she said.

They made their way into the kitchen. Ox pulled out a dining table chair and motioned for Maggie to sit.

"Earl Grey still okay?" He gathered two mugs from the cupboard as the kettle began to whistle.

"Yes, thank you," she said. Bayou sat next to Maggie's chair, waiting for more attention. She obliged, much to dog's delight.

"How is he doing with the therapy training?"

"He has two classes left and then he will be fully certified." Ox carried the mugs of tea over and sat in the nearest chair to Maggie.

"Once he is officially certified, if my MS stays stable, I will launch my small side flying business to help fliers with anxieties."

"I'm so proud of you and Bayou," Maggie said, before seeping on her tea. "Now, are we going to avoid the news I want to hear about?"

Ox swallowed and moved his mug around in circles. "Maggie."

"I'm here, Ox, without Stan. I came all this way on my own. The least you can do is tell me how you're holding up."

With his mug in hand, Ox stood up and paced near the table. "I have good and bad days. The dizzy spells are the same, the numbness as well. I need my cane about two times a week, so no real changes backward or forward."

"And the medicine?" Maggie inquired.

"The first one didn't work for me, which the neurologist said was a possibility. I have yet to try the second one. I admit I'm putting it off."

"Ox, I'm sorry to hear that."

"Me too." Ox stared into his mug.

"Will you give the other medication a try soon?"

"When I'm ready."

Maggie twisted the tea bag's string around her finger. "Do you still have your pilot's license?"

"Yes." Ox sipped his tea and nodded.

"Then that's a huge positive, Ox."

Ox nodded. "So how are you, Maggie?"

"I'm doing well. The house doesn't seem as lonely as it once did. Much to my surprise, I took up the old lady cliché of knitting. I joined a book club through the library, and I go swimming at the community center a few times a week." Maggie sipped more tea. "In addition, I have a weekly dinner date with my friends."

"I love hearing that, Maggie, but I don't think knitting has an age range." He smirked. "Have you started dating?"

Maggie gasped, followed by a giggle. "No, I have not. It would feel weird to say that at my age I have a boyfriend. Who am I? Blanche from *Golden Girls*? Don't get me wrong, I don't want to be alone forever. Stan would not have wanted that, but it's too soon. However, I fear that I'll compare every man I date to my sweetie. Every man will have to live up to perfection."

Maggie and Ox chuckled.

"It's true, Maggie. Stan was one of a kind."

"When I'm ready I will get back out there, but for now, I'm all right." Maggie cleared the lump of Stan memories from her throat. "I shared, now you! Please tell me you have found love."

"Maggie, we talked about this. If I can't be a true man, a healthy man, then I can't be with a woman. I don't want my disease to drag a woman down. A real man can care for himself and the woman in his life. I don't want someone feeling sorry for me."

"What century are you living in? A woman should be able to decide that for herself, Ox. I know you want a family."

"I have a family." Ox pointed at Bayou. "I decided I'm going to be a crazy dog man."

Maggie laughed, throwing her head back. "You can have dogs and humans too."

The phone rang in the tiny office off the kitchen at the end of the hall. Ox went to answer it. "Inn of the Woods." He paused. "Hi, Shawn."

Maggie stood and made her way to the kitchen window. Her rental car was already covered in what must have been a half an inch of snow.

"I'll head over now, thanks. Bye, Shawn." Ox hung up the phone and went for his jacket resting on the back of the kitchen chair. "Sorry, Maggie, but I've got to make a run. Looks like your flight landed just in time. They're closing the airport. Shawn asked me to help out while they prepare to close everything down."

Shawn had been a long time friend of Ox's late father. He owned the Crooked River Airport and Ox had been helping him off and on over the years. In return, Shawn encouraged his employees to send stranded passengers over to inn for lodging instead of to the chain motels in the area.

"Is the storm going to be that bad?" Maggie placed a hand on her hip.

"I guess bad enough to close the airport for the rest of the day and possibly tomorrow morning. Are you okay if I run out? I should be back in a few hours." Ox pushed back his sleeve to check his watch.

"Of course. I'll sit and enjoy the view. Any more guests checking in today?"

"Nope, only you for a few days." Ox gathered Bayou's leash.

"Please, leave Bayou with me." Maggie moved toward the entryway.

"Are you sure?" Ox threaded on his jacket.

"I'd love the company." Maggie patted her leg and Bayou went straight to her and sat.

"Thanks, Maggie." Ox opened the front door and snow floated in. "I'll be back as soon as I can."

Maggie glanced down at Bayou. "What should we do, buddy? I'm hungry. Want to see if your dad has any popcorn?"

Bayou tilted his head. Maggie giggled as they made their way to the pantry in search of a snack they could both enjoy.

"Be safe," Maggie called as Ox closed the door.

Chapter Four

Driving-wise, Kate lucked out, avoiding the snow until an hour into her journey north. The return flight home would be out of the tiny Crooked River Airport. Since they had lengthened the distance of their runway, they could now accommodate some larger planes. She refused to travel on miniature planes, with their exposed propeller spinning like a child's remote controlled toy. Because of her flying research, Kate knew they were called turboprop planes.

The drive from Seattle to her parents' home in Crooked River would help clear Kate's mind. If she had flown into the Crooked River Airport she wouldn't have had two hours to ponder on the open road. Upon her arrival, her parents would throw a rush of hugs and questions at her like a game of hot potato. The entire trip was a grand plan to work on her fear of flying, as well as an attempt to contemplate her career choice. Every day as she walked into her office building, her chest tightened from stress. She had quickly grown to despise her job. In fact, Kate loathed her entire career path as an engineer, wishing she had chosen differently.

Once she entered the Crooked River city limits, Kate could close her eyes and find her way. But with the snow coming down in cotton candy clumps, she firmly gripped the wheel. Her knuckles matched the white of the flakes landing on the windshield. Her fear of flying caused Kate to be well acquainted with driving. Yet the last time she drove in the powder she had been a teenager.

Turning at the mailbox, she made her way down the snow-covered gravel drive. Although Kate had lost track of the last time she had been home, everything appeared frozen in time.

Her parents' home was a pale yellow two-story cottage with navy blue shutters and a porch to fit any rocking chair's dream. Hemlocks and pines surrounded the home like a towering fence.

Her body nearly warmed thinking of the hot chocolate her mom would start making before she even got a chance to remove her coat. As a child, Kate loved coming in from sledding and snowman-making to homemade cocoa. She also loved sitting under a cozy blanket on the porch swing as she watched her dad tinker away with his latest car or outside home repair.

The thick falling snow crunched under her boots as she hurried up the porch steps. Scanning the home, Kate noticed the closed curtains. Both garage doors were also closed, but there wasn't anything odd about that with the snowing coming down.

She pushed the doorbell and then rubbed her gloved hands together in anticipation of seeing her parents' faces when they opened the door. Kate leaned toward the side window, and noticed that the house appeared silent. She couldn't hear noise from the television, voices, or music playing. Since she rarely came home and didn't even live in the same state, she was without a key. Making a fist, Kate firmly knocked. Still the door did not open. Kate removed her cell phone from her pocket. Locating PARENTS HOME in her contact list, she hit the green phone icon.

Inside, the phone rang and rang. *Don't panic. They are probably at the grocery store or running a last minute errand before the snow starts to pile up.* Kate ended the call once she got to the voice-mail.

She scrolled to MOM CELL on the contact list and hit SEND. After three rings, her mom, Josie Wilson picked up.

"Hello, sweetheart!" Josie cheered.

"Mom, hi! Oh good, are you at the grocery store with Dad?" Kate wrapped her free arm around her now shivering body.

"The store? No, sweetheart, Dad and I are on vacation!"

"Vacation? Mom, what do you mean? It's January! Who travels in January?"

"Sweetheart, what is wrong? Are you okay?" Josie asked.

"Mom, I'm home. I came home to surprise you and Dad, as a late Christmas present."

Kate heard her mom cover the phone and mumble something to her dad in the background.

"Mom? Mom? MOM!" Kate clenched her body. "Where are you?"

"Sweetheart, we're in Hawaii."

"Mom, you and Dad never leave home in the winter," Kate reminded her.

"We decided to be young and adventurous. Sweetheart, I'm sorry. If we had only known."

Kate lowered her chin to her chest.

"Sweetheart, you hate flying. Why would you even come to visit? Is something wrong? Do you have a man with you, a boyfriend? Did you bring him home to meet us?"

Before Kate could answer, she heard her mom fail at attempting to whisper to her dad.

"Gene, it might be a man, maybe she is finally getting married. Grandkids, Gene, grandkids!"

"Mom? Mom! Josie!"

"Yes, sweetheart, do you have news?"

"No, Mom, there is no boyfriend. I wanted to surprise you and Dad. It's fine, you stay and have fun. I'll hang out here until my flight leaves next week."

Kate glanced around. "Where is the hide-a-key?"

"We don't have one anymore. Leonard up the road had a hide-a-key and some burglar found it and robbed his home."

"Mom!" Kate lowered her head into her gloved hand, supporting its weight. "When are you coming home?"

"Not for two weeks."

"Mom, it's cold and snowing. I got on a plane. Do you know how hard that was for me? I only slept about an hour last night from all the anxiety. In fact, I'm not sure I can even get on a plane to go back home. Why didn't you tell me that you and Dad were going on vacation? That's something you tell your daughter!"

"Dad left you a voicemail yesterday when we got to the airport," Josie stated.

Kate held her phone out, frantically scrolling through a few screens.

"No, I don't have a voicemail," Kate confirmed.

"Gene," Josie called out, "You left Kate a voicemail about our trip, right?"

Kate heard her dad's voice in the background, but couldn't make out what he said.

"Oh, Kate, I'm sorry. Dad forgot."

"Have fun, Mom. I have to go before I become an ice sculpture on the front porch."

Without waiting for a response, Kate slammed her finger on END and then shoved her phone into her coat pocket. The snow beyond the front porch fell in thick layers, blanketing the ground. Kate had to admit, pushing past the anger, it was a beautiful scene. The evergreens covered in the glistening paint of snow. The car's tire tracks up the driveway were nearly hidden at this point with the newest layer.

"Oh crap!" Kate bolted down the porch steps, stumbling through the snow now coming in over the tops of her boots. She needed to make it back into town. They didn't plow these back roads and Kate could get stranded if she didn't hurry.

She reached the car door and went to yank it open when

she lost her footing. Kate's arms went straight out, circling rapidly to keep upright. Her body leaned forward and then back, and then she centered herself by grabbing hold of the car door for support.

"Phew," she gasped, wrapping her gloved hands around the doorframe.

She sat down, letting her boots hang outside the door and clicking the snow off them like Dorothy before drawing them inside. With the heat on full blast and the windshield wipers pushing the snow aside, she made her way out of her parents' driveway. The plan was to make it to the Crooked River Airport and try to switch her flight to today, if not first thing tomorrow morning. *So much for my self-discovery vacation.*

The tires struggled to grip what they could find of the main road. A few tire tracks already sliced through, but not enough to melt the quickly falling snow. The navigation system informed her that in ten more minutes, she would reach the airport.

Kate gripped the steering wheel as the tires slipped over the surface of the road. On either side of the rental car were towering spruces and hemlocks. She had no plans to become best friends with the trees anytime soon. Kate focused on being grateful for the green lights so she didn't have to stop and then try to start moving again.

"Okay, I'm sorry. I've changed my mind, enough snow already," she pleaded.

Chapter Five

Snow stuck to the top of the Crooked River Airport sign as it came into view. Kate turned into the parking lot which contained only one vehicle, a black truck. *Where are all the cars?* Kate peered around. *Not many people travel in January. Just my crazy parents and me.*

Kate parked the rental car, grabbed her luggage, and made her way to the curb. The airport welcomed fliers with its wood A-framed beams and fancy slate rock wrapped columns. It was a far different atmosphere than the hustle and bustle of the Sea-Tac airport.

The automatic doors eased open. Brushing the snow from her boots on the entrance rugs, she made her way through the empty ticket counter ropes. By the time Kate reached the counter, she noticed there was no one behind it.

Her eyes scanned left and right. There was not another traveler in sight. *How can the airport be so empty? It's Washington. It snows here; it's nothing new! Surely there's someone manning the security check-point.*

Wheeling her suitcase behind her, Kate strolled to the other side of the airport. "Thank goodness," she said as she approached the check-point.

A man with his face covered by a paperback book glanced up at her as though she had interrupted something important.

"Where is everyone?" Kate lifted her luggage for scanning.

"Don't put that there," the man grunted.

"It's not working?" Kate tried to peek around the monitor.

"It works, but there are no flights heading out until the storm blows through." The man set his book down. His eyes were a brilliant shade of sapphire. Kate nearly choked when she swallowed. She knew her mouth hung open, but she did not have the brainpower to shut it. His hair, a dark chocolate brown, was tucked behind his ears, and more than a five clock shadow showed on his jawline.

Close your mouth! But those eyes! If he blinked, she might cry.

"I'm Ox." He approached Kate.

"Ox?" Kate's face twisted, her nose scrunched up.

"Short for Oxnard, I guess either way it's not the best name. It's what happens when you're born in the nineties." He smirked.

"I was born in the nineties too," Kate blurted, immediately regretting such a lame attempt to note their similar ages.

"And you are?" Ox stood.

"Kate," she said, like a shy five-year-old.

"Well, Kate, you won't be flying anywhere anytime soon. Did you not get an alert from the airline?"

"It's been a long day, and I mean, long." Kate slouched. "I hoped to move my return flight up a week, so I wouldn't have gotten an alert," she looked around. "I guess I'll be sleeping amongst the chairs."

"I'm closing up," Ox said.

"Closing the airport?" Kate's hands rested on her hips. "Can you do that?"

"I have the keys, so, yes." Ox waved a ring of metal in the air. "I should have done so about half an hour ago." He held up the book. "But this last chapter hooked me."

No longer able to hold them up from the day, Kate's shoulders slumped. She plopped down onto her luggage. The handle, although collapsed, dug into her tailbone, but she didn't care. This day had been one for the books. One where the pages were worn, torn, and yellowed at the edges. *Don't cry. Whatever you do, don't cry. Just pull yourself together.*

"Are you hungry?" Ox drew near Kate.

Her eyes were on their boots, both pointing toward each other.

"I'm starving." Kate didn't bother looking up.

Ox's breathing filled the silence of the airport. Finally, Kate tilted her head toward him.

"I can't carry your suitcase with you sitting on it." Ox's hand reached out.

Kate stood; their faces came closer than either had planned. Up close, Ox's eyes could wash away all her troubles, even on a day like today.

"I can handle my own luggage."

"I thought women liked chivalry." Ox turned and walked away before she could reply.

"What is it with men and that word today?" Kate jogged to catch up, the wheels of her luggage spun frantically.

They made their way out through the sliding doors. In just a few minutes, the snow had managed to pile up another half of an inch. Ox placed a closed sign on the windowsill, shoved his key into the lock, and entered a code into the panel next to the doors.

Kate could no longer make out where the sidewalk ended and the street started. Surely, her suitcase would not wheel well in the thick snow. Folding the handle down, she locked it in place and picked it up. The traveling and driving had caught up with her as she struggled to carry all the weight. Between the thick snow and her mind focused on her troublesome day, Kate missed the edge of the sidewalk. Flying forward, Kate's luggage slipped from her hand and thumped into the snow two seconds before her face planted next to it.

"Are you okay?" Ox asked, between bursts of hysterical

laughter. She lifted her head out of the snow. Snow matted her copper curls and the collar of her coat. Ox strolled over and grabbed Kate's snow-covered luggage. He faced her and held out his hand.

"Stop laughing," she playfully demanded, taking his hand.

Ox's hand was warm and strong, as though he curled weights with each individual finger. Kate brushed herself off with her free hand and shook the snow from her hair.

On the ground, an outline of a snow angel she created from her fall. Kate caught Ox staring. His eyes were even bluer outside in the brilliance of the snow's reflection.

"Let's get you in the truck and warmed up."

"I have a rental car." Kate pointed to the pearl sedan covered in a blanket of snow.

"We'll come back for that later. Let's take my truck; it's drivable in this mess."

Kate did not argue, she was more than happy to not have to try to drive anymore today.

"Why don't you have a scarf?" asked Ox who was still firmly grasping Kate's hand.

"It's in the trash at Sea-Tac, don't ask." She held tight to Ox's hand. Not only did she not want to fall again today, she could not remember the last time she had the comfort of a man's hand in hers.

How could a hand make Kate feel so at ease and safe? They met minutes ago, yet instantly he felt like a long-time friend.

They made their way to Ox's black truck. It was nothing fancy, but clearly a newer model. Growing up in Washington, Kate could glance at tires and know if they had studs on them or not. Ox's did.

The door locks popped up, and Ox loaded Kate's suitcase into the back seat. He then opened the passenger door and held his hand out to help Kate.

"I'm not that kind of girl," she informed him. Ox backed away, dropping his hand.

Kate placed her left foot onto the running board. As she went to raise her right foot, it slid out from under her on a patch of hidden ice. Before she figured out what to do, Ox's arms reached out and caught her just as she started to go down.

"How long have you owned those feet?" Ox laughed.

Kate rested in his arms, not wanting to move, but also not having the strength to protest. Overwhelmed by her day, she joined in the laughter. Her feet were straight out in front and Ox was holding her under the arms.

"Is this how most of your days go?" Ox asked, momentarily breaking free from the bonds of laughter.

Kate stood and turned around. Yet again, Ox's face closer than she had planned. Those sapphire eyes were the water to her heart's drought.

"Sometimes," Kate whispered as softly as the falling snow-flakes.

"Please, let me assist you. Technically, I'm still on the clock for work. If you sustain any injuries, I could be at fault."

With those blue eyes so close, she could not argue. Ox held out his hand. She took it, using it as leverage to climb into the truck. Once Kate was all the way in, he shut the door.

The driver side door popped open, and in one swift move, he slid into his seat. Ox started the truck and switched on the heat.

Kate placed her nearly frozen fingers over the vents.

"Who names their kid Oxnard?" Kate broke the silence as he navigated the truck out of the parking lot.

"Who goes to the airport in the middle of a snowstorm?" Ox fired back.

She raised her hands up in defense. "Where are we going? If the airport is closed I would think any restaurants in town would be as well."

"Good thing we are not going to a restaurant then." Ox grinned.

Kate's heart rate sped up. *What have I done? I'm an R- rated movie ready to happen.*

She was alone in a truck with a man she just met, plowing through a snowstorm with her current location unknown to anyone else. The setting could not be any more perfect for something bad to happen. *Great way to start the New Year, Kate, getting yourself abducted.*

Chapter Six

"Remind me again, why the airport was empty? I mean someone else must have shown up or gotten off the last flight." Kate's hands remained on the vents for warmth.

"They rerouted the few remaining flights to SeaTac. Everyone who should have boarded a plane out of here was sent away hours ago."

"Then with the snowstorm coming and the airport empty, why were you lingering behind for a book?" Kate asked as they made their way off the four-lane road onto a two-way lane.

"This story has engrossed me completely." Ox placed a finger on the cover of the book, which rested in the center console. It was *Jamaica Inn* by Daphne Du Maurier. The worn cover had a tear at the bottom and a library barcode laminated across the top.

"Didn't Hitchcock make a movie of this?" Kate held the book in her hand.

"I'm impressed that a girl from ..." Ox started.

"I'm from here in Crooked River, but I live in Phoenix now."

"You grew up here?" Ox turned to Kate, taking his eyes off the road. "Did your feet sleep through all the snow days?"

When he refocused on the road, he swerved a few feet before lining the truck back up.

Without thinking, Kate swung her wrist outward, smacking his arm playfully.

"And yes, Hitchcock made a movie of it. So far, I think the

book is better."

"They usually are," Kate remarked.

"Do you have a favorite book?"

"Too many." Kate studied the snow coming down in near blizzard conditions. "Are we close to where we're going? By the way, where are we going?"

"My house." His voice was matter-of-fact.

"Your house?" Fear punched her stomach.

"Every other place will be closed due to the snow. I have food and," Ox flipped up his turn signal for no one else as he turned off the road and said, "I can cook."

Please don't cook me.

"I promise, I'm harmless. I run an inn. Maggie is there. She is a regular guest every January, so you don't have to worry about being alone."

Kate wondered who Maggie was, family or friend. At the beginning of the heavily wooded drive, a sign nailed to a tree read: INN OF THE WOODS

"You run an inn and an airport?" Kate gazed through the windshield, waiting for the inn to come into view. The fear of abduction dissipated as she let out a deep breath.

"I don't run the airport. I help my parents' long time friend, Shawn, every once in a while. He owns the airport. I run my inn."

The truck seemed to part the woods. Before her, as though a pop-up book created it, a log A-framed structure appeared. The falling snow only made it more magical. Kate's eyes widened at the beauty. This was not here before she moved to Arizona.

The snow coated the metal roof, struggling to keep from sliding off. The inn, a glaze of brown wood, looked as though it had been dipped in maple syrup. On the left, there was a parking spot for guests' cars. One sat there, covered completely in snow which disguised the make and model. A three-car garage sat off to the right side of the inn, its roof hidden by snow-covered hemlock branches.

Windows took up the entire front of the structure, as if they were the walls supporting the entire inn. A warm light glowed from within on both levels. The second level balcony held snow-draped chairs.

"So you live here too?" Kate's whole body was nearly up against the windshield.

"Yes, it's an inn-slash-home." Ox drove his truck into the garage.

"Do you have any employees?" She climbed out onto the safety of the snowless concrete floor.

"No, I manage. It doesn't get too busy."

He cooks, cleans, runs an airport for fun, and owns an inn. Not to mention, he has the most amazing blue eyes on the planet. Don't fall for him.

They made their way to the front porch. She wanted to spin around like Mary Tyler Moore, immersed in the beauty surrounding her.

Edison style lights lined the underside of the patio, where Adirondack chairs sat covered in a blanket of white.

Kate stomped her boots on the large rough black mat in front of the Craftsman style emerald painted door. Ox swung open the door and the warmth from inside enveloped Kate in an instant, causing her to smile. She couldn't believe how at home she felt in a place she had never been before.

From behind the door rushed out a blur of yellow fur, a tail frantically waved.

"Bayou!" Ox grabbed hold of the blue collar. "Sorry about that. I forgot to tell you, I have a dog." Bayou wiggled free of his master's grip.

At Kate's boots an excited hundred plus pound dog attempted to hop, but Bayou's two front paws were the only things coming off the ground, but not by much.

"Are you afraid of dogs? He's harmless, just a big boy." Ox patted Bayou's bottom, trying to get his attention. "Sit."

"I'm not afraid of dogs. I just prefer to know when they are going to charge me." Kate reached down, petting Bayou on his blocky head. He looked like a lab, but a lab that ate another lab. "Is he a lab?"

"The vet said he's an English lab." Ox placed Kate's bag on the entry's rug. "It's the reason why he is stumpy and struggles to jump like a normal dog."

Kate giggled as she continued petting Bayou.

"Ox, it's coming down out there. I was getting worried." A slender older woman entered the entryway from the living room. "I thought you said you didn't have any other guests arriving today?"

"Hi." Kate reached out her hand. "I'm Kate."

"Margaret, but call me Maggie." She took Kate's hand and shook it, the other one cupped overtop as she smiled.

"Maggie has been staying here every January for the last five years." Ox closed the front door.

"Who could say no to this view?" Maggie turned and faced the living room. "And Ox's cooking too."

Beyond the entryway, matching windows from the front mirrored the backside. Through the windows, a painting came to life, as Kate walked forward, drawn in.

The inn sat higher up on the land with the view dipping deep into the lush valley of treetops coated with white powder below.

"You're staying then, Kate?" Maggie elbowed Ox out of Kate's view.

"If Ox will allow it, I'm rather stranded. I went to surprise my parents, but they're in Hawaii. Since I live out of state, I didn't have a house key. My return flight is not for another week, but I can't impose that long. I hope to catch a flight out as soon as the snow stops. Although, I dread having to get back on a plane. I loathe flying." Kate gazed out the window, wishing the snow would never stop, stranding her for years.

Maggie rubbed the edge of Kate's shoulder.

"Things happen for a reason," Maggie whispered and then winked. "Stay."

"Dinner should be ready in about thirty." Ox stepped back into the room. "Kate, I have a room for you."

He handed Kate an iron skeleton key. It looked like it once belonged to a pirate's chest. The black patina metal cool and heavy in her now warm palm.

"Take the stairs; it's the second door on the right." Ox smiled. "I'll bring your suitcase up in a minute."

Kate returned his smile. His eyes glittering like two rare sapphire snowflakes. "Are you sure?" Kate asked. "I can pay."

"I'm not worried about payment. Go and take a break, you must be tired. I'll come get you when dinner is ready."

She blushed at his kindness, drawing her head down to keep her flushed cheeks hidden from Ox's view. Kate pivoted and made her way to the steps. Pausing to turn around and thank Ox, the back of Kate's boot caught the bottom of the step. As her arms circled at her side, she did a quick twist, leaned backward and sat ungracefully on the step.

Kate crossed her legs and placed her elbow on her knee. Resting her head in her palm, she sat as though she meant to sit on the step rather than go upstairs.

Ox's head tipped back as laughter burst from him once again. "Maybe I should just bring you dinner in bed."

Pushing her shoulders up and back, Kate grabbed the staircase railing and stood. The sound of Ox still laughing filled the space between them as she made her way to the room, giggling quietly about her klutziness.

Chapter Seven

Ox continued to stare in the direction of Kate long after she disappeared up the stairs. A woman had never caught his heart, mind, and eyes all at once before.

"She is beautiful." Maggie's voice broke through Ox's thoughts.

Shaking the thoughts from his mind, he turned to Maggie. She stood with her hands on her hips. "Don't go down that road, Maggie. You know I swore off relationships. Period."

Pulling out the ingredients for dinner, Ox lined them up on the counter.

"I know you can date. You're the one putting up the roadblock." Maggie leaned against the kitchen island.

"A woman wants a man who can be a man and do man things, not one she has to take care of on bad days." Ox washed the green beans, scrubbed the potatoes, and set them on the cutting board.

"Man things?" Maggie shook her head like a judge hearing excuses. "Tarzan, I mean, Ox, when a woman loves you, she loves you. That includes everything about you. Not every day will be perfect. Stan and I loved each other, but we still had bad days. There were days when Stan and I would not even make eye contact, days when all we did was ignore each other. There were days when we fell ill and cared for each other. But, Ox, there were all the other days too. We had days when we fell in love all over again, and days when we laughed and cried because we loved each other through it all, and that's what mattered."

"Maggie, my bad days are unknown. I might have bad weeks." Ox's vision traveled the direction of the stairs.

"The right woman for you won't care about bad days." Maggie placed a hand over Ox's hand and squeezed the top of it. "Trust this old lady as much as you would your own mother." She kissed Ox's cheek.

As Maggie left the room, Ox's shoulders were heavy with the burden of thoughts. He moved about the kitchen, preparing dinner with rhythmic movements. He followed a recipe he knew by heart, which made it easy to allow Maggie's words to linger.

The thought of Kate's curly copper hair framing her soft, fair skinned face caused Ox to grin. Her inability to navigate surfaces without stumbling made him laugh. Yet Kate's drive of independence stirred something in him, something no woman he had ever dated or known had done.

Ox slammed the onion down on the cutting board, startling Bayou. *Don't go there.* He ran through his list. *One, I have MS. Two, well, crap! There is not number two.* Ox paused to consider things. He raised his pointer finger in the air. *Ahh ha! Two, she doesn't live in the state.* He glanced around, realizing he looked ridiculous with his finger pointing upward.

Bayou rested against the cupboard at Ox's feet, waiting for a green bean to fall. Ox remembered Kate mentioning how much she hated flying. *Perfect! That's number three. I'm a pilot for goodness sake.* As though Bayou could hear Ox's thoughts, he sprang up and placed his paws on the counter.

"Get down, you know better." Ox used his arms to slide Bayou's paws from the counter.

The reflection of Bayou's service vest resting on the hook by the door caught Ox's eye. He frowned and lowered himself to his dog's eye level.

"It's not a sign, right?"

Bayou sniffed the air around the kitchen. Ox pondered his thoughts of Kate, before returning to cook with his mind still racing.

With dinner ready, Ox took the steps two at a time to Kate's room. "Do you think you can manage walking downstairs for dinner?" Ox stood at Kate's open door.

She tilted her head as though to ponder such a thought. Before she could answer, Ox turned, laughed, and made his way back down the hall to the stairs.

The aroma of dinner met Kate's nose at the bottom of the landing. "Where is my television?"

"We have a main television in the living room." Ox carried a bowl of steaming hot mashed potatoes, and another of green beans, setting them on the lace table runner.

"Don't tell me you are one of those distraction free inns?" Kate rolled her eyes.

"We all need a break from time to time, even if you don't think so," Maggie stated entering from the living room.

"She's right." Ox smiled. "That's why she is my favorite guest."

"I thought it was because I'm not a messy guest." Maggie chuckled.

"That too." Ox pulled out a chair for Maggie and then Kate before sitting down.

He passed Kate a serving plate of pan-fried chicken, followed by mashed potatoes, and the green beans. The aromatic warm smells danced in Kate's nose with delight. Even in her mom's kitchen, she had never smelled something so amazing. Her stomach growled with anticipation.

"I hope this is to your liking." Ox poured Beaujolais into their wine glasses and passed them around.

"Oh my!" Kate nearly choked on a bite of chicken as her fork crashed onto the plate. Under the lip of the table she saw

Bayou's head rested in her lap. His brown eyes were wide and focused. For such a large beast his movements were cat-like. He lifted his paw up and tapped Kate's thigh. Drool threatened to slide from his mouth.

"Bayou, go lie down. I'll give you some scraps later." Ox stood and walked around the table taking Bayou by his collar. The lab reluctantly allowed Ox to direct him to his dog bed hidden in the corner.

"That's an interesting name, Bayou." Kate picked her fork back up.

"Oh, I love this story." Maggie leaned forward as Ox sat down again.

"Maggie has heard it only a dozen times." Ox took his wine glass in both hands.

"Never gets old." Maggie smiled.

Kate raised her hand toward Ox in a do tell motion.

He took a sip of Beaujolais and cleared his throat. "About three years ago I had a planned vacation to Louisiana. A large hurricane hit right before I was to leave, Hurricane Laura I think, and for some reason, something nagged me to go regardless. I did some research on organizations that might need a service I could provide by flying my own plane in to help."

Kate held her left hand up. "Wait, you can fly a plane?"

"Yes, a Cessna. It's small," Ox said, as though everyone had the ability to run an inn, fly a plane, and oversee an airport. "I discovered HPR, Hurricane Pets Rescue, Inc. For the first week, I volunteered with the transportation of rescued animals through their Paw Lift program."

Kate found herself smiling at Ox. His cooking skills were on par. Her mouth watered, needing to take another bite of chicken. She desired to learn more about him. *What else does Ox do? Maybe he volunteers in the hospital's birthing ward while dressed as Santa!*

"I had a little bit of free time with most of the stores

boarded up. I'd always wanted to explore the bayous of the state. They are mysterious and beautiful."

Kate stopped eating and rested her head in her hand, leaning toward Ox.

"There was this park with a grand bayou just off the main road."

Every time Ox said the word bayou, Kate could see the English lab raise his head off the bed.

"I got out of my rental car, to take a peek around and maybe get a few photos. The hurricane had beaten up the area pretty badly. I was the only one there, or so I thought. A whimpering noise came from this grassy area, and then there he was, this little yellow lab puppy, covered in mud and Spanish moss. He lay there, and as I approached him, even though he was clearly exhausted, his tail managed to wag. Reaching out to him, I spoke softly, telling him that I would help and he would be okay. He sniffed my outreached hand and immediately started to lick it, his tail wagging rapidly. Your elbow is in your green beans."

Maggie laughed, as Kate continued to stare at Ox, who pointed at Kate's elbow. She peeked down, lifting her elbow from the green beans, her cheeks turning a slight rose color.

"What happened then?" she asked, trying to move past her embarrassment.

"I picked him up, carried him to the car, and went to get him checked out. No tags and no microchip. It was an odd coincidence that I was volunteering for HPR when I found him. The last time I had a dog was during my teenage years, and had not thought about how much I missed the company. In fact, I could not stop thinking about Bayou, and while I knew he was safe, the organization was struggling to find all the lost animals their families or new homes. The vet's back room kennel was already full of other homeless pets from the storm. Because there were hundreds of dogs who needed homes, HPR and the vet agreed without a doubt

I should adopt Bayou."

"So Bayou, because you found him in a bayou." Kate smiled and scooped up some mashed potatoes.

Ox nodded. "For a while afterward I worried that I had taken him away from his family. I left my information with HPR and several animal shelters and at the vet's office just in case, but I never heard from anyone."

Kate glanced over at Bayou, who was now asleep. "I'm sure he is grateful you found him."

Ox smiled. "I'm currently working with a therapy trainer for him. A few more classes and he'll be certified as a therapy dog to help people with anxiety. He enjoys visiting hospital patients undergoing chemotherapy or other similar treatment plans. Mostly, I'm looking forward to him working with individuals who fear flying. Really, anything that gives people anxiety. Although judging by how he nearly gave you a heart attack, maybe he needs a bit more work."

Kate giggled. "You think he can help with flying?"

"Yes, of course. We can work with you, if you like."

"Thanks, but no thanks." Kate's voice was firm.

Once Kate's plate was nearly licked clean, she took her glass of Beaujolais to the living room and gazed out the window. The snow continued to fall in near whiteout conditions.

"Looks like you'll be staying for a while." Maggie came up behind Kate. "I don't think I have ever seen it snow this hard before. Hopefully Winter Wonder Day will still happen."

"I remember my parents mentioned it last year." Kate took a sip of wine.

"Ox enters one of his pies every year." Maggie eased herself onto a plush tan armchair near the window. "He is hoping to finally win this time."

"If his pies are as good as his dinners, I would think he would have won."

Maggie crossed her arms and sank back into the chair. "The other entries manage to have something extra pushing them over the top. Maybe he just needs a little something special to help him win. Do you bake?"

Kate remained at the window, her eyes fixed on the view. "I do."

"Interesting." Maggie's posture alerted. "Apparently this snow had a little plan of its own."

Maggie never left much to the imagination. She reminded Kate of a kindergartener. Kate stood there, wondering if Maggie might be onto something.

"I think I'll have Ox put on some tea." Maggie stood and her footsteps disappeared as another set came toward Kate.

Looking down she found Bayou standing at her side. He stared up at her as if to ask, "Can we go play in the snow?"

"Need any help?" Maggie offered at the kitchen's entry.

"Thanks, Maggie, but I have it covered." Ox took his time washing the dinner dishes. Anything to keep his mind busy and his thoughts off Kate. "Would you like me to bring you some tea?"

"Delightful, you read my mind." Maggie's voice singsonged as she pointed toward the living room. She traced an outline of a heart on her chest.

Ox shook his head, but Maggie noticed the glimmer of a smile. She returned to the living room before Ox could wave her off.

He plunged his hands back into the soapy water, scrubbing the casserole dish long after it was clean. *No relationship. Zero. It cannot happen, so don't even go there. Sure, today was a great day, but you don't know what tomorrow will bring.* Ox had not experienced any weakness or dizziness since Kate's arrival and his cane remained hidden against the wall in his closet.

"I'm not sure how the inn thing works." Kate's voice startled Ox. A dish slid from his hand and plopped into the pool of sudsy water below.

Placing her hand on her heart, Kate gasped. "Ox, I'm sorry I startled you."

Playing it off as best he could, Ox continued to wash the already clean casserole dish. "Are you feeling okay? You took a few falls today."

"Yes, thank you, and thanks for letting me stay here." Kate pushed a curl behind her ear. "I wanted to take a shower before bed."

"Yes, of course. Fresh towels are in the bathroom cabinet. Treat it like a hotel, only you have to share a bathroom. Luckily, it's only Maggie and you, or is it you and Maggie? Without the glaring eye of my English teacher, I can never remember."

Kate leaned against the kitchen island. "I'm not going to judge the order of your 'yous.'"

Ox gave a smoldering glance. "Good. Will you need anything else before bed?"

Kate's smile turned down. "No, I'm okay. Thank you, Ox. Goodnight." She made her way up the stairs.

"Night," Ox mumbled, caught off guard. *Why did she suddenly leave?*

Ox rested his hands at the sink's edge and stared off at the empty staircase. He told himself to turn away but he could not. Kate's presence caused him to completely forget about his diagnosis. Even when up in the air, in control of his Cessna, his diagnosis bombarded his mind. At this point Ox was both elated and worried about Kate's being grounded at his inn.

As Kate reached the top of the steps, her heart hurt at Ox's sudden hint to get out of his space. How quickly he mentioned bedtime. Reading men could be hard, but Ox proved to be an over the top challenge. She entered her room, closed the door, and leaned against it.

"You can't fall for him. You don't live in the same state." Her voice was low and wobbly. "He can't even stand to have you in the kitchen."

The view from Kate's room overlooked the woods on the east side of the inn. On the bed, a peach chiffon quilt rested on top of the cream-colored satin sheets. The nightstand held an antique Tiffany style lamp and several classic Mark Twain books. A stack of hardcover Edgar Allan Poe books sat upon the five-drawer pine dresser. A mason jar of dried lavender kept a mini lamp on the nightstand company, while a woven rug of mixed sea blues covered the hardwood floor.

She removed her cell phone from her pocket and unlocked the screen. The low signal meant she could not make a call. Kate wanted to talk to Ali; however, a text message would have to do. She could try emailing but didn't know the inn's Wi-Fi password.

KATE: i have a problem. it's a man. need help. advice?

ALI: Why? How did you find a guy at your parents' house?

KATE: long story, tell you later. i'm staying at an inn run by a … well, he is gorgeous

ALI: What's the problem then?

KATE: i don't live here anymore

ALI: I've always supported you, Kate, and I know that you have not been happy lately.

KATE: i haven't?

ALI: …

Kate hung her head, re-reading Ali's text messages.

Ali never hid her opinions. She told you if your dress was hideous or when you had broccoli between your teeth. Come to think of it, Maggie and Ali were similar.

While most people preferred texts, especially Ali, Kate preferred phone calls. But tonight Kate preferred text. Ali would not be able to hear the tone of her voice and make her create the dreaded list.

She moved her fingers over the phone, finally ready to reply.

KATE: i'm sure it's some pre-midlife crisis. i'll be fine once i'm back home

ALI: I remind you every time you ask me a question you already know the answer to. Give your mind and heart equal opportunities. Kate … Please stop lying to yourself. Now, it's late, goodnight.

KATE: goodnight

Chapter Eight

Even though the clock on the nightstand had both hands on the twelve, Kate's eyes were not heavy. She kicked her legs like a frustrated child and rolled over in bed. Moonlight broke through the shifting clouds outside the window. The snow had stopped.

The weight of depression sat heavy on Kate's chest. She thought coming back home would help her sort out what had been plaguing her mind for months, maybe years. A part of her never wanted to return to Phoenix. Another part of her wrestled with why she had those feelings.

Her thoughts wandered. Thinking about her job caused her to feel like a stress ball ready to pop. She flipped over in the bed again with a heavy sigh thinking of her lifeless and lonely home. Her life seemed as empty as her house. *There is nothing wrong with being alone.* Kate loved Arizona, at least the first few years. Lately she dreaded the summers and longed for the seclusion of the deep evergreen woods. All I need is time to rest and recharge, to step back and reevaluate my life. Then I will appreciate going back to Phoenix.

A low whap, followed by a whap, whap on Kate's door interrupted her thoughts. She bolted upright in bed.

Whap, whap, whap, whap, whap.

She tossed back the blankets. Making her way to the door, she opened it enough for a crack of light to come in. Kate peeked out, not seeing anything. The door pushed open with a large amount of force. When she looked down, Bayou nosed his way past the door.

"Come on in then." She ushered with her hand.

Bayou pounced his front paws onto the bed, his back end still on the rug. Kate stood with her hands on her hips staring at him.

"Can't you get up on your own?" Bayou remained half on the bed, half on the floor, his tail wagging gently. Kate got behind him, placing her hands under his hips and lifted.

"My goodness, Bayou," she laughed. "You are rather hefty."

Using his front paws, he hoisted himself the rest of the way onto the bed. Bayou did a circle and made himself comfy with an exaggerated flop.

"Welcome." Kate crawled back under the covers. The weather's cold dampness seeped into her bones. One positive of Phoenix, it was as dry as a dog's bowl after dinner.

Bayou glanced at her from the corner of his brown eyes as if she had disturbed him getting into the bed, versus the other way around. Kate stared at the ceiling with such intent that her vision blurred. The mattress shifted as Bayou army-crawled closer to Kate. His front paws rested in the crook of her arm.

"I'm happy," she asserted, rubbing the top of his head. Am I happy? Thinking about home gave Kate a sudden pang of anxiety, moving through her chest like heartburn. It was searing, uncomfortable burn. She wondered if being here sparked something more in her, something she had pushed aside for years. Would she feel this way if she were in her parents' home?

Bayou shifted his body weight up against Kate. As she sank her fingers into his yellow fur, peace washed through her.

"Have I ignored myself?" she asked Bayou. "Pushing my unhappiness to the side, thinking I could outrun it forever? It seems to have caught up to me now."

Bayou yawned, his eyes drifted closed. Kate yawned too.

Curled up with Bayou, she slept as though she had not slept in months.

When Kate's eyes opened in the morning, Bayou's large blocky head leaned over her. His pink tongue hung, drool threatened to drop down and splash her face. She sprang up, the drool hitting the pillow below.

Bayou attempted to dismount the bed. His front paws on the ground, his back legs still on the bed, a near yoga pose. Kate could learn a thing or two from the big yellow mound of fluffy fur. Together they made their way downstairs to the smell of eggs and French toast.

"There you are, buddy." Ox greeted Bayou by rubbing his ears. "I thought he had snuck out to sleep with Maggie. I hope he didn't bother you too much."

"No, actually." Kate finger brushed her hair. Her eyes widened as she glanced down noticing she had not changed out of her ice cream cone pajamas. *Too late now to run back up and change.* In an attempt to hide at least half of her pajamas, she took a seat at the table. "I slept amazingly well. He does snore a bit though."

Ox bent down to Bayou's level. "Nothing like a dog's snore to drown out the noise of a busy mind."

As he stood, their eyes met from across the kitchen. "And good morning."

"Good morning."

"Good morning, Kate." Maggie entered the kitchen. She poured herself a cup of coffee before sitting down. "The sun is shining. It looks as though you can make your early flight home."

"Actually," Kate loaded her plate with eggs and French toast and said, "I want to stay, keep my flight the same, if Ox is able to accommodate me for the full week."

"Absolutely, but only if you are willing to help me with the pie contest." Ox placed food in Bayou's bowl. "Maggie mentioned that you bake."

"I do, but I don't know how much help I can be," Kate paused. "But I'll try. Maggie, maybe you would be a better help to Ox than I."

"Why? Because I'm an elderly lady?"

Kate choked, patting her chest. Taking her coffee mug in both hands, she took several sips. "No, because you're wiser in your years." Kate grinned hoping to redeem herself.

Maggie winked at her from across the table. Kate breathed a sigh of relief and took a bite of her eggs.

"I'd like to do a few trial pies today, if that's possible." Ox wore a charcoal long-sleeve shirt, dark stone washed jeans, and tan boots. His muscles were concealed beneath the sleeves, but Kate knew they were there, strong and capable. His face, unshaven yet again, caused Kate to wonder if he owned a razor. Pulling out a chair, Ox sat at the table with Maggie and Kate.

"I wanted to do a bit of walking around since the sun is out." Kate tried not to sound too standoffish, but she needed to do some soul searching.

"Of course, you're on vacation." Ox peered down as though embarrassed he mentioned it.

"As soon as I return, I'd love to help," Kate said, hoping she could undo the disappointment on his face.

"Why don't you work on pie prep after breakfast, then show Kate where that trail is? When she comes back, you can work on baking the pie." Maggie suggested.

"Great idea," Ox and Kate said together.

They smiled in unison, and warmth spread through Kate. It reminded her of the same coziness as seeing a family decorate a Christmas tree. *How can I feel so at home with two complete strangers?*

"I'd like to send Bayou with you on the trail. With all that snow out there, it can become disorientating. Also, he knows his way home." Ox sprinkled pepper onto his eggs.

"Sure, I'd love the company." Kate sliced off a bite of French toast with her fork. "It's not too deep for him?"

"Not right now, it's rather compact."

Comfort filled Kate's heart knowing that Ox cared enough to send Bayou with her. Having grown up around here, she knew that with everything covered in snow one could get disoriented quickly. Plus, the care he showed for Bayou proved he was more than a pet. He was family.

"This inn wasn't around when I grew up. I would have remembered it for sure." Kate wrapped her hands around her coffee mug.

"You didn't attend college here?" Ox asked.

"No, I left right after high school."

"That's why. It's only been in operation for about eight years. We probably started building just about the time you left." Ox's eyes traveled around the kitchen. "It's really a work of art. They would be proud of its upkeep."

Before Kate could ask a question, she caught Maggie and Ox sharing a glance. Loss filled Ox's eyes as he cleared his throat. With a sigh, he poked at his breakfast. Only the sound of forks scraping plates filled the expansive kitchen.

Without a word, Ox stood and cleared the empty breakfast plates.

"Thank you, the French toast was delicious." Kate's chair dragged across the hardwood floor as she slid it out.

The dishes clinked as Ox rinsed them.

Kate headed up to her room to dress for the day. The embarrassment of her pajamas no longer at the top of her list. As she dressed, her thoughts drifted to how Ox easily switched himself off. At times, her own mom had those days where something would cause silence through the home. Yet in less than twenty-four hours, Kate appeared to have hit several of his nerves. Having just met him and knowing so little, Kate could not fault Ox. It was far too easy to make judgments. She could be reading him all wrong.

As Kate descended the stairs and reached the kitchen, Ox's eyes drew upward. To say he was taken aback by Kate's simple beauty would be an understatement. Her thick mint colored sweater hid her small figure, as it appeared to nearly reach the tops of her boots. She wore limited, if any makeup and her curls were tied up and off her face. Without doubt, Kate took his breath away.

Kate joined Ox at the counter. In front of them were three apple pie recipes, which Kate studied. The cards were covered in stains and worn soft from bakers' greasy hands over the years.

"I know that something is missing from the recipe for this apple pie, but I can't figure out what. I'm wondering if I should nix the apple pie all together," Ox questioned.

"Have you tried experimenting?" She pivoted, facing Ox.

His eyebrows arched as though Kate asked him a question about astrophysicists.

"That's a no." Kate giggled.

Ox crossed his arms. "I have learned with baking that if you experiment things turn out inedible."

"Baking does have its own set of individual quirks. Cooking allows for a bit more leeway," she leaned against the counter, "but you can get away with a few tweaks to spice things up."

"You will help me with that, right?" Ox asked, as though he feared her answer.

"Of course." Kate tapped his arm with the back of her hand. "Now, this recipe," she said while holding up the closest one and waving it, "have you tried different types of apples for it and different spices?"

"I did and either the pie tasted sour or the flavors didn't mix well." Ox's shoulders slouched.

Kate stepped closer until their sleeves touched. They felt

the warmth of their arms connecting and their rapid heartbeats pumping in their bodies.

"Depending on the apple, a sour taste can happen." Kate lifted another recipe card. "Usually recipes call for Granny Smith apples, but you can use a few others. Local ones are often good, which might be what your competition does. You can make any type of pie for the contest, correct?"

"Yes, I've always done apple because it's a classic. I'm stuck in my ways."

"Has anyone done any type of odd pie and won the contest?"

"Odd, like mincemeat? No, the winners have been an apple, boysenberry, and a key lime pie."

"I have a recipe. It's unique and might be exactly what you need to win the competition. However, I've only made it once."

"What is it?" Ox leaned in as though Kate had the code to unlock Pandora's box.

"Green tomato pie."

Chapter Nine

"I want to win the competition, not lose as the laughing stock of the town." Ox filled a glass with water.

"It's unexpected and should give you an edge over the other pies." Kate pressed her palms on the counter.

"It doesn't sound good in the slightest." He gulped the water in one long swig.

"What's the worst that can happen? You lose … again?"

Before glancing out the kitchen window, Ox gave Kate a lip curl that would have made Elvis proud. The snow melting from the roof gave the appearance of rain outside.

"There is no way you have the recipe with you, so I guess I'm out of luck." Stiffening his posture, Ox crossed his arms.

"I have it saved in my email, but I need to use your Wi-Fi. My network signal is weak in this part of town. I can send texts and possibly make calls, but nothing else."

Kate pulled her cell phone from her back jean pocket and waved it at him.

"I don't have a wiffy. Remember, distraction free inn, no bedroom televisions and no phones."

"It's Wi-Fi." Kate giggled. "Wait, are you joking?"

"No, I'm not big on technology. Having constant tabs on everything seems unnecessary to me. The library and airport have wiffy if you need it badly enough."

"Wi-Fi," she corrected him snidely. "How do people make reservations?"

Ox's lips questioned Kate, his eyebrows arched. "By phone."

"People still do that?"

"You have been without an internet connection since you arrived. Can you tell me that you've missed it?" Ox tapped his foot waiting for a reply. "Are you more relaxed?"

The thought had not crossed her mind. She shrugged her shoulders. "Sure, it has been a little more relaxing, only a little though." She would not admit any more to a man with such a smug look across his face.

"Great, now for this green pie." He focused on the empty pie pan, his elbows resting on the kitchen island.

"I do remember the basics of the recipe. You make it as though the green tomatoes are apples. One issue I had when I made it was over-cooking it. The tomatoes broke down during baking and were pudding-y."

Ox's head lowered into his palm.

"What?" Kate pivoted toward him.

"Just trying to figure out what a 'pudding-y' substance is."

Kate threw her head back in an over exaggerated laugh, preparing to talk back. "You know what I mean."

Ox shook his head. "No."

"They tasted good, but lacked structure. The real question is: does the grocery store here sell green tomatoes? They can be tricky to find regardless of the time of year, but especially challenging in the winter."

"Are green tomatoes ones that are not ripe?"

"No." Kate laughed. "Have you never had one?"

Ox shook his head, making the face of a five-year-old with a mountain of cooked broccoli in front of him.

"You've missed out." Taking Ox by the hand, she dragged him toward the front door.

"Where are we going?" Ox stumbled behind her.

"You're taking us to the grocery store to find green tomatoes," Kate directed, without turning around. "I can go hiking when we return."

The roads were clear enough for Ox to drive into town without his truck ice-skating across the pavement. He found an open parking spot near a pile of blackened snow. Their boots made imprints in the slush as they approached the storefront.

Without warning, Kate's left leg went forward and her right leg when back. Her arms waved, trying to keep herself up-right. The slush was too slick. She did half a pivot and went down, slamming her butt into a mound of snow.

"Are you okay?" Ox reached his hand down for Kate. She grabbed Ox's gloved hand, and pulled herself up.

"I'm okay." Kate brushed the snow from her rear end. "I think when we're out I should hold your hand. The last thing I want to do make a trip to the emergency department. I detest hospitals."

Kate peered down, Ox's hand offered a secure, yet gentle grip.

"Should we ask an employee where they are?" Ox questioned as they wiped their wet boots on the entry rugs with the store logo plastered across them. They glanced at their hands still held together and reluctantly dropped them to their sides.

"No, if they have them they will be with the other tomatoes."

"Are you sure there is not some special green tomato section?"

Kate glared at Ox for his sarcastic comment. He copied, frozen in a staring contest. Within seconds, they both broke into laughter.

"How is it that you run an inn, plus cook all the meals, yet have never before used or seen a green tomato?" Kate asked, as they made their way to the vegetable section.

"I probably have, but thought they were just unripe

tomatoes."

"Yes!" Kate's arms went straight up as though she had crossed the finish line in a triathlon. A small pyramid of green, red, yellow and orange heirloom tomatoes sat on the corner near a stack of red and green bell peppers.

Kate sorted through the green tomatoes, placing several in Ox's hands and the rest in her own. "I cannot believe the selection they have here. You have all the other ingredients to make the pies, correct?"

"I thought I already did." Ox smirked, as they headed toward the checkout.

"You won't have this attitude when you finally win the pie contest."

They placed the tomatoes on the conveyor belt.

"I'm sorry, Kate, you're right. We do need something different to win. Even if we don't win, at least you helped me to think outside of the box."

The way Ox kept using the word "we" made Kate smile. He saw them as a team. She had craved a "we" for some time, but every date proved to be a "never ever" or a "what was I thinking" ending.

"What's with the pouting?" Ox asked, as Kate climbed back into his truck.

"I'm not pouting," she declared. "Maybe this is my resting face."

Ox turned the key in the ignition. "Your face is not a permanent pout. I've known you for less than a day, but that," Ox pointed, "was a pout."

"I must have been reliving the moment when you mentioned you are stuck in the nineties without a wiffy."

"Wi-Fi," Ox mumbled.

"I knew you would get it right."

Staring out the window, Kate saw the snow glistening in

the sun. Happy feelings mixed around inside her heart causing a smile to develop on her face as they headed back to the inn.

"Why don't you and Bayou head out for some exploring? Remember to use your feet in a walking motion, versus a falling motion." Ox suggested, as they pulled into the garage.

"Yes, boss." Kate rolled her eyes.

"When you get back, we can start on the pie. I have a few inn things to handle first."

"Perfect."

Bayou dashed off the front porch with as much grace as a bull disguised as an English lab could. He sat at Kate's side, formal and posed before leaning back into a sloppy sit.

"Hi, buddy." Kate petted his head and scratched under his chin. "Let's go."

Bayou glued himself to Kate's leg as they stepped through the soft snow around the side of the inn and down the slope in the backyard. The tall pine fortress prevented the sun from reaching the landscape below.

Kate paused, allowing the stillness around her to soak in. Bayou stopped too, sniffing the air.

"You are a great guide dog, Bayou. Lead the way."

Their steps were easy and their breathing was the only noise. When Kate turned around, she could no longer see the inn. All that filled her view were evergreens and snow. As a child, she enjoyed living here. However, once she became a teenager, the itch to leave grew with each passing year until the need to escape, to see and do something different, overwhelmed her. While some of her friends went overseas on graduation trips, Kate remained focused on packing for the move to Arizona. Nothing could get her on a plane flying over an ocean.

"What's happening to me?" Kate asked Bayou. "If my teenage self could hear me now, it would kidnap me until I came to my senses."

He raised his head, focusing his huge brown eyes on Kate as if in an effort to understand.

"Living in a state with eight months of spring and four months of summer gets to you after a while."

Bayou let out a bark before weaving forward through the hemlocks.

"Wait up," Kate called.

Kate reached a clearing in the trees and found Bayou taking in the view. The valley dipped further down as only the tops of snow-covered pines were visible. It appeared as though the valley took a deep relaxed breath, its limbs resting.

Kate breathed in the crisp air, returning upon it her warm breath. Peace surrounded her like a knitted blanket. *How have I managed to push aside my own feelings for so long? Am I even bold enough to take a leap and move back home?*

She closed her eyes, heightening the silence of January all around. Her mind cleared as she took a renewing breath. Yet moving back home represented failure to Kate. She didn't see it as a positive.

Kate eased opened her eyes. Removing the cell phone from her pocket, she snapped a picture of the view. Then she squatted down to Bayou and held the phone level with their faces and took a selfie. Out of habit, Kate swiped to pull up her social media account but remembered the poor signal and Ox's words from this morning. Kate shook her head and smirked before shoving her phone back in her pocket.

"Shall we go home?" With that, Bayou trotted forward. His tail swayed to the beat of his steps.

Chapter Ten

"Thank you." Kate wrapped her ice-cold fingers around the mug of hot chocolate Ox had set in front of her.

She swiveled side to side on the bar stool at the kitchen island. Bayou rested in his nearby bed. He fought to keep his eyes open but finally succumbed to defeat. With a striped black and white dish towel, Ox dried a few pots.

"Okay, boss lady, I'm ready for my pie instructions." Ox placed the pots, now clean and dried onto the stove for dinner.

"You have enough green tomatoes to make two pies. Use half for the trial run pie and the rest for the contest pie. If you decide this is the one you want to make, of course. Otherwise, you can use the green tomatoes for dinner or a lunch."

"Did you have a nice time out with Bayou?" Ox removed a cutting board from below the island.

"I did, he lead me to this vista overlooking a lower part of the valley. It helped clear my head and oddly enough, Bayou is a great listener." Sipping her hot chocolate, the melted marshmallows stuck to her upper lip.

"Indeed he is, but I didn't know you had to clear your head."

Kate's smile wrinkled. "I'm good at ignoring things."

Ox turned the water on and began to wash the green tomatoes. "I think if something in life is easy to ignore, most people do." He glanced at Kate, their eyes locked.

The kitchen around them faded from Kate's peripheral. She couldn't look away unless Ox did first.

"So," Ox's eyes still locked on Kate, he asked, "what do I need to do?"

Kate's thoughts went several different directions.

"About the pie." Ox leaned on the counter, his palms at the edge.

Kate shook her head of the thoughts. "Make the pie as you would an apple pie."

"With cinnamon, sugar, cloves, and nutmeg?" Ox questioned.

Kate laughed into her mug, wiping away the chocolate mustache she created.

"Yes, green tomatoes have this buttery taste to them, so I don't add any butter. We will add the spices and some lemon juice. We want to marinate them for maybe a few minutes in the bowl as they soak up the flavors. Just enough to coat everything."

Kate slid down off the bar stool and made her way over to Ox. She stood close enough to smell Ox's mint and evergreen scent.

"Tomatoes hold more moisture than apples, so we'll need a little bit of flour to help soak it up."

Ox grabbed the flour, spices, and lemon juice, and set them down next to the bowl. Kate cored and sliced the washed green tomatoes as though they were apples. She placed them in a bowl.

While Ox sprinkled in the spices, Kate gently folded everything together. Then in another bowl, he mixed the ingredients for the crust.

"If you don't mind me asking," Ox began to roll out the dough, "Why did you move to Phoenix? You seem relaxed and at home here."

"I do?" With a wooden spoon, Kate folded the tomatoes three more times before letting the mixture sit. "I moved to Phoenix because I wanted to start something new. My best friend, Ali, and I met our senior year of high school. We were both accepted at Arizona State so we decided to take the leap together. I don't know if I could have moved to a new state on my own. Even the thought of it now pings my anxiety meter."

"Does your meter have a setting for your walking ability?"

Kate placed a hand on her hip. "You're not funny."

"I know." Ox smirked. "Bayou is being trained to help others with anxiety. I'm only trying to make you laugh. I'm well aware of the seriousness of it." Ox's voice was straight. "Maybe your 'pudding-y' and my seriousness can meet up for dinner."

Flashing Ox a devious smile, she rubbed her hands over the decorative vine embellishment on the outside of the bowl.

"When you're someplace new, you grab hold to anything that helps you feel less alone. College was just that and soon took over, pushing Washington into the past. I had been incredibly sheltered as a child and found the real world exciting and shiny. And once you fit in, at that moment, you dare not leave. I didn't think I missed living here nor did I think I hated my career. I guess it takes removing yourself from a situation to realize things. What about you, are you from here?"

Ox lifted the crust into the pie pan with the help of the roller. "I'm from Alaska, born and raised into a butt-head of a child."

Kate laughed. She could not see Ox as anything but a mellow child.

"My parents thought my teenage behaviors were because I had too much freedom." Ox pressed waves into the pie crust edge. "As an only child, my parents hovered since they didn't have any other kids to discipline."

"My parents too. Only-child syndrome is a lot worse than

others think." Kate leaned up against the counter facing Ox. "This town seemed small to me as a child and has not changed a lick, outside of your inn and the remodeled airport."

"It's been the same since my parents moved us here. Of course, compared to where we lived in Alaska, this town was huge. We had one stop sign for the entire town. Oddly enough, someone kept cutting it down every time they replaced it."

Kate folded her arms. "Did you happen to be that someone that kept stealing the stop sign?"

Ox chuckled and put his finger to his lips. "Anyway, when my parents decided to open an inn, they found this land through their long-time friend, Shawn. He owns the airport now, and at the time had lived here for a while. My father sketched out the plan for the inn with my mom. We moved, and I spent my college years building this inn and then helped them run it."

Kate's eyes scanned the kitchen. "You helped build this?"

Ox nodded as though he had built a simple Lego house, not an entire inn.

"Did your parents sell you the inn? That's why you run it now?"

Kate poured the marinated tomatoes into the pie crust.

"It was given to me in the estate." He laced the lattice on top of the pie.

"Estate?" she questioned.

"They passed away," Ox ran his fingers through his hair, "in a car accident."

"I'm sorry to hear about your parents," she said.

"Do you think you might move back here?" He held the oven door open as Kate slid the pie onto the rack and set the timer.

"I'm pondering a lot right now," she said. "So was your career plan to run an inn?"

Ox smiled, his gorgeous eyes catching the sunlight

coming in through the towering kitchen windows. "I wanted to do something during my downtime from flying. Flying was always my main career goal, but the unexpected switch worked out okay too."

"Oh, I forgot to show you." Kate removed the cell phone from her back pocket.

Swiping through to the photo gallery, she held her phone so Ox could see the selfie she took with Bayou.

"That's beautiful." He took Kate's phone and held it closer to examine the picture better.

"The view really is amazing out there," she added.

"I meant you and Bayou." Ox's eyes focused on the picture for a second longer before he gathered the courage to meet Kate's eyes. "I guess cell phones can be useful."

Her cheeks flushed red as he handed the phone back.

"I have some things to do around the inn, but I know Maggie would enjoy your company for a movie. I have a large selection of classics in the living room." Ox held tight to the counter and paused.

"Sounds nice." Kate half smiled, noticing Ox's sudden change. "Everything okay?"

Ox nodded as his hand let go of the counter, but then leaned his body on it for support.

"Popcorn is in the pantry, Maggie knows where." Ox took a few shuffles away from the counter. "And thanks, Kate, for the help with the pie. If I don't hear the timer would you mind pulling it from the oven?"

"Of course, I'll keep an ear out for it." Kate followed him out of the kitchen.

Bayou crept from his bed to join Ox, nearly tapping against his side. She gave Ox a small wave as though he were boarding a train out of town, instead of just going down the hall.

Kate placed her face into her palm and scolded herself. *Could I be any more cheesy? I'm lucky he didn't turn around and see me!*

With her hand, still covering her face, Kate turned to the living room. She missed the step down into the room, and her right foot stomped down with a jerk. Pain shot up her back. She was grateful to keep her balance.

"That was close," Maggie stated from the lounge chair. Her fingers worked the needles around the baby blue yarn square.

"I have already fallen once today. I think I'm at my quota. My fall protection kickstand should have been activated by now."

"Do you think maybe your mind is busy doing everything but being in the moment? Maybe that's why your feet keep trying to take you out." Maggie focused on looping the yarn.

Take me out? What is this, a mob hit? Kate sank into the couch, tucking her feet under herself. "I do have a lot on my mind, probably more than I did a few days ago," she answered.

"Maybe something has changed your thoughts, Kate. Perhaps something you never expected?"

Kate tilted her head toward Maggie.

"Something magical almost." Maggie placed her knitting in her lap and smiled at Kate. "Let's watch *It Happened One Night*. I haven't seen it in ages."

"I have never heard of that movie." Kate stood back up and searched for it on the entertainment center shelf.

Maggie strolled past Kate, reached out, and placed a hand on her shoulder. "I'll get the popcorn, you get everything set up. Those fancy remotes always frustrate me."

"Maggie." Kate held the movie case. "Is Ox all right? His gait seems a bit off balance today and he appeared weak when we were making the pie."

Maggie peered down the hall toward Ox's bedroom. "You'll have to ask him." Maggie left Kate standing there, but Kate caught the sweeping sadness across Maggie's face.

Ox rested his hand on Bayou's neck, just below his blue collar. He continued to replay the moments he had with Kate. How grateful he was to be able to make it to his room before Kate saw anything more. Clearly, she noticed something since she had asked him if he was okay.

His body went from great to bad in minutes, weakness cutting through him like a knife. Yet he needed the reminder, especially in Kate's presence. A reminder that because of his diagnosis, he could not be in a relationship with anyone, especially Kate. He would not ruin Kate's life by dragging her down with him.

Ox shifted in bed, trying his best to rest, but every time he closed his eyes, he saw Kate. He saw her smile, her eyes, and he heard her laughter echo around him. Kate was perfect in every way. Heck, he mentioned his parents passing and she didn't even dig at him with questions. Ox could tell his stories when and if he wanted to. Even Maggie had never allowed him to do that. A tinge of guilt swept over him. Maybe he owed Kate an explanation. The way her lips frowned at times, he knew she must be confused.

Ox wiggled his head on his pillow, getting more comfortable as the weakness grew deeper throughout his limbs. Bayou shifted his body, snuggling up against Ox. Along with the weakness came anger. This disease had taken his future away, the future he hoped for and wanted.

He used the last of his strength and smacked his fist into his open palm. Startled, Bayou popped his head up.

"Sorry, buddy." Ox petted Bayou until he drifted off to sleep.

Ox knew he had to nap during the bad times so he could hopefully function properly later on. Or, at least, have enough strength to give the illusion of being all right. He drifted off to sleep with the memory of Kate's sweet sunshine scent in his nose and her smile on his mind.

Chapter Eleven

"Do you smell smoke?" Maggie arched her body in the chair.

Pushing pause on the remote, Kate eased her body upright on the couch.

"Oh no!" Kate sprang from the couch. "The pie!"

Kate bolted into the kitchen, sliding to a stop on the hardwood floor with her socks. She grabbed the island to brace herself, swinging around to the oven. Snatching the potholders off the counter, Kate flung down the oven door, reaching into the smoke. She placed the pie on the trivet and fanned the remaining smoke. She was too late; the smoke detector sounded. Covering one of her ears, Kate continued to fan the smoke.

Ox and Bayou came charging down the hall. Ox threw open the front door, his movements stiff. He then proceeded to crank open each of the windows. Bayou assisted by barking at the smoke detector.

"What happened?" Ox shouted.

"I didn't hear the oven timer over the movie," Kate yelled back.

Finally, the smoke detector shut off, and Bayou stopped barking.

"I'm so sorry, Ox," Kate pleaded.

"Maybe it's a sign." He slouched on the nearby barstool.

Ox believes in signs?

Kate glanced at Maggie as if to hint for her to step in and help her out of this mess.

"Ox, it's not a sign." Maggie peeked at the pie. "It's called two ladies distracted by a movie."

Doubt spread over Ox's face. His forehead creased and his lips pouted.

"I'm really sorry, Ox," Kate repeated. "We have enough green tomatoes for one more pie."

"We need those for the contest." He ran his hand over the back of his neck.

"We are not down and out yet." Kate rubbed her arms as the chill from the open windows hit her.

"I think you were right, Kate. I need something to stand out and this was it. Yet without being able to taste it, how will I know?"

The word "we" had already disappeared from his vocabulary. Kate's heart sank.

"You know what, Ox? Maybe this is a sign you don't need a trial run pie," Maggie interjected. "A sign to trust Kate's green tomato pie."

"Maggie is right. I mean it's only a pie contest. I generate buzz for the inn just by participating," Ox said. "But to enter a contest with something I've never tried before, I should know what I'm presenting tastes like."

Kate examined the burnt pie. "I know I only made it once, but I promise it tastes great." Trying to find at least an inch of it that they could taste test, Kate found nothing outside of what a mouse might enjoy.

"We could always go traditional with the fruit you already had picked out," Kate suggested.

"No, like I said, this is what I need to win. I just need to have faith," Ox mentioned. "The contest is in less than forty-eight hours. If I lose, then I'll just double the rate of your room, Kate."

Her entire body slouched with a deep sigh. Ox leaned his head back in a laugh. Standing, he placed both hands on

Kate's shoulders. Immediately, she straightened her back, her heart nervous by Ox's sudden closeness.

"Don't give up on us," Ox said. "The pie, I-I mean, don't give up on our pie."

Her face flushed immediately, and she focused on her socks to avoid Ox seeing her red cheeks. When Ox removed his hands from her shoulders, it was like a wave going back out to sea.

"What movie were you two watching that caused such a severe sidetrack?"

"*It Happened One Night*," Maggie answered. "Kate had never seen it."

"That's a good movie. It's been a long time since I watched it." Ox made his way to the windows and began to crank them closed.

Kate noticed Ox move from window to window. His legs were stiff with limited movement at the knees, and he shuffled slightly between each step.

"Join us, we are only about half way through it," Kate suggested.

"I'd love to, but I have a few more things to get done around here. With the roads clearing up, I'd like to take the Cessna up for a bit tomorrow."

"Why don't you have Kate join you?" Maggie interjected.

Kate's eyes widened, and she glared at Maggie. Her fists clenched tight with anxiety. "First, I never fly on tiny planes. Second, it took me years to get up the courage to fly out here to surprise my parents."

"It's a beautiful view from the air." Ox opened the refrigerator.

"It looks just fine from the ground. I saw it all on the way in, and I will see it again on the way out. I don't need anything in between."

"Bayou could come with." Ox poured himself some iced

tea from the pale blue pitcher.

Hearing his name caused Bayou to tilt his head in their direction.

"He does need more practical training to finish his certification."

Kate glanced at Bayou from the corner of her eye. "I don't think a dog, even one as wonderful as Bayou, can help me when it comes to flying."

"Think about it. Okay, Kate?" Ox patted his leg for Bayou to come to him. "I'd love to show you around from the sky. It's only a bonus if we can help lessen your fear of flying." Ox downed half of the glass of tea in one large gulp.

"Thank you again, but I simply can't."

Even the thought of airplanes caused tightness in Kate's chest and shoulders.

"You can." Ox nodded. "I believe you can."

Kate started to open her mouth to reply when Maggie interjected again. "Kate, think about it. Now, let's go finish the movie." Maggie took Kate's hand as though without it Kate would sink into the unseen anxiety quicksand.

"How about just taking off and landing?" Ox and Bayou followed close behind.

With Maggie still holding her hand, Kate spun around as best she could. Ox's face was mere inches from her's. His jaw line strong, yet something behind those brilliant sapphire eyes flickered a secret on the edge of escaping.

"What do you mean?" Kate asked, in a near whisper.

"We can takeoff, make a circle over the airport, and then land. We would only be up in the air for about three minutes, tops."

"Three minutes?" Kate's eyes narrowed in question. Ox nodded, his eyes focused on Kate's lips. "I guess that doesn't sound too bad. It's the only part of flying I like."

"Great." Ox stepped back. "Tomorrow it's on."

Maggie turned to Kate. "Take it easy on my hand."

Kate didn't realize it, but she was squeezing it.

"Sorry." She released Maggie's hand.

They made their way into the living room, the movie still paused on the screen. The current scene took place at night. Clark Gable had pulled hay from the haystack to make a bed. Kate's thoughts went to Ox, then back to the plane, and then returned to Ox.

"You can ponder your life during the movie too," Maggie whispered.

Kate sank into the couch and pushed play on the remote. Within seconds, Kate's focus was no longer on the movie, but on the moment she had with Ox. Kate wanted to spend all her time with him. She wanted to find out more about him, ask Ox about his life, his dreams, his everything. She craved to know more, but she wasn't sure if Ox wanted to share. So far, he had only shared enough to get by in brief conversations.

Will going up in his plane and getting him alone allow me to learn more about this tight-lipped ox of a man? Will he open up to me on a deeper level being in his element? She covered herself back up under the soufflé colored blanket and actually considered the plane ride.

Chapter Twelve

Mid-morning the following day Ox stood framed in Kate's open door. "There is a woman downstairs who says she's your best friend."

As she peered up from her magazine, Kate's eyes squinted. She pointed to herself. "Me?"

Ox nodded, "Yes, who else?" He laughed and turned to head back downstairs.

She reached the bottom of the steps and hugged her best friend, swaying her back and forth. "Ali!" Kate shrieked. While Kate had only been away from Washington for three days, it felt as though she had not seen Ali in weeks.

Ali's sleek shoulder-length licorice black hair complemented her pressed black blazer and matching boot-flared dress pants. A hot-pink blouse added a pop of color to her outfit. Ox held Bayou by his collar to keep him from getting dog hair all over Ali's outfit.

Finally, Kate released her best friend from the hug. Ali responded by smoothing out her blazer. Kate did not take offense to Ali's dislike of physical affection.

"What are you doing here and how did you even find me?" Kate reached for Ali's arm and gave it a squeeze of excitement.

"I had a connecting flight in Seattle before I leave for work in Shanghai. This being the only inn in the area, I took a chance. You were right, Kate. This place is beautiful."

"Thank you," Ox said. "Will you need a room?"

Ali gave the entryway a once over like a queen might judge

her garden. Pivoting to take in each area from one single spot, she was pleased with what she saw from a distance.

"No, thank you." Ali hit the side button of her cell phone for the time. "I have to be back to Sea-Tac by six p.m."

"I'll let you two be." Ox turned to Kate. "Let me know if you need anything, I'll be in my room. If you decide on flying, we can move it to tomorrow." He held Bayou at his side.

"Still undecided." Kate frowned.

As Ox headed to his room, Kate's eyes remained on him.

Ali leaned toward the hall mirroring Kate's focus. "He is gorgeous."

"Shhhhh!" Kate returned her focus to Ali and hugged her once again. "I cannot believe you're here!"

"Should we do lunch? So I can talk some sense into you?"Ali straightened her blazer yet again. "I have a rental car, but follow me in yours. That way if our lunch runs long I won't be late heading back to Seattle."

Kate gasped. "My rental car is still at the airport. Actually, I need to return it. I don't think I'll need it anymore." It had slipped Kate's mind to go back and get it after Ox brought her to his inn.

"No problem." Ali made her way to the front door. "I help you return it and drop you off on my way out."

"Let me grab my purse." Kate took two steps at a time. Ali did not wait for anyone, even her best friend.

Ali and Kate enjoyed the same music, movies, television shows, books, and food. Their differences fell on the bigger ticket items such as career and family. In college, Kate took her time to engage in classes that had nothing to do with her degree, such as early childhood education and culinary classes. While Ali went straight for classes that were on her degree list, rolling her eyes at Kate's suggestion to take a class for fun.

Ali's family arrived Chicago at the end of her junior

year of high school. She had already lived in Texas, Alabama, and California. Ali's parents relocated to Florida after she left for college. Due to all the moving of her childhood, Ali did not have attachments to where she spent her childhood days. For her, being back in Washington meant nothing. One might think Ali would crave a permanent place, but that wasn't Ali's personality.

Soon, Larry's Restaurant came into view. The parking lot, which consisted of crushed gravel and no white parking lines, welcomed visitors to a relaxed setting. If not for the restaurant sign, the building could easily be mistaken for someone's home. Ali and Kate had spent a good chunk of their senior year of high school at the popular mom and pop restaurant. Kate worked as a server, Ali did not. Kate and her parents were regulars for Saturday dinners at Larry's; and nearly everyone at Crooked River High School found themselves there in the afternoon. She hoped the menu had remained the same.

The outside of the deep gray building looked the same as it did when Kate last visited. However, the sign had faded more so than before. When Kate pushed open the door, which was heavy with years of layered red paint, a bell jingled. Inside had been remodeled with new banquettes and tables. The light fixtures were modern, but the mahogany bar and swivel chairs remained frozen in time. A haphazard stack of old newspapers filled the edge of the bar's counter.

"Welcome to Larry's, table for ..." The waitress spun around. "Kate? Ali?"

Kate examined the woman in a long sea blue dress, a thick rose cardigan over top, and black SAS shoes. "Faye?"

Faye reached her hands out, and Kate grabbed them as Faye pulled her in for a hug.

"I have not seen you gals in years!" Faye drew her shoulders to her ears and showed off a grand mile smile. "You're getting a hug

too, Ali."

Ali's eyes rolled up as Faye's arms wrapped around her. When Faye released her, Ali gave a hint of a smile.

"It's been a long time." Kate continued to observe the restaurant. "I'm happy to see this place is still here. I know how hard it is to keep hometown restaurants in business with all the big chains forcing everyone out."

Faye snagged two menus from the stand. "Larry and I had a few close calls, but we've managed to survive."

Ali and Kate followed Faye to their table. They slid into the currant-colored booths as Faye placed the menus on the table. "What brings you gals back home?"

Ali held out her cell phone for a signal. "A work trip layover, and to talk some sense into Kate."

"I had planned to surprise my parents, but they're out of town." Kate opened the menu, already starving with the familiar aroma in the air. "Do they still come here?"

"Every Saturday." Faye smiled. "Where are you staying?"

"Inn of the Woods."

"Oh, yes, I heard that place is wonderful. Rumor has it that the owner's cooking is as good as ours." Faye winked. "I'll let you gals review the menus, although I don't think it has changed much since the last time you were here." Faye shifted on the balls of her feet and went to check on the nearby customers.

Ali read the menu several times over before placing it on the table. Kate continued to ponder. Mac and cheese sounded good, so did the chicken pot pie, and so did a cheeseburger, and the Sloppy Larry's (the restaurant's homemade version of the popular canned variety).

Ali pulled down the top of Kate's menu. "I know you already know what you want."

Kate dropped her menu on the table, folding her arms and pouting as though she were a seven-year-old. Before Kate could respond with a smart aleck comment, Faye approached the table.

"Do you gals know what you want to order?"

"I'll have the cheeseburger, no mayo, light cheese, and overcook the burger." Ali handed the menu up to Faye, "And a diet Coke with lemon. If you are out of lemons, I'll take a lime."

Faye peered over the edge of her glasses at Ali. Kate was most likely thinking the same thing as Faye. Some things never change.

"May I please have the chicken pot pie and lemon water?" Kate handed the menu to Faye who shoved it under her arm with the other one.

Faye headed to the kitchen window and stuck the order form into the ticket holder for the cook. Kate leaned onto the table, her chin resting on the palm of her left hand. "Can you believe the menu is exactly the same?"

"I can. This town is not one for change I suppose." Kate laughed. "Can you believe I don't miss being tethered to my cell phone?"

"Yes. I texted you three times and even called to tell you I was stopping by to see you."

Kate's face scrunched up. "Oh, I'm sorry. I haven't been checking my phone much. It's been nice to use it only when I want to. Good riddance. The world needs more quaint towns with limited cell service."

"Good riddance?" Ali placed her cell phone upside down on the table. "You're home less than two days, and you've already reverted back to your teenage self."

Kate sighed as Ali removed a small notebook and pen from her purse.

"Let's make a list." Ali made a line down the middle of the notebook page.

Kate groaned. "Not the list!"

Ali's go to for solving all problems in life had always been and remained with "THE LIST." She made one for every life choice she ever faced. Soon after they became best friends, Ali forced the practice onto Kate. The list had two columns, one labeled GOOD, the other BAD.

"Good reasons for staying in Arizona?" Ali held her pen at the ready.

"I already live there." Kate grinned.

Ali glared at Kate, but wrote it down because with the list, you wrote everything down. "Now, something less obvious." Ali raised an eyebrow.

Kate slouched in the bench. "I don't know." She rolled the paper napkin into a tube.

With a beaming smile, Faye delivered the diet Coke with a lemon and lemon water. "I'm so happy to see you gals."

"Thank you, Faye." Ali grinned but kept her eyes on the list.

Kate removed the straw from its white paper wrapper. "I have a great job in Arizona and I would need to land a new one here."

"Great." Ali scribbled in the both columns and then removed the end of her straw's wrapper, twisting the remaining end.

"Let's move onto the other column, maybe it will help with exploring both sides." Ali placed the straw in her mouth and blew the wrapper. It hit Kate right in the middle of her left cheek.

"Immature," Kate stated. No matter how stiff Ali came off, Kate knew that her fun side always popped through. The unexpected laughs she provided reminded Kate of what a great best friend Ali was.

"No distinct seasons. I've grown bored with my job. I don't feel alive." Kate twisted her empty straw wrapper around her pointer finger.

"These are great." Ali reviewed the list. "Not great, great. You know what I mean."

"Arizona doesn't have Ox," Kate whispered, immediately taking another sip of water.

"Thank you for admitting that before I had to drag it out of you."

Lacing her fingers together, Kate grinned and batted her eyelashes. "But Arizona has my best friend."

Ali closed the notebook. Her eyes wandered and her lips formed a frown. She sighed. Kate leaned forward. "What?"

"I'm moving." Ali feared Kate's reaction.

"I'm guessing it's not here to Washington."

Ali shook her head. "The branch wants to open another corporate office and they want me to run it."

Kate reached her hands out and took hold of Ali's. "That's amazing! Congratulations! I'm so happy for you."

Ali squeezed Kate's hands and then retracted her hands from Kate's and wrapped them around her notebook. She fanned the pages. "It's in Shanghai."

The smile on Kate's face fell like melted butter. "Shanghai? The city over the ocean? The other side of the world?"

Ali nodded.

"That's a huge decision. Not to mention a completely different culture and lifestyle. And, might I reiterate, on, the, other, side, of, the … ocean!"

"It's been overwhelming trying to decide."

Faye approached, placing the lunch plates in front of them. "Let me know if you gals need anything else."

Ali lifted the bun off the burger and added a copious amount of ketchup. She placed the burger back together, raised it to her mouth and took a huge bite. Ketchup oozed onto her manicured nails. Kate followed next by cracking the top of her pot pie with her fork; creamy chicken sauce poured out and steam rose to her grinning face.

"Don't eat that without blowing on it. You always burn your tongue," Ali warned Kate.

"Yes, Mom." They laughed and shared a smile.

"It's great seeing you happy, Kate."

"I am." Kate took a bite of pot pie. "Ouch, owww."

"I warned you." Ali raised her right eyebrow sarcastically.

Kate fanned her tongue with her hand. "I know you've already made up your mind about Shanghai."

"I have not. I've only kind of decided." Ali shoved a heap of ketchup-covered French fries into her mouth.

Kate rested her fork on the plate. "We've been best friends for how many years, eight or nine? You have always been full of adventure, especially regarding your career path. Your love of flying is the polar opposite of mine. Your career is the love of your life, climbing the ladder and doing new things, bold things."

"And you want a picturesque house with a white picket fence and a family who travels the states in a Winnebago." Ali sipped her diet Coke.

Kate smiled and attempted to keep from burning her tongue on a second bite of pot pie with a few blows. "You're right, I'm not happy in Arizona, but I can't base a move on a guy, let alone a guy I just met. I don't know if he likes me or if he wants a family. I know nothing about him, other than I'm completely and utterly falling for him faster than an anvil after a coyote." Kate rested her head back on the booth. "I'm so in over my head, Ali."

"Have you asked?" Ali took another bite of her now half-devoured cheeseburger.

"I can't just ask Ox that. He is nice one minute and then the next he turns into this stand-off man. Plus, something is going on with Ox. Maggie clearly knows what it is, but I'm not in on their secret. I can feel it; they are hiding something."

"Do you want me to ask for you?" Ali flipped her phone back over and checked the time. "I'm swinging by the inn anyway to drop you off."

"No, Ali, thank you. Do I need to remind you about Ethan from last year?"

"You dated two Ethans last year."

"Ethan R."

"Was he the one that cheated on you or suddenly decided he didn't want a relationship?"

"Suddenly disappeared, same thing as didn't want a relationship in my book. See, if it's meant to be, it will be. Oh gosh, listen to me. We aren't even dating. Had my parents been home, none of this would be happening. See? Plane trips are bad."

"Well, Ox is Ox, not Ethan one or two. Focus on the list."

For as long as Kate had known Ali, she had never been the type to need a relationship. Even in college, Kate could count on one hand the boyfriends Ali had.

"Kate, we've talked about this. You have the family and the babies. I'll spoil them with gifts, from a distance."

Kate nodded her head. "Speaking of your so-called work babies, what is this business trip for anyways?"

"The company wants to show me around the new office and where I would be living." Ali held her hand up in defense. "I didn't decide until my flight landed in Seattle today that this is something I want to do. So don't jump down my throat about not telling you."

"Without seeing it first?" Kate asked between bites of pot pie. "That's not like you at all, Ali."

"My list was strong." Ali winked. "The whole thing has invigorated my mind and my heart. Maybe I read too many self-empowerment books, but there is something about finding a career and life outside of what I'm used to." Ali turned her face toward the window, as though she could see her future outside.

"Are you scared?" Kate asked. "Even thinking of moving back home causes me anxiety."

Reaching into her purse, Ali removed a baby wipe, cleaning her ketchup-covered fingers. "I'll admit, I'm scared."

"That they won't have ketchup?" Ali rolled her eyes, her lips in a straight line.

"No, because it's a big step, even for me. I'm not moving to another state, but to a whole different country and an entirely new culture."

"I wish I could be you." Kate held her hands together in a fist, willing the anxiety to stay at bay.

"I wish you could be okay being you. Kate, you know the answer already, list or no list, you know. Don't let your self-made hurdles hold you back. Ox or not, this is home for you, and I promise to visit you whenever I get the chance. I don't expect you to get on a plane and fly over the water, but I expect you to be a better you." Ali took a sip of soda. "To be you."

Kate leaned back in the bench, and Ali did the same. True friendships are honest and awakening. True best friends push each other to be their best just as Ali always did.

"What will I do with you so many miles away?" Kate frowned. Hopelessness seemed to fill the air around her.

"It's not final yet, but it's five thousand, seven hundred miles, give or take five miles." Ali smirked. "We will do what we always do, only with modifications. I'll even allow video chatting while we munch on popcorn and watch movies. Think of all the great new recipes I can try and then share with you!"

They reached out and held hands. Tears filled both of their eyes. They were tears of anxiety, happiness, and new experiences. Ali's visit shocked energy into Kate, and she knew Ali was right.

"Give me my list." Kate provided a weak smile.

Ali tore the page from her notebook and handed it to Kate. "Start by doing something new."

Kate sighed. "Ox's plane."

Chapter Thirteen

Kate's best friend stopping by for a surprise visit could not have come at a better time. Thank goodness for unplanned visits. Ox used his cane to lower himself onto the bed. Every muscle in his body was either stiff or tingled with numbness.

Yesterday his weakness had been off and on, but today as the day wore on, it punched deep in body and radiated through it.

"Here." Maggie entered Ox's room with a bowl of soup resting on a platter. She placed it on the nightstand for him.

"Maggie, please don't wait on me. You're a guest." Ox snatched the slice of sourdough bread from the platter and struggled to tear off a bite.

"Don't you dare boss me around, young man." Maggie raised her eyebrow at him and sat at the edge of his bed. "You need to rest today. I wish you would tell Kate what is going on with you. She was worried enough yesterday to ask me."

"You didn't …"

Maggie raised her right hand. "No, I didn't say anything, but you need to."

"Kate is a guest and nothing more. The only reason why you know about my MS is because you are a nosy lady who relentlessly seeks out the truth until her victims cave in." Ox grinned.

Maggie grinned back. "Nothing wrong with being nosy to learn the truth. The truth is: you need to tell Kate. Who, by the way, is more than a guest. I can see it in your eyes."

"She can't be."

"Eat your soup, Ox. That way you can't talk back as I give you advice." Maggie stood, handing him the spoon.

Ox moaned in disagreement but his stomach could not argue. He scooped some soup into his spoon and blew on it.

"The right woman for you will not care about your diagnosis. In fact, the right woman would be downright upset that you are acting like such a fool about it. If your parents were still here, they would say the same thing."

Ox set his spoon down and petted the top of Bayou's head. "Would they, Maggie? I wonder how different life would be if they were still alive." Ox's eyes scanned his room, ending on the view out the window. The memory of the police officer standing on the front porch, his hands sliding in and out of his pockets, solemness etched across his face. Ox had ridden in the passenger seat of the patrol car, the blue and red lights flashing without the sirens as it rushed him to his parents' bedsides. He had insisted the nurses move their beds together so they could hold hands. They were both in a coma, so Ox linked their fingers together knowing they would have wanted it that way.

Ox refocused on today. "However, regardless of them being here or not, my diagnosis would be the same."

"Yes, but they might knock some sense into you about Kate." Maggie crossed her arms. "Ox, I see the way you two gaze at each other. I see how the world around you fades from your eyes. Even Bayou is already falling for her."

Ox chuckled and tilted his head at Bayou, who could care less as drool formed waiting for a scrap of sourdough to come his way.

"Maggie, I wish I knew how to approach Kate with the diagnosis." Ox shook his head. "No, what am I thinking? I cannot be in a relationship, not now or ever. The disease might be at a standstill, but I'm not getting better."

"What about the second medication?"

"I don't want to be disappointed. If it doesn't work, I'm out of options."

Maggie pointed at Ox's soup. "Eat up and listen to me. First, you are not dying, not even close. Second, medication is not your final option. Research will continue and new prevention through those studying it in the field will come about too. What if you had joined the Army and returned without your leg? Would that change your dreams?"

Ox's lips parted in contemplation. "I've never thought of it that way."

"Love is love. It sounds as cheesy as mozzarella, but it's one hundred percent true. Love will overcome anything and everything if it's strong enough. With Stan, it was true. We met late in our lives, when I had given up on finding love after my divorce, and I was stubborn. Stan had his work cut out for him."

Ox took a few sips of soup and ate some bread. "And after all that you are ..." Ox stopped himself. He didn't need to bring up the obvious.

"Yes, Ox, I'm a widow, but I wouldn't change a thing, even if I knew I would lose him again. Even through the pain, I hold the memories close to my heart. I can say my life is complete having loved a man like Stan, and having him love me. Don't allow the problem to cause a burden." Her eyes filled with tears.

Ox handed Maggie a tissue from his nightstand, and she used it without hesitation. He didn't know what to say to make her feel better, so he finished his soup. For a long time, the room remained still.

"Maggie, it goes beyond love. I have to worry about how to support a family. Look at me." Ox pointed to himself. "I own an inn. I can't run it from bed. You understand and put up with it because it's not too bad right now, but what about when this happens more often? What if my bad days grow from once or twice a week to five days a week?"

Maggie stood and observed the photos on Ox's wall. "That's exactly why you should allow love to happen. Love is supportive. Love will carry you through all the downs."

"Love is not always roses, Maggie."

She turned to Ox and let out a long breath. "Right, Ox. It's not always perfect and happy, but nothing is, not even Bayou. Remember when you first brought him home, and he was puppy bonkers? Stan and I were here and saw him chew through an entire table leg. We had to eat with TV trays until you got a new table. Now, Ox, you loved him just the same, even on his bad days."

Ox sighed and let out a chuckle thinking about the pile of shredded table leg and Bayou's clueless face about what he did wrong. "Maggie, I get your point, but Bayou is a dog, not a wife."

"Tell that to the dog who hogs half your bed and steals your sheets." Maggie pointed to Bayou sprawled out on what was clearly his side of the king-size bed. "Please, Ox, think about what I'm saying. I know your parents would agree with me."

Maggie took the empty bowl and platter from Ox. "Great love is important, regardless of how long it lasts, and everyone needs to experience it. Everyone deserves it. Remember, the neurologist has not suspended your pilot's license."

"I know." Ox shifted in bed. Maggie had a point for sure. If the MS affected him enough, he would be grounded from flying.

Maggie nodded her head and winked before she made her way to the bedroom door. When the door shut, he sank down lower into his bed. His thoughts on Maggie's words and his heart wrapped up in thoughts of Kate.

Chapter Fourteen

The next morning, sitting on the edge of her bed, Kate applied her lavender oil and slid on the motion sickness wristbands. She took a swig of water to wash down the Dramamine.

"You got this," Kate whispered. "You can do this."

A thud, low and firm, smacked on her door. Then instantly, whap, whap, whap, whap. Kate stood and walked over, opening the door to see Bayou raising his paw for another smack. He wedged his body through the door's crack, pivoted, and sat on top of Kate's feet.

She bent down, petting his head. "Thanks, Bayou, but you're squishing my toes."

Ox peeked his head around the corner of the doorframe. "You both ready?"

"Not particularly," she replied, "Hey, doesn't Bayou get motion sickness?"

"No!" Ox yelled already heading back down the hall.

Kate began trembling by the time Ox pulled the truck into the hangar just off the airport runway. Kate kept fidgeting in the seat in hopes of keeping Ox from noticing.

"Walk around the plane with me," Ox instructed, climbing out of the truck.

He opened the truck's rear door. Bayou leapt down into a pile of snow that had been shoveled off the main entrance. Kate and Bayou followed Ox as he ran through his pre-flight checklist which took about ten minutes.

"I filled it up with gas after my last flight, so we are set to go."

Ox popped open the plane's door and Bayou put his paws on the bottom of the frame.

"Why are the controls on the wrong side of the plane?"

"It's the right side, don't worry. It's the opposite of cars on some small planes. One, two, three." Ox lifted Bayou's back end level with the bottom of the door and eased him onto the plane's floor.

Bayou climbed up onto a small pale blue seat behind the two front seats, a pro in his natural habitat.

"He really has a thing about only getting in on the driver's side of everything, doesn't he?" Kate followed Ox around the plane to the other side.

"He has been that way since I brought him home. I guess I don't even think about it anymore." Ox held out his hand to Kate. "Did you need me to count for you too? One, two, three."

She faked a laugh and using Ox's hand for leverage as she placed one foot into the plane, she boosted herself up. Kate slid into the seat as though she had done it a thousand times before. Ox latched the door closed.

"I'm okay. I feel great," Kate whispered, as Ox started up the plane. Bayou leaned forward, placing the tip of his chin on her shoulder.

"Good boy," Ox said, sliding on his aviator sunglasses. "You keep Kate calm. Here, put this on." He handed her a split-pea green headset.

After placing it over her ears, she took one deep breath after another, but it didn't help at all. Her heart thumped so loud she thought it might break a rib.

"I've changed my mind." Kate's body went rigid in the seat. "I can't do this. I'm about to hyperventilate."

"I have never crashed a plane yet," Ox smirked and

glanced at her. "Not a good time for jokes?"

"I can't do this," she said louder than before. Kate could feel Bayou's chin pressing firmer onto her shoulder.

"Three minutes, Kate. You can even time me."

With shaky hands, Kate pulled her cell phone from her front jacket pocket. She scrolled through the apps to find the timer. *A perfect distraction.*

"Once the wheels lift off the runway, hit start." Ox flipped switches and spoke into his headset.

Bayou's breath was warm on the back of Kate's ear. She twisted her arm back, awkwardly patting his head. Kate gazed down the path of the runway, and her trembling increased. Sweat formed around the line of curls on her forehead and her teeth clenched. Ox reached his hand over and placed it on her knee, only making her heart race more.

"You can do this," Ox calmly said into the headset.

Kate picked up Ox's hand from her knee and placed it back onto what she imagined was the steering controller. Ox laughed.

"You need both your hands. Focus on your job," she sneered. "Not killing us."

She reached for her seat belt, a three-point harness contraption, and tightened the straps. *I can do this. I can do this.*

The plane sped up, the force pushing Kate snug into her seat. She wrapped her left hand around one of the harness straps, her right hand held the cell phone. The plane swayed left to right, the wheels no longer touching the runway. Kate's stomach dropped for a second as though she were floating up in her seat. With a trembling finger, she pushed start on the phone timer.

Treetops appeared outside the windshield as they climbed higher into the air.

"This seems high enough," Kate shouted into the headset.

Bayou took his left paw and placed it over Kate's arm, his

bottom barely on the back seat. Ox banked the plane to the left as they started to circle around the outside of the airport.

I'm good. I feel great. Kate stared down at the timer. One minute had passed. Two to go. *I'm okay.*

"Look at the view, Kate. It's amazing on such a clear day." Ox nodded at the side window.

Even with the plane leaning, Bayou kept his weight on Kate's shoulder and his paw in the crook of her arm. She caught a peek out of the window and had to admit it was a beautiful view. The sun had melted all the snow from the tree branches but it remained on the ground in patches. With one hand firmly gripping the seat belt, she used her other hand to swipe up to the phone's camera. She snapped a picture before returning to the timer. One minute to go.

Ox leveled the plane back out and Kate could see the run-way coming into view. He radioed the tower for permission to land.

The plane dropped lower to the ground, the timer read thirty seconds. The view of treetops turned into tree middles. Tires skipped onto the runway as they bounced in their seats. The plane slowed to the speed of a car in a neighborhood. The timer beeped at zero.

"Perfect timing!" Ox cheered, turning the plane toward the hangar.

Bayou lifted his paw and head off Kate's shoulder where it had been for a solid three minutes.

"I'm proud of you." Ox patted her shoulder. "You did it! Wonderful view and you made it through. We will do five minutes next time."

"Next time?" she shrieked. "No, I gave you three minutes."

"The only way to overcome your fear is with practice. Don't you want to travel the world?"

"No, I'm perfectly fine seeing what I can by car, thank you."

Ox brought the airplane to a stop. "You have to fill your remaining days here with something fun, why not do both?"

"Both?"

"Fun and fear conquering. What else will you do with your five remaining days?"

"Enjoy being on land."

"Think about it. We have the pie contest tomorrow, but otherwise we have plenty of time."

Kate didn't want to admit that although petrifying, the plane trip had not been too terrible. She scrolled through the few photos she took. She was able to enjoy them better from a grounded plane.

Suddenly, it dawned on Kate that she brought her expensive Canon camera. The plan was to take photos at her parents' place and around town. For some reason it slipped her mind. She could get some amazing shots from up in the air, as long as she could control her shaking. In February, *Photography Life* magazine held its annual photo contest. She thought about entering if she managed to capture something worthwhile on vacation. Her local road trips never provided anything too spectacular.

"For someone who hates planes, you sure don't want to get out of them." Ox stood with the door open, his hand out.

Lost in the photos on her phone's camera roll, Kate didn't notice Ox getting out of the plane or hear the door open.

"My mind was elsewhere." Kate took his hand to step out.

"And where is that?"

Scanning the area for Bayou, she located him rubbing his nose back and forth in the snow. "There is a photo contest for *Photography Life* magazine every year. I have never entered it before. I thought about entering this year, so I brought my Canon."

"You have a Canon, and you're taking pictures with your

cell phone?" Ox laughed, locking up the hangar.

"When you have a cell phone, like a normal person," Kate stated, "you forget that actual cameras exist."

"Even if you bring them with you on vacation?" Ox jabbed her with his elbow.

"Yes, smart aleck." Kate jabbed him back.

"Smart aleck? Did we step back in time? Is this the nineties again? Now, take my arm," Ox said. "We don't need you slipping and falling."

Without hesitation, Kate wrapped her arm around his, slightly tighter and closer than needed. "What is your biggest pet peeve?"

Ox's eyes narrowed, pulling the thought from somewhere deep. "Fake garlic seasoning. It's fresh from the clove or don't bother."

"Oh yes, that's a good one."

"And yours?"

"Fake snow in movies and television shows. I know budgets can be tight, but with high definition televisions you notice immediately."

"Really?" Ox's face twisted.

"Yes, that's why books are the best. No fake snow."

Ox's smile spread beyond his face to his heart. He could actually feel it warming. They headed back to the truck with Bayou squeezing between their legs.

Chapter Fifteen

Kate bent down, snapping several photos of Bayou as he leaned back into the perfect lab sloppy sit.

"I thought you were helping me with the pie," Ox said impatiently.

"Just a few pictures of Bayou won't affect the pie making."

Kate stood, placing the camera on the counter. Doubt about the green tomato pie beginning a winning idea filled her mind.

"This time, I'm in charge of the timer." Ox washed the green tomatoes.

Kate crossed her arms and sighed. "I said I was sorry. Maybe I'm bad luck."

"I know." Ox grinned.

"What does that mean?" Kate's body recoiled as her jaw clenched.

"You're not bad luck, but I will not let you live it down."

"What time do we need to have this pie ready?"

"Winter Wonder Day opens at ten a.m., but the judges must have the pies submitted by two p.m."

"Why do they have a festival in the dead of winter?" Kate sliced the tomatoes, a quarter of an inch thick and placed them into the bowl for Ox to add the spices.

"As you remember, while it often drops below freezing, it does not normally snow to the degree it has been this week. I think the festival is about getting the residents out for a bit, breaking their cabin fever, snow or no snow."

"True, when you've been held up inside it's nice to have an excuse to finally get out."

"I was wondering," Ox sprinkled the cinnamon in and said, "if you wanted to drop the pie off early and then walk around at the festival."

Kate stirred the tomatoes, gently folding the spices together. "I'd like that actually, viewing the town from land. I could get some great shots with my camera too."

"You did well in the plane, Kate, honestly. Next time five minutes."

"That's still up for debate." Kate held up a finger.

"Why do you hate flying?" Ox's eyes narrowed.

"I'm not going to tell you. I don't need you laughing." Kate's lips turned down, her shoulders hunched over.

"Don't be stubborn. Something must have happened to create your fear."

Kate breathed in through her nose, her nostrils shrunk in at the sides.

"Fine. When I was," Kate gazed forward, "four or five years old, my parents decided it would be a grand idea to go on a trip to Minnesota. My mom's sister and her family live there."

Ox pinched the pie crust around the edges of the dish.

"We got on the plane, and I know it seems odd that I remember all this being so young, but it's as though it happened last week."

Ox's vision focused, his lips parted in anticipation of the story.

"My mom packed everything I needed, crayons, coloring books, toys, my favorite doll and blanket. Dad snuck me a few chocolates. I even had the wings from the pilot."

"Everything sounds like a great trip."

Kate held up her hand. "Yes, until the turbulence hit. I

didn't know the word at the time; I called it 'the bumps.'"

Ox chuckled and swiftly covered his mouth, his eyes still giving his laughter away.

"The turbulence lasted for what seemed like hours, felt like hours." Kate rubbed her hand on her arm, half hugging herself at the thought. "Everyone around us was puking and crying, and then I started puking and crying."

Kate's heart raced. Ox reached for Kate, his hand on her arm.

"I thought that plane would never land. I thought we were going to die." Kate's voice cracked as the emotions came roaring back.

Ox continued to rub his fingers on Kate's arm as she started to tremble. "You landed and you are here, everything worked out, you're okay."

Kate turned her head toward Ox. "But I didn't know that as a kid. I knew I was scared. I knew I wanted to get off the plane and never get back on one ever again."

"You did though, Kate. You got on one, and you came here." Ox took both of Kate's hands in his. "Plus, you got on my plane. You did it, and you will continue to improve and overcome your fears."

"Ox, I did it because I had Bayou. I did it because I knew it would only be three minutes. A real flight doesn't take three minutes."

"You can build on that and work on it." Ox smiled. "That's what Bayou and I can help you with."

Kate's smile lasted half a second before her eyes squinted and her lips frowned. "It's easy for you to say. You love flying. You're a pilot."

"I didn't always like flying."

Kate's eyes widened. "What?"

"My father used to take me up in his little single engine

as a child all the time. In Alaska, the only way to get around was by plane. If we needed to go anywhere important, say to see the doctor or go clothes shopping, we had to do it by plane. I remember timing him from takeoff to landing. It helped soothe my nervousness."

"That does not sound like the same level of fear I have."

"You're right, but there were other fears living in Alaska that I had to overcome. Together they all added up to what you deal with for flying."

Kate rested her hands on the mixing bowl's rim. "I don't believe you, but I appreciate the effort to make me feel better."

"At nine years old, I had a bear chase me."

"What?"

"That was the day I discovered I was a pretty fast runner." Ox chuckled.

Kate laughed. "Okay, I don't have that fear. What changed with the flying? What caused your fear to end?"

"Practice, plain and simple. I kept going up with my father every opportunity I had, working on positive self-talk. I would ask myself questions about the plane's safety and then answer them. I used to lie in bed and remind myself that flying was the safest form of travel. I wanted to see the world and the only way to do that was by plane. Talk about self-talk! You would have thought I had an imaginary friend in my room."

Ox laughed and Kate joined in, envisioning Ox as a kid giving himself a pep talk.

Kate poured the pie filling into the pie plate. "Did you ever experience turbulence?"

"In the summer time mostly."

Kate jumped in with her well-studied knowledge. "The air temperature is always different from the ground temperature. However, in the summer months there is a greater distance between the two temperatures and therefore more turbulence."

"Especially in a tiny plane," Ox added.

Kate's face twisted.

"Sorry, no, I mean it's not bad in a little plane. Actually, planes like mine never have turbulence."

Kate smacked Ox's arm. "I'm afraid of flying. I'm not stupid."

"How is the pie coming?" Maggie stepped into the kitchen.

Kate sprang back into her circle of personal space.

"Looks great," Maggie offered, while Ox and Kate were still clearing their thoughts.

"It actually doesn't look half bad." Ox placed the pie into the oven. "Maggie, will you be joining us at the festival?"

"My back has been bugging me some, so I think I will stay here and work on the sweater I'm knitting."

"Can I bring you back anything from there?" Ox asked.

"If they have any kettle corn, I'd love a fresh bag."

"It would be my pleasure." Ox smiled.

Bayou strolled over and dropped two tennis balls at Kate's feet. "What's this buddy? We are inside, we can't play fetch inside."

"That's where you are wrong Kate; we most certainly can play fetch inside."Ox reached down and grabbed the balls off the floor.

He backed up as Bayou remained standing next to Kate.

"Ready, Bayou?" Ox asked, as he tossed one ball underhanded toward the dog.

Bayou's front two legs leapt up as he snatched the ball from the air. He instantly dropped it just as Ox released the other ball underhanded. Bayou caught it with his slight leap. Then, he dropped the ball from his mouth.

Ox walked over, picked up the two tennis balls and backed up again.

"What's going on? This doesn't look like fetch. Bayou is not even moving from his spot."

"It's Bayou's version of fetch. Dad fetch." Ox chuckled.

Kate giggled. "If we're leaving soon, I better go get ready and leave you two to Dad fetch."

Kate hurried up the stairs. Pausing, she turned around, hand on the railing. "Besides, I want to be as far away from the pie as possible. We don't need a repeat."

Ox and Kate caught each other in a glance. Shy smiles glided across their faces, and Kate's smile stamped in Ox's thoughts. He tossed Bayou many more rounds of fetch with Kate distracting his mind and a smile plastered on his face.

Chapter Sixteen

Kate reminded herself not to fall for Ox. Not only did she live in another state, but she had only known him a mere five days. Plus, the biggest factor, he was a pilot, and she wanted nothing to do with flying. Besides, he didn't even own a computer. *Does he even have a cell phone?* Now that Kate thought about it, she had never seen him with one. *A business owner without a cell phone, how is that possible?* She chuckled aloud about the whole thing.

Sure, he matched everything Kate wanted in a man. He had a nice build and gorgeous eyes. He made her laugh, and he knew his way around a kitchen and the garage. A dog had not been something Kate thought about until she met Bayou. Now, she would add it to the list of things she wanted in a relationship for sure. Dog Dad. Had she unknowingly created one of Ali's lists in her mind? If so, the good column was rather full.

Smiling, she weaved the comb through her curls. Next, she added mascara and lip gloss to her look. She felt just dressed up enough to come across spiffier than this morning, but not overly dressed for a festival.

Today's forecast meant she would need a scarf, which was back in the trash at Sea-Tac. She wrapped herself in her deep cherry red jacket, zipping it up as high as it would allow. Hopefully, they would have some outside heaters spread about. Sliding her gloves into her pocket, she headed downstairs.

Kate entered the kitchen to find Ox pulling the green tomato pie from the oven.

"Smells good," she said.

"It does, doesn't it?" Ox agreed.

When Ox glanced up from the pie, he was reminded once again of Kate's beauty. Heat rushed to his cheeks. "You look …"

Kate tried not to blush at Ox's flushed face, clearly giving away his thoughts.

While Ox had called her beautiful earlier, she was still taken aback by his embarrassment. It had been over six months since her last date and none of the men acted as infatuated as Ox. Actually, all of her dates were more like roommates hanging out at a restaurant. Dating had not been Kate's strong suit. Besides the Ethans, she'd struck out for so many different reasons she had lost count.

"I'm going to get ready while this cools," Ox stammered. "Then we can head out." He fled the room in a great effort to keep from staring at Kate.

She made her way into the living room, remembering to watch the step this time. Maggie had fallen asleep in the armchair. Her knitting rested in her lap, her fingers still on the needles. The television off, only the sound of the fireplace crackling filled the room.

Kate viewed the living room from a new perspective knowing that Ox had a hand in building it. The view from the oversized rectangular windows remained breathtaking, even without the falling snow. A heavy forest spread in the distance, traces of snow painted here and there. Yet, in the backyard, the snow remained deep, untouched by the sun. Her inner-child called out for a snowball fight and snowman making.

"Are you thinking what I'm thinking?" Ox whispered from behind Kate.

She clutched her hand to her chest. "You startled me."

"Sorry, didn't want to wake Maggie."

"What are you thinking?" Kate whispered, pivoting

toward Ox.

She spied Bayou waiting at the edge of the living room step.

"Snow angels. Isn't that what women want to hear?"

Kate smacked Ox's arm. "Say what you want to say, not what you think you should say."

Ox over exaggerated the pain, clutching his arm as he mouthed, "Ouch!"

"Snowball fight," Ox whispered.

"Nothing above the neck."

They eyed each other and then walked as quickly and quietly as possible to the front door, both trying to make it there first. Bayou joined in the fun.

The three of them bolted around the side of the inn. Ox took cover behind a young Douglas fir and Kate behind a bare Maple. Bayou remained at Ox's side.

"I'm already outnumbered!" Kate gathered snow and started forming snowballs.

"Bayou doesn't have opposable thumbs, he doesn't count!"

Kate made a good stack of snowballs in a short time.

"On the count of three," Ox shouted. "One, two, three."

She heard Ox rise in the snow and a snowball smacked the Maple tree trunk. But she remained crouched down.

"I said three, Kate!"

"Yes, the prefect warning count!" Kate sprang up and fired two snowballs in a row at Ox.

Bayou barked as the snowballs flew between them. They moved closer with each throw. Kate had run out of premade snowballs and reached for handfuls of snow to toss. She waded through the thick snow, laughing as she tried to stand up but could not.

Ox reached out for her, as they stumbled forward, tangled up with Bayou who attempted to save them. Their laughter filled the late morning air. They lay in the snow sprawled out, gasping for breaths between the laughter.

"We should probably get to the festival," Kate reminded Ox.

"Bayou is busy making a dog angel, we should wait."

Bayou rubbed his chin against the snow, then his face against it, massaging left and right. He flipped onto this side and wiggled his back end like a fish at sea.

Kate moved her arms and legs in and out. She lifted her head to find Ox doing the same thing, with Bayou in the middle still wiggling around.

They made two snow angels and one dog angel. Kate rested her head and stared up at the white cotton clouds as they drifted above, her body and mind happy. *Sure, I'm on vacation, but this is beyond vacation happiness, beyond rest and relaxation.* With her soul comfortable, a smile came instantly and easily, creativity filled her thoughts.

She closed her eyes and breathed in nature's peace. Hearing boots crunching in the snow, she opened one eye.

Ox hovered over Kate and reached his hand down.

"No, I don't want to go," she whined.

"Yes, you do," Ox insisted. "We have a contest to win."

Kate stretched her hand up to Ox and allowed him to lift her to a standing position. As they brushed the snow from their clothes, a knock from above caught their attention. Maggie stood at the window, waving with a smile. They waved back before making their way inside the inn.

After changing out of their snow dampened clothes, Kate and Ox once again met downstairs.

"Don't forget this," Maggie said, handing Kate her Canon.

"I hope we didn't wake you, Maggie." Ox draped plastic wrap over the pie.

"Don't apologize," Maggie said. "Do you need me to watch Bayou?"

"No, I thought he could come with us," Ox remarked.

"Why don't I watch him, give you two sometime to focus on the contest. The last thing you need is Bayou eating his way through the festival."

"Thank you, I'd appreciate it," Ox said.

"Come on, Bayou, let's go watch a movie and have a bone." Maggie tapped her leg. Bayou trotted toward Maggie, accepting her offer.

"Let's do this." Ox held the pie firmly in his hands and shot a wink to Kate.

Chapter Seventeen

"I think the timing of the Winter Wonder Day is perfect," Ox said, hunching forward and taking in the view out the front windshield. "Those clouds are substantial; maybe another storm is rolling in."

"Another one? So soon?"

Back to back snowstorms didn't happen in Washington, at least not that Kate could recall. A second storm coming at just the right time might mean she could delay her trip back home a little longer. It would give her more time to think, sort out her thoughts some more. And, as a bonus, not have to get on a plane. If only her parents were here, she could talk to them in person. Talking over the phone would only cause her mom to have an attack of questions and what-ifs.

"Thinking about something?" Ox switched on his turn signal. "You seem more distracted than normal."

"I do?" Kate's brow lifted.

Ox nodded his head as he turned onto the main road.

"Have you ever stepped back from something and realized it was not what you thought?" Kate asked. "Or that you were willing to give up something stable for something that made you happy? Even if it involved a huge risk?"

Ox wrinkled his face. "I don't think it's easy for everyone. In fact, it might be rare. I struggle with it myself. Each day is its own. It's important to move past yesterday and focus on today."

Kate thought about her move to Arizona. It had been a get out of Dodge or bust type situation. Then she grew stuck in her ways, fear setting in as a normal emotional default. And, if she dared to upset her defaults, it would spike her anxieties. Yet comfort doesn't equal happiness, nor does it mean stability. Coming back home would mean starting over. It would be a do-over, far from simple. In fact, moving back might not be the answer to finding her happiness.

"What brought you here for vacation?" Ox braked at the light.

Kate pressed her hands around the pie plate. "Deep down I needed a break from work and wanted to talk to my parents about my job. Plus, I wanted to prove to myself I could get on a plane."

"Is there a problem with your job?" Ox asked.

"No," Kate sighed, "Yes. I mean, it's a great job, but it's not me. Every time I approach my office building it's as though an elephant came and sat on my chest. There is this crushing anxiety in my chest."

"African or Asian?" Ox grinned.

Kate rolled her eyes at his attempt at a joke. "They are both large elephants."

Ox laughed. "Sorry." He turned the radio on, low and soft, the sounds of a piano and guitar filtered elegantly through the speakers.

Kate rested her head back on the seat. For the first time in a long time, she told herself not to worry about any of her thoughts. She hummed along to the radio. The green tomato pie, the bottom still slightly warm, rested in her lap.

After parking, Ox and Kate navigated their way to the judging area for the pie contest. Kate carried the pie with both hands, the remaining heat keeping her hands warm through her gloves. According to the morning weather report, it would only warm up to about thirty-five degrees. The piles of leftover snow and their chilly breaths reminded them winter was far from over in Washington.

As they turned the corner, Kate's right boot started to slide on a patch of black ice. Her hands squeezed the glass pie dish, as she saw her entire life flash before her eyes, or at least the entire pie's life. She shifted her weight to her left foot hoping to keep balanced. Ox grabbed hold of her arm, keeping Kate's body upright. They froze, rooted to their spots, both fearing to move until they knew the pie was safe.

"Why don't I carry that?" Ox snatched the pie from Kate.

"Probably best." Kate's teeth clenched.

They reached the judging tent, and Ox handed the green tomato pie to the gentleman with the clipboard. Ox filled out the baker's information on a card. As Kate leaned near his shoulder, she noticed he put both of their names down as the bakers.

"Why did you add my name?" she questioned.

"Because we're a team." Ox handed the card to the gentleman. "The type of pie was your idea and you assisted making it, seems only fair to list you as well."

Kate blushed. "Thanks."

"And that way if I lose, I can blame you." Ox flashed a wicked smile.

"Hey." Kate grabbed his arm.

Ox used this opportunity to his advantage and took Kate's hand, wrapping it around the crook in his arm. They strolled down the path; festival booths lined both sides with their worn white canopy tops. Kate recalled the July Fourth Festival, August's Blueberry Festival, and September's Apple Festival from her childhood. The rest of the year, the grounds remained empty awaiting the crowds.

One booth offered fuzzy teddy bears for knocking over snowman painted cans. Local honey and homemade chocolate-covered nuts occupied a following stand. The sweet aromas sent Kate's thoughts back to childhood and her family trips to

Leavenworth, deep within the Wenatchee National Forest. She adored the quaint town, which presented itself as though it were a town nestled into the Alps. Even as a child, she loved to visit these mini-replica towns since she knew she could never fly to see the real places. Although Winter Wonder Day was only a strip of booths, the feeling warmed her just as Leavenworth had.

"Scarves." Ox pointed and directed them to a nearby booth.

"I do need a new one. This time no tassels."

"Let me know if you're looking for something in particular," the woman behind the display offered.

Kate would guess she was in her mid-fifties. She had her long gray hair pulled into a bun and a multicolored wool sweater hung over her slender frame.

"Did you make all of these?" Kate inquired, examining each one.

"Yes, it's something to keep my hands busy in the evening," the woman replied.

"They're beautiful." Kate ran her fingers over the soft fabric.

Each one had a different pattern and color theme. They were made of a strong cotton material, yet they felt as soft as cashmere. Kate pulled one from the pile and held it up. It was as elegant as a painting. It was black at the edges, with baby blue and gray squares sprinkled throughout.

"I'll take this one." Kate reached for her wallet. "How much?"

Ox handed the woman some cash before Kate could pull out her credit card.

"You don't have to pay for my scarf," Kate stated.

"I know." Ox smiled. "Put your wallet away."

The woman handed Ox his change. Kate wrapped it around her already chilly neck.

"Thank you." Kate smiled shyly.

"You're welcome."

Ox straightened Kate's scarf mere inches this way and that, clearly without purpose. Their eyes met as Ox's hands remained on the scarf. Immediately, Kate was lost in the moment, all the noises around her disappeared into a perfect silence. As Ox's fingers rested between the scarf's folds, comfort and peace washed over her. However, Kate felt connected and lost at the same time. She felt a desire for love, yet also feared rejection.

"It's beautiful on you. It brings out the color of your hair." Ox used the scarf to draw Kate closer.

"You mean eye color?" Kate smirked.

"No, hair."

"That's the oddest comment ever, but thank you, I think."

They were so close that a filled pie dish could not slide between them. Taking a strand of Kate's hair, Ox twisted the curl around his pointer finger.

"The blue of the scarf forces the copper color of your hair to stand out."

Shivers traveled through Kate's body. *Kiss me, Ox.* In such anticipation, Kate held her breath. Ox's eyes remained lost in Kate's, his finger still wrapped gently around a curl; the other hand remained on her scarf.

A teenager on a skateboard whizzed behind them. Ox's hand moved, sliding around Kate's waist as he pushed her out of the way.

"Sorry!" the skateboarder called.

Ox stepped back and dropped his arms to his sides. Kate's heart sank with disappointment.

"Sorry about that. Teenagers." He straightened his jacket.

"Look! There's one of those 'Your Face Here' things." Kate pointed, trying to break free from her heartache.

Two booths over a wood cutout of a girl and boy snowman

held holes for people to stick their faces through.

"I'm not doing that." Ox crossed his arms.

"Come on," Kate pushed him toward the cutouts. His body was rigid and his arms remained crossed.

Kate approached a man in a puffy navy ski jacket standing at the next booth. "Excuse me, could you please take our photo?"

Kate prepared her camera and handed it to him. Ox arched his eyebrow over his right eye and dropped his arms to his side in defeat. She yanked him by the hand, as he reluctantly stuck his face through the hole of the boy snowman. Kate pushed her head through the cutout on the snowwoman.

"One, two, three," the man said. "One more, just in case."

"Thank you." Kate took her camera back from the man.

"You're a nice looking couple."

"Oh, we aren't a couple," they echoed.

"Not yet." The man smiled and walked off.

Ox took Kate's hand and wrapped it around his arm once again. "Safety first."

"Of course." Kate blushed.

They strolled forward, passing by a salmon toss game. Kate watched as a little boy tried to toss a ball into one of the bowls containing salmon instead of goldfish. *How Washington of them.* Even the prize was a plush stuffed salmon.

"Are you hungry?" Ox asked.

"I'm famished."

There were several food vendors, and their aromas filled the air with deliciousness as they approached. It had been far too many years since she enjoyed a teriyaki chicken plate. Arizona had restaurants that served it, but nothing like what she grew up with here.

"Do you think they have a teriyaki vendor?" Kate's mouth watered at the thought.

"I'm not sure, let's walk around a bit more and see if we can find one."

They passed a wood carving stand, an acrylic artwork stand, and a smoked salmon stand. Next, they passed a gourmet hot dog stand and a lobster vendor, both of which had been recently highlighted on a popular reality television show.

"If we can't find teriyaki, then we need to come back for the lobster." Kate yanked on Ox's arm for emphasis.

"Deal." Ox placed his hand on top of Kate's, still snuggled in the crook of his arm.

Then at the end of the line of booths, a banner in black writing read: TERIYAKI NOW!

Kate leaned back, stopping Ox from taking another step. She raised her free hand into the air. Triumph! Nearly yanking Ox's feet from his boots, she dragged him toward it.

"May I have a chicken teriyaki bowl with extra sesame seeds and sauce please?" Kate asked the cook.

"I'll have a Beef Yakisoba."

"And to drink?" the cook asked.

"A soda please," Ox said.

"Make that two. Lemon in mine, please."

"You like lemon in your cola?" Ox grinned.

Kate nodded her head. "I know, it's odd. My best friend, Ali, the one you met, started it. I like lemon in everything."

"Actually, it sounds refreshing." Ox smiled. "I'll have a lemon in mine as well."

As quick as a gunslinger from the old west, Ox had his cash ready.

"Let me, please." Kate shoved his hand of money out of the way.

She began to wonder if Ox owned plastic at all. *No internet, no cell phone, and no credit cards. Does he use cash to pay at the grocery store too? Maybe he's running from the law, trying to stay under the radar.* Kate shook her head and smirked to herself.

A woman appeared from inside the food truck, taking Kate's debit card. Kate waved off her receipt, slipping her card back into her wallet.

The festival had set up a few picnic tables for people to sit and enjoy their food. On a nearby stage, a solo guitarist strummed an unknown song; the sound drifted peacefully around them. Ox claimed a bench over to the side of the food truck.

With their sodas in hand, Kate approached Ox, whose vision was fixed in the distance. Kate remained silent. He appeared to be concentrating, and she didn't want to interrupt. In front of them, a forest of evergreens grew with snow-draped mountains in the background.

Kate set the sodas on the edge of the nearby table and removed the cap from her Canon. Positioning herself so she could fit Ox and the view perfectly in the shot without any festival banners proved a challenge. Leaning a bit to the left, she knelt just enough. The shutter of Kate's camera clicked as she captured each shot. They looked perfect as she took a quick glance at them through the viewfinder.

Kneeling a bit lower, Kate leaned forward to make sure she didn't catch the edge of the hot dog stand in the shot. Every time the shutter clicked, it took with it a memory from that moment. Feeling her upper body start to wobble, Kate pushed forward on her heels, but it was too late. Her bottom smacked the cold ground below as her legs shot out in front of her. Kate's arm held the camera high to protect it from hitting the ground. Thankfully, Ox was still focused on the view, and he didn't see Kate fall.

She pushed herself up off the ground, peering around. No one seemed to have noticed. Kate sighed and brushed herself off.

"It's ready," the cook called out, holding the teriyaki

containers. Already standing, Kate went to gather the meals.

"Here you go." Kate placed the container in front of Ox.

Breaking out of his thoughts, Ox's vision locked onto Kate. His eyes had depth behind them as though he were trying to peer into her soul. "Thank you for the food."

"Everything okay, Ox?"

"I had," Ox shook his head, "déjà vu. I never believed in something so ludicrous before because I've never experienced it, but I swear it just happened."

"You've never had déjà vu?" Kate popped open her teriyaki container, pouring one of the extra sauces over top.

"Never." Ox took a sip of his soda.

"I probably have déjà vu at least twice a year. What was yours about?" Kate shoved her loaded fork into her mouth. "Mmmmmmm!" The sauce was just as she remembered it.

"You," Ox stammered. "Us, this."

He opened his container and picked at his food with his the white plastic fork, then glanced back at Kate. She took a sip of soda to keep her facial expression at bay. *What does he mean, us?*

Kate could not hold back. "Really?" she asked, breaking the silence.

"Yes. This moment, here. It's as though it happened before. It's familiar. Silly when you think about it, I guess. So tell me," Ox continued picking at his food, "do you enjoy photography? Does it make you happy?"

Kate took a second bite of her teriyaki, letting the flavors linger before she spoke. "I do, and it does immensely, but it's hard to make a living solely as a photographer. I love baking to. It's all creative. It's not easy to be creative and make it sustainable."

As Kate spoke, the words caused sadness to envelope her heart. The thought of going back to work was on her mind.

"I'm lucky that I love what I do and can make a living, but you never know when life will throw you a curveball and threaten to take it all way." Ox took his first bite of food.

"Someday I will make it all work, I just don't know how yet. I always thought that with age came wisdom, but so far, it just brings more questions. It makes me feel like I'm running out of time to make my life happier. Do you agree?"

He nodded. "Time surely is slipping away."

Ox and Kate let out a collective sigh as they stared off at the pines. They shared in the silence; their container lids the only thing touching.

Chapter Eighteen

"The winners of the annual Winter Wonder Day Pie Contest will be announced in a few minutes. If you entered a pie, please make your way over to the judges' table."

The announcement came over the speakers from the nearby stage. Ox and Kate headed toward the judging table, no longer linking arms as the sun started to dip behind the trees and clouds. It was not even five p.m., but in the winter it grew dark around four in the afternoon. The sun, a rare gift in January, allowed for a bit more lingering light.

They approached the table where other contest hopefuls stood around rubbing their hands together in a desire to win or to keep warm. There were a total of six pies. Deep berry colors spilled from the edges of three pies. The three judges stood behind the table.

Kate worried after seeing the judges and the other entries that maybe green tomato pie had been too much of a stretch. The judges appeared to be true Washingtonians. None of them donned gloves or acted chilly. Kate had already grown accustomed to Arizona and, therefore, was freezing. These judges were clearly the type who preferred a spin on a traditional pie, not something bold and unusual.

"Tough decision this year, folks," one of the judges announced, his voice raised over the crowd. The other two judges nodded in agreement.

"In fact, I think this year's winner surprised us all."

A woman standing next to Ox and Kate, clapped her hands softly. "Oh, I think it's my pie," she whispered. "Apple and berries. I wanted to do something different, and I believe it worked."

Ox smiled at the woman. "Sounds delicious."

"The winner of the fifth annual Winter Wonder Day Pie Contest is …" the judge paused, "Ox and Kate for their green tomato pie."

"What?" the woman with the apple and berry pie whined. "Green tomato? That's a vegetable."

Ox snatched Kate's hand and drew her forward to the table.

"I think your pie partner helped seal the deal this year, Ox." The judge shook Ox's hand and then Kate's. Ox winked at Kate.

"Indeed." He collected the blue ribbon with a picture of a pie embossed in gold on it and the remainder of their pie.

"Ox," the judge asked. "Do you mind if I cut another piece? My mother might enjoy this."

"Of course." Ox lowered the pie plate back to the table. The judge cut a heavy slice and served it onto a paper plate.

Ox took hold of the pie dish and held his elbow out for Kate. Smiling, she slid her hand around his arm.

"Seems to be just enough for us to try." Ox beamed. "Since the trial one ended up a tad bit … smoky."

"My goodness, I've apologized." The weight of her mistake crept back into her mind.

Ox bumped against Kate. "I'm giving you crap, loosen up."

"Well, stop."

"That's not any fun." Ox's lips rose at their edges.

She loved it when Ox smiled. It's as though his smile radiated through his entire body and stretched out toward those around him. Ox led the way to his truck and opened the door for her. Once in the driver's seat, he popped open the center console and pulled out two fast food forks wrapped in plastic. Ox balanced the pie in his free hand as they each cut a bite with their forks.

"It's actually good." Glee twisted through Ox's face. "I mean, wow!"

"Told you." She grinned. "It's just as I remember." Kate licked the fork clean.

"Why weren't you taking any sunset pictures this evening?" Ox inquired.

"Sunsets are beautiful, but it's too common a picture to take. I enjoy photos that tell a story. I want to capture something that causes the viewer to pause and feel an emotion. Don't get me wrong, sunsets can tell a story, but everyone does them, and I'm not everyone."

Ox nodded his head, his lips held back a smile. "You make a good point." He shifted in his seat, turning his body toward Kate. "Have you spent time focusing on your photography or even your baking? I know we spoke about this over teriyaki, but I mean really focus."

"With work I don't have time, and when I do, I'm — well, I guess I don't feel like doing much of anything. Being here, away from work, I have more energy than I have had in Phoenix the last few years."

"Good thing you stayed then, even if nothing went as you planned." Ox handed the blue ribbon to Kate.

"It's yours, you keep it." Kate shoved it back in his direction.

"You did most of the work." Ox shoved it back.

Kate had never won anything before. Giving in, she took the ribbon, the material silky between her fingers.

"Something to remember your trip by," Ox added.

"I have plenty of memories already, far better than a

ribbon." She gazed over at him. "But thank you."

She didn't know how long she had been staring at Ox. The features of his face were sharp and rough. Kate could describe every aspect to a portrait artist.

"You have pie on your scarf." Ox's voice snapped Kate from her trance.

Glancing down, she spotted a dime-size pie crumb in one of the folds of her new scarf.

"Oh shoot, I hope it didn't ruin it." She quickly picked off the piece and brushed the scarf with her finger.

"I'm sure it's fine." Ox's voice was soft and near.

When Kate looked up, Ox had moved his face closer. His sapphire eyes held the sparkle she had seen when they first met at the airport. *Kiss me!* She placed her hand on his arm. The memory of Ox's unsteady gait interrupted her desire.

"Ox, I noticed the other day ..."

"Today has been special and great." Ox turned away. "It's been a long time."

"What has been a long time?"

Ox turned the key in the ignition as Kate's hand slid from his arm. Setting the empty pie plate in the corner of the dashboard, he put the truck in drive.

"Ox?"

He maneuvered the truck out of the parking lot and onto the main road. The streetlights lighted the way. Ox's lips parted enough that Kate waited for the reply. She needed a reply.

"The last time I felt like this," Ox finally spoke, "had this kind of connection, it only made me realize I cannot let it happen again."

"What happened, Ox?" Kate ushered.

Ox remained tight-lipped until they made their way down the side streets taking them to the inn. The drumming of Kate's fingers on her knees was the only sound.

"Let's just say it has been years, and that's how it will remain. Honestly, I should not have mentioned it." Ox pulled into the garage and shut off the truck. "I can't allow myself to be a part of a relationship. I feel that's what's happening with us. Not only do you live in another state, but I can't fall in … I can't. It's good you are leaving in a few days."

"It's good?" Kate's words cracked in pain. "You said less than a half hour ago that my staying is a good thing." Her breathing grew shallow, her chest heavy. "Now it's good that I'm leaving?"

Kate leapt from the truck, the first place ribbon floated onto the concrete below. She didn't bother to pick it up.

Bayou greeted Kate at the door. She gave him a quick pat before rushing up the stairs to her room. The English lab followed behind, taking the steps like he barreled through the snow earlier, and nosed his way through the door Kate attempted to close.

"Fine."

By the time Kate shut the door, Bayou already had his front paws up on the bed. She lifted his hind legs as he pulled himself up the rest of the way.

Kate crawled into bed and curled up, trying her best not to shed a tear over someone she met only a few days ago. *This is stupid.* She rolled over onto her back. *If my parents were here, none of this would have happened.* Kate grabbed a pillow, covered her face and let out a grunt of frustration. She contemplated calling her parents to get their advice but didn't want to bother them on vacation. Besides, her mom would hog the phone and she needed to talk to her dad, who hated using the phone. Her plan all along had been to come and have a heart to heart with her dad about her job and about how unhappy she felt. He understood her the best and would know just the right words to say to make her feel better. While her mom would tell her not to worry about it and that she needed to simply get out more and take more "me" time.

Bayou inched closer, his paws on Kate's pillow, his head on

her chest. "Your dad is stubborn."

Bayou lifted his head, whimpered, and placed it back on Kate's chest. Why had she let this happen? She should have known better. Kate ruffled the fur on Bayou's head. "Why does Ox not want to be in a relationship? Is it me?" she asked Bayou. "Listen to me! I'm going on about something that never even existed, to a dog."

Kate curled up around Bayou. "Why do I always fall so hard?" A knock at the door startled them both.

"Come in." Kate, attempting to collect herself, sat up.

Maggie leaned her head around the door. "Are you sure?"

"Yes, come in."

Maggie entered and took a seat at the edge of the bed. Bayou lowered his head with a groan. He rolled to his side, his back pressed up against Kate.

"What happened?" Maggie asked.

Her tone told Kate she could not get away with a simple "I'm fine" or "nothing's wrong.'"

"I was foolish to think something good might be happening between Ox and me." Kate drew her knees to her chest like a small child. "We had this moment where I swear he was about to kiss me and then he didn't. We were driving back here, and everything in him switched off. Actually, we almost kissed twice. "I didn't even know skateboards were popular anymore."

"Skateboards?" Maggie crossed her arms.

"A kid came by on a skateboard, interrupting what assumed I would have been a kiss."

Maggie nodded.

"And I do have other things on my mind, besides Ox. Don't think it's only a silly lust thing."

Maggie continued to nod.

"It's like a switch went off. He said it's good that I'm leaving because he couldn't fall for me, that he could not have a relationship. We weren't even discussing relationships, and he's already against it." Reliving what transpired in the truck caused Kate's heart to overflow with sadness.

"Did he say why?" Maggie asked.

"No, only that he can't be in a relationship. Something about him not letting it happen again."

"Oh dear."

"Maggie, do you know something I don't?"

Maggie scooted closer to Kate and placed her hand on Kate's knee. "I feared he would do this, but I never thought I would see the effects though. Ox has always struck me as the type of guy who falls hard and fast for someone. It hurts more if things don't work out for one reason or another and causes someone like Ox to withdrawal."

"I can't speak for Ox, but I feel like I fell in love the instant I saw him." Kate threw her hands up. "Literally and physically."

Maggie grabbed Kate's hands and gave them a squeeze.

"Can you believe I'm considering moving back here?" Kate shook her head. "Not here to the inn, but back here to live. I wanted to ask my parents if I could stay with them while I searched for a job. I didn't realize how much I missed it here and how unhappy I am in Arizona. I loathe my job. It's wrong of me to say because it's good income, but it's not me, and it's not my happiness. Coming here made me realize how unhappy I am in Phoenix. Maybe I'm confused."

Kate took a gasping breath, resting her back gently against Bayou who remained asleep behind her. An immediate wave of peace moved through her. "Maybe it's vacation fever."

"And?" Maggie asked.

Bayou snored softly, the sides of his lips flapped with each exhale.

"And I realized what a silly thought all of it is in the end. I'm so confused I even considered going back up in that tiny death trap for a five minute flight." Kate chuckled at the thought.

"Go," Maggie said.

"Go? Why would I? Clearly, any feelings I had were for nothing. I'm excited to return home, home to Arizona. I might even head to the airport tomorrow to try to catch an earlier flight. Home," Kate repeated, throwing her head into her open palms. "I am home." The words mumbled through her hands. She missed her parents, the seasons changing, the park with the trail around the lake, and the forest green hills..

"Kate, dear." Maggie's eyes pleaded with softness and concern. "Don't let life do that to you. Regardless of Ox, you realized you're unhappy in Arizona. You feel happy here and know you want a new job. You are home. That means something."

Kate reached over to the scarf piled on her nightstand, running it over her hands and wrapping it around them. The supple fabric felt smooth and cool between her fingers.

"I know, Maggie. But ..." Kate paused.

"No, don't do that to yourself. Don't waste a day of your life not living it to your fullest. If my Stan taught me anything, it was to stomp the grapes of life."

Kate tilted her head, her eyes narrowed, brow furrowed.

"Yes, really stomp life's grapes. Get all the juice out, because otherwise they just end up bitter and wasted."

"If I don't get everything from life, then I waste it?"

"Smart gal." Maggie stood up. "Speaking of grapes, how about some wine?"

"That sounds perfect actually, but I don't know if I can face Ox."

"You have a lot to learn about men, dear." Maggie took Kate's hand.

They hugged before making their way out the door. Bayou did his long-hold yoga pose off the bed, before catching up to them.

Chapter Nineteen

The sound of Kate slamming the passenger door continued rattling through Ox's body. A slam so intense he feared the door would never open again. Ox sighed, he knew he came off rude, but he could not be in a relationship.

The only light filling the cab of the truck came from the garage's overhead lights. Ox smacked his palms twice on the steering wheel and then grabbed hold, squeezing it until his knuckles went white.

Ox couldn't believe how quickly he had fallen for Kate. He wished she had never walked, or truthfully fallen, into his life. He laughed thinking of all her clumsiness in only a few short days.

A knock at Ox's truck window caused him to nearly hit his head against the roof.

"Sorry, Ox, I thought you would have heard my truck coming up the drive."

"Richard, how have you been?" Ox climbed out, firmly shaking hands.

Richard, a friend of his late parents, was pushing the big seven-o this year. His brown hair had been losing the battle against the gray hairs for some time now. He wore his staple red and brown flannel jacket over a red and white flannel shirt. Ski gloves kept his hands warm. Richard's wrinkled jeans were tucked inside his black rubber boots. Ox enjoyed Richard's visits; he always had a great story to tell about his late parents.

"Good, now that the snow has melted off the roads."

Richard's red Chevy had seen better days, so had the tires. "How are you?"

Ox leaned up against his truck's bed, eyeing the inn. "I would say a beautiful woman has gotten my mind into a bit of a conundrum."

"That's always the case, especially when you're married to a beautiful woman." Richard laughed.

Ox smirked. "What brings you by?"

"Speaking of ladies, the missus has been relentless about putting in a new shower. The old one is leaking pretty badly. She's not a fan of using four towels for one shower. I hoped you might have some free time to come and help me out. Chloe will bake you anything you want in return."

"Sure, Richard, I can swing by next week. Let's say Thursday in the morning."

"Thank you, Ox. Are you sure you are up for it? How is the body holding up?"

"Good days and bad days, but I will be there to help you out." Ox stepped forward. "Mind if I ask you a question?"

"Shoot."

"Kate, my unexpected guest, oddly enough grew up here. The snow and her vacationing parents led her to me." Ox dropped his hands to his side. "Forget it, it doesn't matter."

"You know your father came to me asking about your mother the very same way," Richard rested his weight on the bumper. "He knew the moment he saw her that it was over. Over in the sense that he could never move past her. That she must be his wife."

"My mom always said they met overseas when my dad was in the Army," Ox shifted his weight to one foot and crossed his other foot over top.

"They did." Richard smiled. "Your mom turned him down when they met at the bar. She wanted nothing to do with …

How did she put it? … 'No bar hopping fool.'"

"I didn't think my dad drank!" Ox laughed.

"He didn't, but his friends did, and he tagged along with them. Your mom shot him down, and he walked off wondering what could have been. He never stopped thinking of her. Even a month later, when he saw her on the streets of Munich, his eyes were like cartoon hearts."

Fate had brought them together again. Ox's mouth turned up at the thought. "What changed her mind after saying no?"

"Your mom could not stop thinking about him either. They decided the best story of how they met was love at first sight on a foreign street over your mom's comment about him being a bar hopping fool."

Ox thought about the story as he crossed his arms and uncrossed them, gazing off at his inn. A great story, but it was missing one component, his parents didn't have multiple sclerosis.

Richard pushed himself off the truck's bumper and turned to face Ox. "I think you had a question to ask me?"

Ox sighed, shoving his hands into his jeans pockets. "I like Kate, but I know that I can't be in a relationship with her or anyone." He ran his hands against his facial scruff. "But Richard, she's amazing."

Richard glanced at the inn, then back to Ox. "Make yourself happy now. Let later worry about later. Nothing is guaranteed. Don't let your life be guaranteed unhappy because of your pride."

Richard held out his hand to Ox, who shook it. "See you Thursday."

Ox waved as Richard left the driveway. Noticing the edge of the blue winner's ribbon on the concrete, he picked it up before heading inside.

When he entered, Maggie and Kate were standing around the kitchen island.

"Who won the pie contest?" Maggie uncorked a bottle of Sangiovese.

"We did," they said in unison.

Maggie poured three glasses of wine with a smirk on her face. Silence filled the kitchen as they sipped from their glasses. Ox's heart twisted in confusion as he couldn't help but stare at Kate.

Chapter Twenty

"I'm sorry about earlier." Ox's soft voice filled the space between them.

They sat together on the living room couch facing the snow-frosted evergreens beyond the window. Maggie had hurried off to bed immediately after dessert. The lamps were off and the fireplace had grown cold. Only the full moon produced shadows across the carpet. Bayou lay between their feet as Kate held her empty wine glass as though it were full.

"Don't worry about it." Kate tried to keep Ox from hearing the lump in her throat.

"No, it came out rude, and I didn't mean for it to. I think you are beautiful, funny, and intelligent. I don't want you to think that this is about you. If I could be in a relationship, I would."

"I never said I wanted one," Kate fired back, her voice slightly raised. "You don't need you to keep beating me over the head with the fact that you don't want a relationship."

Ox shifted his body toward Kate, but quickly regretted it seeing the moon's light on her lips. He swung his chest back around and faced the window.

"I wanted to thank you for the help with the pie contest." Taking a deep breath, he exhaled his frustration.

"No problem," Kate mumbled.

Ox had not fooled Kate with his sudden switch in topics. While it irritated her, she was not able to suppress her feelings for him. She needed to take that into consideration if she moved back to the area. What she couldn't explain was why she remained next to him on the couch, as though she could not bear to walk away.

Her mind drifted back to their teriyaki dinner, the sunset view, and the excitement of winning the pie contest together. Kate had yet to go through her camera shots, but she hoped there were some great ones of Ox and the mountains in the distance.

"I still want to take you up for a five-minute flight tomorrow." Ox took a long sip, finishing the last of his Sangiovese.

"I don't know, I think I should just get to the airport and see if I can catch an earlier flight."

"Please, Kate." Ox's eyes now fixed on her.

She felt his stare and turned toward him, their eyes once again shy with each other. The reflection from the moon's glow rested softly across Ox's face.

"Kate, please, let me take you up in the plane tomorrow. You can get some great shots and continue to work on overcoming your fear."

Kate swallowed hard. She wished her wine glass wasn't empty so she could take a sip and wait to answer. "Why? Why should I?"

Ox shrugged his shoulders, staring at his empty glass, turning it in circles between his fingers. "Can we forget what I said in the truck?"

"No, we cannot." Kate's frustration lines creased her forehead. "You discarded me. You made me feel irrelevant."

"Kate, I want you to stay, please. Please stay."

"I want you to tell me the truth."

Ox grabbed the back of his neck and squeezed it, letting his hand slide down over his chest as he leaned his head back. "It doesn't matter. It won't change anything, because I can't change the outcome."

"You have control of your life." Kate's words echoed through her, nearly smacking her upside the head. She had control of hers too.

Ox focused on Kate. A strong pull to tell her everything lay in front of him like an unopened gift.

"I have control over my life." Kate stood, her shoulders back. "And so do you. This whole time I've kept my focus on what I hated and what I feared."

"We don't have control over everything in life, Kate." Ox leaned forward on the couch, reaching for Bayou. He petted Bayou's back, his fingers disappearing into the mass of yellow fur.

"But, Ox, we do. Look at my fear of flying."

"Which you don't have control over," Ox reminded her.

Kate held up her pointer finger. "I know I have to work on it. And I will, because I'm trying my best. If you plan on helping people overcome their fear of flying, you need to be aware of that."

Ox's elbows rested on his knees. He clamped his hands around the stem of his wine glass. "Kate, I do think you can overcome your flying fears, but not everything can be changed."

"Yes, Ox, it can."

"If you had a disease, a disease that might take away your strength and your ability to care for others and yourself, could you change that?"

Kate's smile dropped, her shoulders slumped. Sighing as her lips parted, she paused to give herself a few more seconds to think of the words she wanted to use. Thoughts of her aunt who passed away from cancer filled her mind. She thought of Ali's older brother who spent three days a week at a dialysis center at the young age of thirty-five.

"Ox, are you sick?" Kate's voice shivered as though it just came in from a blizzard.

"I don't know how long I will be able to run my inn, fly my plane, or be me." Ox stood, going to the window. "I don't know long I have to do simple tasks like chop wood, make dinner, and walk Bayou." His right hand covered his mouth as though trying to keep the words from coming out.

Kate went to Ox, placing her hand on his back. He flinched, startled by her touch. Kate remained silent, even though she wanted to ask more. Guilt flowed through her as her hand continued to press against Ox's back. She had pushed and pushed, when she should have let him tell her when he was ready.

Ox felt as though Kate's hand prevented his entire life from sliding like sand through her fingers. He was not ready to tell her about the MS, unsure if he would ever be able to. She would be leaving at the end of the week anyway. He could not have her feeling sorry for him for the rest of her stay. It would not change anything between them.

Kate removed her hand from his back and shoved it in her pocket. "I won't ask anymore of you. Goodnight."

Ox closed his eyes. His hearing focused on the sound of Kate's steps leaving the living room. He heard the creak on the third step that he should have fixed last month.

Finally, the sound of Kate's door latching closed caused Ox to place his hand on the window frame for support.

"If I could change it, I would. I would change it for you, Kate," Ox whispered.

Chapter Twenty-One

In the morning, when the sunlight spread through the windows, Kate covered her head with the duvet and let out a moan. *How am I going to face Ox?* Rolling over onto her stomach, Kate inched her head under the pillow, pressing it firmly down. When she couldn't breathe anymore, she sat up, her curls a knotted mess. Kate kicked the covers off and paced the room. Her stomach craved breakfast.

"I can do this," she whispered. "Don't look into his eyes and you will be fine."

She sighed, returned to the bed and perched on the edge. *It's not your place to inquire about what's happening to Ox. If he wants to tell you, he will. Otherwise, move on.*

Happy with her pep talk, Kate stood, snatching her hairbrush off the dresser. She attempted to control her curly tornado. After she shaped the curls into order, Kate dressed in jeans, a long sleeve white shirt, and a blue sweater. She would not be showing up to breakfast in her pajamas again. Then she took in a strong breath and exhaled, opening the bedroom door.

Before she could take a step out into the hall, a gift at the threshold greeted her toes. Picking up a vase of purple and yellow roses, Kate closed the door. A white envelope rested in the middle of the bouquet. Kate placed the vase on the dresser and opened the envelope.

The front of the card was a photo of orange and yellow California poppies; inside, the message was written in thick cursive black ink.

Kate,

Having you as a guest has brought up feelings I had hidden inside of me. I knew the second I saw you that it would be hard to deny them. You are a snowflake. You might think all snowflakes are beautiful, but every once in a while, there is that one that is incomparable to all others for so many reasons. I apologize for myself, and I hope you understand this has nothing to do with you. It's me. You deserve to smile. Ox

Kate read the card once more before setting it on the nightstand. To be honest, she had wanted to run away last night. She wanted to pack her suitcase and drive, but with Ali's help, she had already returned her rental car. And something inside her heart told her not to flee, to shut her eyes and sleep on it. She had tried, but couldn't sleep with the dreaded thoughts of the plane trip home racing through her mind. She dared not make it happen sooner than needed. The thought of renting a car to get to Phoenix crossed her mind many times, but the snow over the passes would be too dangerous this time of year.

"Why did I even decide on this trip in the first place?" she whispered, throwing herself back on the bed. But she knew the truth and had avoided it on purpose. For years, she simply ignored it. Over time she hid the thoughts so well, even she even had trouble finding them. Kate knew avoidance could take you far in life.

A thud at the door drew Kate from her thoughts.

Whap, whap, whap, whap.

"Hang on, Bayou." Kate made her way to the door.

Whap, whap, whap.

Kate swung the door open as Bayou barreled through, wrapping himself around her legs in excitement.

"Hi, Bayou." She laughed, bending down to give him a

morning hug. "Are you here to escort me to breakfast?"

Bayou leaned his head on Kate's legs; his eyes stared up at her. "Okay then, let's go."

As Bayou and Kate entered the kitchen, Maggie leaned over the steam of her mug at the table. Ox stood at the stove cooking something in a skillet.

"Good morning," Kate announced.

Ox turned and smiled. "Morning, Kate."

"Morning, Ox." Kate pulled out a chair and poured herself a cup of coffee from the carafe.

"Can you believe the sun is shining?" Maggie beamed. "The weather report said snow today."

A plate of muffins and fresh fruit in the middle of the table made her mouth water. Ox finished scooping Bayou's food into his bowl and took a seat across from Kate. As Ox sat, he lowered a dish of steaming scrambled eggs onto the table.

"Thanks for the roses," Kate mouthed.

Ox smiled and mouthed back, "You're welcome."

In an attempt to stop staring at Ox's eyes, Kate turned to Maggie. "Are they still saying snow?"

"That's correct." Maggie took a sip of her coffee. "But the sun clearly had other ideas."

"You know by now how the weather is here, Maggie. The forecast is only about ten percent correct," Ox said, "about ten percent of the time."

Kate nodded her head and chuckled. "I spent many childhood days thinking school would be canceled because of the snow, but it rarely happened. Or I didn't bring my jacket because they said sunshine and it would rain."

"The joy of the Pacific Northwest." Ox smirked.

Kate scooped some fluffy warm eggs onto her plate. "I remember having to use my jacket to wipe down the slide, versus wear it." Kate laughed at the memory.

"Why would you do that?" Maggie pushed her fork into a slice of kiwi. "When I was in grammar school in California, if it rained, we stayed inside."

"Not here." Kate sipped her coffee. "As a kid you knew how best to use your thirty-minute recess. If the slide was wet, as it often was, then someone had to volunteer to wrap their jacket around their waist and go down first to dry it."

"It's a slide," Ox stated. "How wet could it have been?"

"The top area was flat so it puddled there and then again at the bottom. The rest was simply damp." Kate took a bite of muffin.

Ox nodded, but Maggie's head remained tilted. "Didn't you get your jacket dirty by doing that? I'm sure the parents of the child who volunteered didn't like that."

"That's why it was hard to get someone to agree to do it."

Ox glanced up from his plate. "I'm guessing you were volunteered the most."

Kate nodded. "Yes, but I also knew how to work the washing machine when I got home. The benefits of being a latchkey kid."

"Those were the days." Ox leaned back in his chair and gazed off as though watching his younger self through memories playing on the wall. Kate took the opportunity to study his face without him noticing.

"So," Ox said, coming out of the fog of his memory, "since it's nice out, I'd like to take you up in the plane today, Kate, unless you have other plans?"

Kate focused on the food on her plate. If she caught even a glimpse of Ox's sapphire eyes, she knew she would say yes.

"Kate?" Ox asked.

"Yes?" Kate lifted her head. *Dang it!*

Ox smiled, his eyes captured her. Why could she not go back to her youth? When a crush meant nothing more than waiting for a note in her locker. When the biggest worry she faced was how late her parents would let her stay out and what vegetables she had to choke down at dinner. A simple, youthful life, not this wondering and longing.

"Kate?" Ox asked again.

"Yes, I would like to get some shots from above of the town and wilderness. As long as Bayou goes with, of course. Five minutes, right?"

"Yes, I promise." Ox smiled.

A tingle ran through Kate's body. Could she be excited to get on a plane? She did want to get some additional shots. Maybe that confused her true feelings. Her heartbeat sped up just thinking about it.

Once the muffins, eggs, and fruit were devoured, Kate prepared herself for the day. She swallowed the motion sickness medicine, dabbed her essential oils on her scarf, and slid her motion sickness bands onto her wrists. Next, she checked the batteries on the Canon and made sure she had easy access to the filters.

Ox and Kate made their way out to the truck with Bayou wedged between them the entire way.

"Thank you again for the roses," Kate said. "You didn't have to."

"I know."

"Ox, you have a wide vocabulary." Kate laughed.

"Yep." Ox opened the passenger door and Kate stood back to allow Bayou to climb in. "Kate." Ox ushered her with his hand.

"I'm waiting for Bayou," Kate said.

"He won't get in on this side, remember?"

"Oh, I forgot about his behind the driver status." She giggled as she slid into the passenger seat. Ox closed her door and walked around to the driver's side. Kate leaned back and observed.

Bayou placed his paws up on the floorboard, just like he did with the bed. Ox hoisted his back legs up and Bayou pulled himself all the way inside.

"I'm not sure why he is the way he is, but he's worth it." Ox smiled and started the truck. "I would agree. And I keep meaning to ask, why did you decide to train Bayou to become a service dog?"

"I would take him to the dog park when he was young, but all he did was sit next to owners, waiting for attention. He didn't seem to care about other dogs at all. One time I had him out with me and he took off when he spotted this lady in the parking lot. She was in the middle of a panic attack next to her car. The lady lowered herself to the ground and Bayou snuggled up against her until she'd calmed down."

"Wow." Kate glanced back at Bayou fast asleep.

"I guess you can say he told me he wanted to be a service dog."

Ox kept his focus on the road, as they headed toward the airport, clouds started to build. The snow remained piled high in the shady spots along the side of the road.

"Think it might snow after all?" Kate leaned forward, observing the sky. A part of her wanted it to snow. Let the clouds roll in and let loose another massive snowfall. But part of her worried, because it might ground her past her allotted vacation time, forcing her to put more thought into what she needed to do about moving back home. Yet, on the plus side, it would allow her to not have to be in the air for three hours and not have to return to work. Maybe Ox's viewpoint would change. She struggled to switch off her feelings for him, which continued to grow uncontrollably in her heart.

If something was wrong, for whatever reason, he might need her, and she wanted to be there for him. Kate had lain awake late into the night contemplating what could be wrong with Ox.

What is he facing that is so big he doesn't want to share? She asked herself questions and debated her own answers. The airport came into view and Kate started her mantra, repeating it until they boarded Ox's plane.

Chapter Twenty-Two

"You promise only five minutes?" Kate spoke into the headset.

"Five minutes." Ox straightened the yoke with both hands.

Kate breathed deep as cold air filled her chest and held it before exhaling. The plane's wheels lifted off the runway, and Bayou's chin felt heavy and warm on her shoulder. This time she had fewer tremors and her breathing was not as labored. The plane's ascent eased her back into the seat.

Kate placed a filter on the Canon and took a few shots out her window, holding her hands as steady as possible. She had to focus on her passion, to create something from her photography. But first, she needed to stop the trembling or her photos wouldn't turn out. Gazing out the side windshield caused her to shake more.

Kate turned around, surprising Bayou, who lost his headrest. "Sit back, Bayou," Kate instructed.

Bayou leaned back on the aquamarine bench seat, as though he understood Kate. Bayou's back legs stretched forward in a V shape, his front legs straight and centered between, holding him upright. Kate clicked off a few shots before repositioning her Canon and clicked some more.

Turning around, she replaced the filter and snapped the flash on top. Now Bayou's eyes were focused out the right side of the plane.

Kate snapped her fingers, but Bayou continued to gaze out the side window.

"Can you get Bayou's attention?" she asked Ox.

Savannah Hendricks

"Sure, I don't need to fly the plane."

"You don't have to turn around, just call his name or something so he will look in your direction. He's ignoring me."

"Bayou, front," Ox raised his voice over the noise.

Bayou turned and tilted his head. Kate's camera clicked off in rapid succession.

"Perfect, Bayou. Perfect!" she cheered.

Kate scrolled through the shots on the viewfinder and beamed. Replacing the lens cap, she lowered the camera to her lap. When she returned her vision out the plane's windows, the town didn't appear below them anymore.

"Where are we?" Her jaw tensed. "You said five minutes."

Kate's heart rate increased as her nausea peaked.

"I wanted to take you out a bit so you could get some less populated shots."

"I want to go back. We're going to be over the five minutes," she choked between panicked breaths.

Ox placed his hand on Kate's knee. "It's okay, we can head back, but I thought you might like this. Look out your window."

Kate's eyes squeezed shut. "No, I can't. It makes me dizzy."

"Remember what you told me last night?"

Kate opened her left eye, but continued to squeeze her right eye shut. "Yes."

Ox patted her leg.

"I have control." Kate opened both eyes, her focus shifted to his hand on her knee.

While the warmth of Ox's hand provided additional comfort, it also caused a severe distraction. Kate lifted his hand and placed it back on the yoke. She counted down from five, and then did it again, placing her scarf with the lavender oil to her nose.

Calmness rolled through her, starting at her shoulders. Bayou shoved his chin into the bend in her arm, getting as close to her as he could from the backseat.

Glancing out the window, Kate could see what Ox meant by some great shots. She steadied her hand and lifted the Canon back up. Shades from hunter green to olive filled the valley below. An outline of a single-lane road appeared to wrap around white patches of remaining snow like spilled ice cream.

"Is that the Nooksack River ahead?"

"You remember well, Kate." Ox smiled. "Are you ready to turn around and land?"

"Maybe a few more minutes in the air will be okay." Kate's voice wavered.

Kate swapped out the filter on the Canon and pointed it toward the Nooksack. After a few clicks, Orcas Island came into view. Kate focused on each shot, zoning out everything else around her. The ever-expanding view held a mix of blue and green with hints of pearl white.

Without warning, Kate's anxiety returned, racing through her body, weakening everything. No longer able to hold the Canon up, her vision blurred and dizziness swept through her.

Bayou whined, alerting Ox, who glanced over at Kate. "Are you okay?"

Fear caught up to her mind. "You need to land," she whimpered. "We are too far out. Take us back!"

Ox called into the tower, carefully banking the plane in one swift motion, and turning them back toward the airport. Kate pushed her hands up to her eyes.

"It's all right, Kate." Ox's voice steady and reassuring. "You will be fine."

"I feel good. I'm doing great," she whispered. "I'm great, wonderful, fabulous."

She opened her eyes and saw the airport coming into view

through the windshield. Kate gathered her breath. It filled her chest and then she exhaled. But she noticed the plane's nose was not dipping like last time.

"Why are we not lining up with the runway?" Kate shrieked.

Ox spoke into the radio. Then there was silence; then he spoke again.

"We can't land. There are two planes before us. I have to loop back around."

"No, no, no!" Kate's breathing went into short gasping puffs.

"Kate, you're okay, I'm here. Bayou is here too. Nothing will happen." When Ox glanced over, he saw the tension and terror on Kate's face.

"How c-could I say I have con-t-t-rol over my life? I can't change any-th-th-ing. I'm not in con-t-t-rol of m-me." Tears formed at the edge of Kate's eyes.

"You have changed, Kate. You have control. You just need to remind yourself. You made it twice as long as your first trip." Ox placed his hand over top of Kate's and squeezed. "Be proud of yourself, stop knocking yourself down."

"B-but look at me!" Kate used her right hand to wipe the tears that had escaped her eyes.

"Yes, Kate, look at you. You're in a plane, working through your fear, facing it."

Kate rotated her hand under Ox's and squeezed it back. "I feel safe and happy," Kate whispered. "I can do this."

The airport runway returned into view.

"Oh good, we can land!" Kate cheered.

"Sorry, Kate, once more around." Ox pointed. "We are after that last plane coming in."

Kate sighed and pushed her head up against the headrest before shutting her eyes.

Ox's reassuring voice filled the plane. "You can do this, Kate. I believe you can. Bayou believes you can. You should too."

Ox remained in the holding pattern and once again circled the airfield waiting for the tower to confirm permission to land. Clouds moved in, filtering the sunshine.

"I should never have said yes to another plane ride! What was I thinking? I must have lost my mind over a far-fetched dream! This is crazy. I hate flying, why would I ever say yes?"

Bayou pawed Kate's arm as though he was knocking on her bedroom door. The plane straightening out again. A feeling of warmth and comfort came over her. She grabbed hold of Bayou's paw and held it like a human hand.

"You will be all right, Kate. Be proud of yourself, you have been in the air for twenty minutes now."

"Please land this plane. I'm not all right."

Ox confirmed his clearance into the radio, lined the plane up with the runway, and began its descent. Bayou pushed up against Kate as best he could. Her entire body was damp and clammy.

The wheels skidded on the runway and her stomach shifted back into its proper location. *Land, oh glorious land at eye level!*

Ox braked the plane and steered it toward the hangar.

"I'm sorry, Kate. Sometimes the runway gets busy this time of day."

"No, you knew that flying away from the town would put us out longer than five minutes."

Ox shut off the engine. Kate remained frozen in her seat, waiting for her blood pressure to go from full boil to slow simmer. Ox climbed out, lowered Bayou onto the ground, and walked around the plane to pop open her door.

Ox undid her seat belt. "Kate?" Her head eased its way toward Ox. She twisted her body and reached for him like a scared toddler, sliding from the seat into his open arms.

Kate's body shook with fear. She buried her head into Ox's

shoulder, trying to keep from crying.

Once she gathered herself, she pulled herself out of Ox's grip.

"Sorry for freaking out." Kate stared at her boots.

Ox's hand reached for her chin and lifted it up. "You did great, Kate, don't be sorry."

Their eyes locked for what must have been minutes. Puffs of steam from their warm breaths lofted around them.

Bayou's bark interrupted their near kiss. They turned toward him. Outside the hangar, the clouds had covered every spot of blue sky as the snow started to fall.

Chapter Twenty-Three

The snow landed in wet clumps as they made their way to the truck. The temperature must have been right at freezing. The droplets could not decide if they wanted to be rain or snow.

"I don't remember any storms rolling in this fast before." Kate's jacket was moist from the snow as she slid in the passenger seat.

"I can't recall one either. It's almost bizarre." Ox flipped on the wiper blades.

Bayou shook the moisture from his coat, sending a shower of damp dog hair sprinkles everywhere.

Ox pointed at the windshield. "It's trying hard not to snow."

Kate reached for her phone. "If I can get a signal before we are too far into the woods, I can get the local weather. See? Technology is not so bad." She thumbed the screen, swiping to the weather app.

"Even if we know the weather, what will that do?" Ox stopped at the red light. "Weather will happen. All we need to know is if a tornado or hurricane is coming. And there is only a five percent chance of that happening in Washington. You can tell if a road is not drivable by walking out to your vehicle and seeing how slick it is under your shoes."

"Well, I still think it's good to know," she stated.

Sure, he was correct, if it snows, it snows. With her flight not for another four days, the snowstorm would surely be over by then. She returned the phone to her pocket.

The snow would force her to spend a few days relaxing, on land with the carpet between her toes. Plus, if they were snowed in, maybe Ox would finally tell her what was going on.

"I hope my two other guests, Matthew and Ben make it in." Ox observed snowflakes melting as they landed on the windshield.

"You have others checking in today?" Her heart sank knowing they wouldn't be alone now.

"Yes, a long time … friend is coming and a new guest, Matthew," Ox mentioned, his voice lifted and happy. "Both flights were to land in the afternoon. Although," Ox leaned into the steering wheel. "I'm not sure what is happening with the flights now. We left the airport just in time. I'll have to check with Shawn."

The truck crept up the driveway to the inn, the tires etching tracks in the newly fallen snow.

"Wait here." Ox climbed from the driver's seat. "I'm leaving the truck out. I'll let Bayou out and then come get you. It's slick, and I don't want you falling."

"I can climb from a truck," she reminded Ox, but he had already lifted Bayou out and shut the door.

Ox pulled open her door. "I can do this myself. I'm not that clumsy."

He raised his right eyebrow in complete disagreement. "I nearly slipped walking around."

Ox held his hand out. Kate glared at him and pushed his hand to the side. She placed her right foot down on the driveway, and then followed with her left foot, when her right slid. Ox wrapped his arms around Kate as both of her feet went sliding under him like the Wicked Witch of the West when the house landed on her.

"One of these days you will heed my advice." Ox pulled her to standing again.

Ox's words echoed in Kate's mind. One of these days? For someone who wants nothing to do with a relationship, why does he keep referring to a future on some level?

Flinging Kate's camera bag over his shoulder, Ox reached out his hand. She grabbed hold without a protest.

The air, moist and chilly, caused Kate's breath to form tiny clouds in front of her. Bayou dashed around them in circles, excited to romp in the fresh snow collecting on the grass.

"Bayou," Ox called, "calm down, buddy. I don't want you slipping."

Maggie swung open the door. "I'm so glad to see you both!"

She wrapped her long violet cardigan tightly around her body. The warmth escaped from inside as they reached the front porch.

"This storm came out of nowhere." Maggie pulled them inside, closing the door inches from their heels. "I already put the kettle on."

"Thank you, Maggie." Ox removed his coat. "I have two guests scheduled to arrive this afternoon, Matthew and Ben. I will need to check with Shawn to see if their flights have been cancelled." Ox headed to his office. "Save me some tea, Maggie."

"How did you do, Kate?" Maggie steeped the tea bags on the kitchen island.

"Let's just say I have finally stopped trembling. Ox flew us out a bit from town, so I could get some shots of Orcas Island. Yet when we went to land, we weren't able to. Two planes were in front of us. He had to circle around twice. I panicked." Kate buried her head into her hands. "I cried, Maggie. Even talking about it right now makes my heart rate."

Maggie handed Kate a cup of tea. She accepted it and wrapped her hands around the mug. The two women made their way into the living room, where a crackling fire added some much needed extra warmth. Sinking into the couch, Kate tucked her feet under her, and gazed out the large windows. The snow instantly stuck to the tree branches.

"Well, you made it back." Maggie took a seat in the nearby armchair. "That's what matters."

"I shook all over, terrorized from the plane not being able to land. I don't think I can get back in a plane again, ever."

"Now tell me, Kate, if you are not going to fly again, how will you get home? How will you explore the world?" Kate shook her head, taking a sip of tea, letting the flavor fill her mouth.

Bayou appeared and made an ill-attempt at jumping onto the couch. His front half made it, his back end dangled. After pawing the cushion with his front legs, his bottom finally made it up a few seconds later.

"You're insanely graceful, Bayou." Kate petted him as he circled the cushion and curled into a ball.

Ox entered the room, a mug of tea in hand, and stood at the window. "I spoke with Shawn. The airport is still open and no flights have been canceled, yet."

Kate secretly wished the guests' flights were delayed, maybe even all together canceled. She loved how cozy and homey the inn felt with only the three of them.

"Kate informed me she is never flying on a plane again," Maggie blurted out.

Kate's head snapped toward Maggie, her eyes wide as if to scold her.

"I hope that's not true, Kate. Look." Ox pointed at living room window. From beyond the thicket of woods in the backyard, three deer wandered in. "I left some apples out there before we left this morning."

Maggie observed the deer munching on the snow frosted apples. "Once she has calmed down, I'm sure Kate will change her mind."

"No." Kate interjected sternly, her free hand petting a snoring Bayou.

Ox turned to Kate, but before he could say a word, the front door swung open as if a gust of wind had taken control. A breeze of bitterly cold air stretched its way into the living room causing Kate to shiver. Bayou remained unfazed other than a brief lift of his eyes before returning to sleep.

"Hello," a figure called from the doorway.

The whiteness of the world beyond the figure caused it to appear as a shadow. It moved forward and closed the door. A man dressed in a desert tan scarf wrapped up to his ears and a charcoal colored peacoat stood on the large Oriental rug at the entryway.

"You must be Matthew." Ox made his way over to shake hands with the new guest.

"Yes, please call me Matt." He raked his fingers through his black hair, cut shorter on the sides than the top. "Seems as though I made it just in time, but barely."

Matt grinned, his ear pierced with a flattened ebony stud. Kate noticed is eyes were such a deep brown they appeared black as he placed his suitcase on the rug. He brushed the snow off his shoulders, before stepping onto the hardwood floor.

Maggie and Kate headed to greet Matt, but Kate's foot caught on the living room step. She double hopped, catching herself, but spilled her tea on the floor. Thankfully, the tea spilled on the hardwood floor rather than the carpet.

"Kate struggles with walking." Maggie shook hands with Matt. "I'm Maggie."

Ox brought Kate some paper towels from the kitchen.

"Thank you, Ox." She wiped the floor dry. "I'm Kate." She waved, heading upstairs to change and bury her head under the covers.

"Hi, Kate." Matt waved. "Nice to meet you." Kate gripped the handrail just in case her feet decided to deceive her again. When she reached the landing, she peeked back downstairs. Kate remained in sight of the entryway, but out of view from everyone downstairs. Ox and Matt faced each other continuing to chat about the storm. Maggie stood nearby, her hands loose at her side as a sluggish Bayou joined them.

Two handsome men together in the same inn, this could be the best snowstorm of her life. She wondered when the other guest, Ben, would arrive. A smile turned up the sides of her lips.

A frantic triple knock sounded at the front door. Ox hurried to open it.

"Ox!"

"Ben!"

Kate saw Ox throw his arms around … *her.*

"Simply lovely weather you're having, unreal I made it here in the rental." Benjamina's British accent put a fresh spin on vowel sounds.

"You should have called me." Ox held Benjamina at a distance with his arms. "You look as wonderful as ever. Please come in."

He snatched up Benjamina's luggage and closed the door.

Benjamina wore black leggings, a red sweater with a puffy neck and matching red lipstick. Her black leather boots added a few inches to her height. Without an introduction, Benjamina hugged Matt and Maggie.

"These are my other guests, Matt and Maggie. This is Benjamina. Kate is upstairs, and that's Bayou."

Hearing her name she ducked, trying to avoid being caught spying.

"Lovely to meet you both." Benjamina removed her pearl gloves. "You too." She nodded at Bayou.

"Ben, short for Benjamina." Maggie crossed her arms. "It seems as though you know Ox."

"Yes." Benjamina swung around to Ox and placed her

hand on his arm. "We courted a few years back."

Benjamina pivoted on the rug. "Ox, your inn is lovely indeed!" Her British accent stood out like Big Ben's chimes at noon. "Such a delight to be here."

Ox lifted up Matt and Benjamina's luggage. "Let me show you to your rooms."

Benjamina wrapped her hand around Ox's arm as they made their way up the stairs.

Before Kate slipped into her room she noticed Maggie remained in the entryway with her arms crossed and her shoe tapping the floor.

Chapter Twenty-Four

Kate heard boot heels clumping down the hall, followed by giggles and the muffled sounds of a conversation. She cracked open her door just as Matt, Ox, and Benjamina strolled by.

"Hello." Kate flung the bedroom door open wide and stood in the frame.

Benjamina spun around. "You must be Kate." Benjamina embraced Kate, who was taken by surprise by the hug. "I'm Benjamina. Lovely to meet you."

"A- and I to you too," Kate stammered, "I mean, it's great to meet you too."

Kate managed a crooked attempt at a smile, which looked more like an Elvis twitch.

Taking several steps backwards into her room, Kate waved and shut the door. *And I to you?* She cradled her head and sighed.

She then went to the mirror, checking on her hair. The mess of copper curls that once seemed cute and fun, now resembled the aftermath of an electric shock. She patted down the sides with her fingers and tried to calm the frizz without any luck. Her shoulders lowered in defeat.

An idea came to Kate with a gasp, and she went to her purse and started digging through it. She removed the eyeshadow, eyeliner, mascara, and lipstick before returning to the mirror. Leaning forward, she swept the maple gold eyeshadow over the tops of her lids. Then she penciled on the eyeliner, followed by several swipes of mascara. Lastly, she pressed the mauve lipstick over her lips. Kate stood back examining her polished face.

"Why do I look like a clown?" Kate asked the mirror. "Ughhh."

Riffling through her purse again, she found her travel pack of moist wipes. She rubbed off her unsuccessful handy work. *Now I'm plain, again. Too plain.*

Taking great care, Kate reapplied the eye shadow, eyeliner, mascara and lipstick. Why do I look like a kindergartener who got into my mom's makeup bag? Once again she wiped her face clean with a moist wipe. Kate observed herself in the mirror, her face red around the eyes and lips from all the rubbing. She sighed and rolled her eyes. *Forget it!*

After checking her clothes for lint, she took a deep breath and exited the room.

"What happened to your face, Kate?" Maggie stood outside her door. "It's red in spots."

"I had a little makeup mishap," she whispered.

"Makeup? You've always been beautiful without trying to play it up." Maggie took hold of Kate, yanked her into the room, and shut the door.

"What are you doing?" Kate stood in the middle of Maggie's room.

"Covering up all the red. You are beautiful, but right now your face resembles someone who has been out wandering the Sahara desert without sunscreen. Now sit." Maggie pointed at the bed.

Doing as instructed, Kate sat while Maggie pulled out a compact and proceeded to powder up Kate's face.

"Much better. Now we can go to dinner." Maggie linked arms with Kate as they headed down the steps.

In the kitchen, Ox leaned over the stove. Benjamina glided around the table, setting a napkin in each spot perfectly. Matt stood at the kitchen window, hands in his crisply ironed khaki pockets. Bayou made his way over to Kate and sat at her feet waiting for his evening petting. He pushed his weight up against Kate's legs as she leaned down and rubbed his head with both her hands.

"Kate." Matt turned. "Ox tells me you are up here from Phoenix?"

"Yes, I grew up here. Came back to visit my parents, but they're out of town."

Matt rocked back and forth on his heels. "And you didn't stay at their house?"

"Poorly planned surprise." Kate shrugged.

"I see, well, I live in Tucson."

Ox twisted his upper body toward Kate and Matt, his wooden spoon stopped mid stir. "Well, how about that."

"Ox and Benjamina used to date," Maggie chimed in. "Is this the time I mention it's a small world?"

Kate paused, her hands on Bayou's ears. "You dated?" *You called her a long time friend in the truck.*

"Years ago," Benjamina stated, her accent caused years to sound like ears.

"How exactly did that happen?" Kate crossed her arms.

Bayou pivoted his head up as though to ask Kate why she had stopped petting him. When she didn't make eye contact, Bayou lay down, his bottom covering her feet.

"I was on an extended holiday with my aunt and uncle who lived in town at the time." Benjamina added the silverware on top of the napkins. "Where was it we met? The airport, I believe."

Ox turned off the stove. "Yes, I was working on my pilot's license and you were there helping your uncle with the skydiving class."

Benjamina brought her hands together in prayer form, as her smile lit up her entire face. "Yes, that's it! Oh, how I miss those jumps. It feels as though it has been ages since I last threw through the clouds."

Kate cleared her throat, her self confidence lodged like a rock. Maggie patted Kate's back.

"You like planes?" Kate pushed past the lump.

"Oh, yes! Flying is delightful, an utter joy." Benjamina carried a basket of warm bread and the butter dish to the table.

Kate provided a weak smile. "That's nice."

"Ox is helping Kate overcome her fear of flying." Maggie motioned for Kate to make her way to the table.

"It's Bayou who is actually helping." Ox cut the foil on a bottle of 2010 Cabernet. Kate pulled out a chair; thoughts swarmed her mind like bees around a hive.

"Splendid." Benjamina smiled and pulled out a chair next to Kate.

The five of them sat around the table, a lasagna in the middle, flanked by rolls and steamed vegetables. Ox poured them each a large glass of Cabernet, as candlelight danced on the kitchen island.

Kate took a long sip of wine. Benjamina took a roll, breaking it open over her plate, the steam rising from inside. *Of course, she can eat bread. Benjamina can probably eat the whole basket and not gain an ounce. Then after dinner she can fly around the world and still be as put together as she is right this instant.*

"How lovely you grew up here, Kate." Benjamina slathered butter across her roll. "Did you know Ox before moving to Arizona?"

"No, I moved to Arizona to go to college just about the time Ox moved here." Kate set her wine glass down and faced Matt. "What brings you up here, Matt?"

"Skiing. Do you ski, Kate?"

"I did as a child, but it has been years since I snapped on a pair." Kate scooped a serving, strings of mozzarella stretched from the dish to her plate.

"I didn't know you skied," Ox stated in a firm tone, as though Kate had left him out of some secret society.

She nodded her head. "There are a lot of things I enjoy doing, even if they don't involve everyone's obsession of flying."

Bayou finished his dinner and made his way over to the table. He squeezed between the table leg and Kate's leg, lying on top of her fuzzy socks.

"You should join me, Kate. I'm heading to Mt. Baker tomorrow." Matt smiled at Kate from across the table for what seemed like minutes.

"Sounds great. I'd love to go." Kate smiled back.

"You would?" Ox asked.

Kate took a sip of wine to keep from having to reply immediately. Truth be told, she didn't know if she could hop right back into skiing after all these years. But it would be a great place to clear her head, away from Ox. Not that Matt would help; maybe she could sneak off to the lodge and sip hot chocolate while he ran the slopes.

"Yes, I'll need to get a pair of rental skis." Kate set her wine glass down. "I have a set at my parents' house, but I can't get to them."

Ox hung his head as though Kate had turned him down for the prom.

"I'm sure Benjamina would enjoy going too," Maggie suggested.

"Why don't you join us, Ox?" Matt added.

"Yes, Ox, let's all go," Benjamina cheered as though they had been invited to the opening of an ice cream shop.

"Ox probably has inn or airport things to do," Kate interjected.

"I'd love to go." Ox glared at Kate. "I don't have a thing to do. Besides I have studded tires on my truck and neither of your rental cars out there will make it to the freeway, let alone the base of the pass."

"Good point, Ox. I had thought to pick up some chains on my way to Mt. Baker, but studded tires work just as well. Thank you," Matt added.

"Great, so tomorrow we'll all go skiing. Maggie, would you like to join us?" Ox asked.

Maggie laughed, shaking her head. "Unless you plan to pull me around in a sled, this lady will not be partaking. I'd like to take my original hips to my grave."

The table erupted in laughter.

"Benjamina, what brings you here? Your family?" Kate interjected.

"For Christmas my mum gifted me with a winter holiday." Benjamina took another roll from the basket. "I spend two days here, then two in California, then three in Hawaii. I have a few work things to do on the side, but I'll manage."

"That's a lot of flying, and Hawaii too, flying over water." Kate snatched a roll.

Benjamina chuckled. "Since I came from London, I'm used to flying over the ocean."

Kate lowered her head and shoveled a piece of roll into her mouth. She prayed the powder Maggie had covered her face with hid the extra red flush spreading across her face.

"I'm not a big fan of flying." Matt prepared a bite of vegetables onto his fork.

"Thank you, Matt, it's nice to not feel so alone." Kate raised her wine glass in a toast to him only. Their glasses clinked as wicked smiles formed.

"I don't let it stop me, but I'm grateful when the wheels touch down."

"You two are lovely." Benjamina lifted her wine glass. "Indeed a delight to meet you both. And how dare I forget Maggie.

Cheers to us all."

With a forced smile, Kate tapped her glass amongst the others. Then returned her focus to the meal, finishing up in silence.

"How about some green tomato pie for dessert?" Ox scooted back his chair and stood.

"That sounds horrible, Ox. I'll pass." Matt wiped his mouth with the napkin.

"Oh, it's scrumptious," Benjamina said.

"You've had green tomato pie?" Ox's eyebrow raised.

"Who hasn't?" Benjamina stood, carrying her plate and swiping Kate's plate.

"I didn't know you had made another pie," Kate took a sip of wine.

"Late last night when I couldn't sleep, I ran out and bought more tomatoes. I was surprised they had a new shipment in." Ox returned to the table with the pie.

Ox took a stack of plates to the sink and returned with dessert plates. Benjamina made herself at home, opening another bottle of Cabernet before taking it to the table.

"I thought I heard someone in the kitchen." Maggie drained the last sip of Cab from her glass.

Kate wondered why Ox hadn't been able to sleep last night. But then again, she had spent last night tossing in bed more than sleeping. *Had we been thinking the same thoughts?*

"Why couldn't you sleep, Ox?" Maggie asked. "Everything okay?"

"It's nothing, Maggie. Now would you like a slice of pie?" Ox held the pie server like a gavel.

Maggie frowned, as if disappointed in Ox's general response. "Yes, do you think it turned out as good as when you and Kate made it?"

"I hope so." Ox winked.

"I'll leave you all to the pie." Matt stood. "Ox, if you could let me know the wireless password, I'd like to get a few things done for work."

"Sorry, Matt, there isn't one. I do have it listed as a distraction free inn." Ox passed the plate of pie to Maggie and glanced at Kate.

"Ox, that's lovely." Benjamina held out her plate for Ox to place a slice of pie on. "Technology can be overbearing and intrusive. I always welcome a break."

Ox handed a plate to Benjamina, and then sliced Kate a piece of pie.

Kate couldn't stop thinking about how much Ox and Benjamina had in common. She could see why they had dated, but she needed to know why they had stopped.

Matt hovered at the base of the stairs. "Is there a coffee place nearby that has internet?"

"There is." Ox handed Kate her dessert plate. "But you can't go out in this weather. Your rental care would never make it."

"I think I'll just go to bed early then, get ready for tomorrow. Thanks, Ox. Goodnight, everyone." Matt took the steps two at a time.

"Yikes." Ox sat down with his piece of pie. "Matt is not happy about that. Kate, do you remember how taken aback you were when I told you I didn't have internet?"

Kate chuckled. "I admit, I panicked a bit."

Maggie licked her fork clean before the next bite. "This pie is divine, Ox."

"It's different not having constant access to everything and everyone." Kate sliced off a bite of pie with her fork. "At first, I found myself reaching for my phone. Now I wonder if I will ever go back to my old ways."

Ox smiled as he took a sip of his wine.

"That's great, Kate." Maggie yawned and stretched her

neck.

"This pie is scrumptious." Benjamina had already eaten three-fourths of her piece.

"Yes, Kate, you must make sure I don't leave without getting this recipe," Maggie said.

"Of course, but, Ox, where did you find a recipe?" Kate forked off another bite.

"I remembered the one you gave me." Ox winked.

If Kate had not been sitting down, she might have needed to grab onto something to keep her legs from folding. *That wink! Does Ox owe the electric company for the sparks he creates?* Kate focused on her pie. Even in the low kitchen lights, she didn't want Ox to see her face flush or for Maggie to boldly point it out.

"Would you like to watch a movie, Kate?" Ox took a bite.

"Me?" Kate placed her hand on her chest as though there was another Kate behind her.

"Of course you, Kate," Maggie stated from across the table.

"Sure," Kate mumbled.

Why did he only invite me? Why didn't he ask Maggie and Benjamina? Bayou shifted on Kate's feet and stretched out his paws in a yawn. These first few days of vacation had been a ping-pong match of emotions and now it had grown even more complicated.

She broke from her feelings and glanced down at Bayou under the table. One thing was certain, she adored the yellow fur ball. Growing up Kate had zero pets but had spent many years begging for a cat or at the very least a hamster. Her friends had pets, but Kate's parents were not keen on the idea of fur all over their home. They used Kate's busy childhood as an extra excuse to not allow pets. Weekends were filled with activities, weeknights were for homework, and after dinner meant strolls through the neighborhood with her dad.

"I'd invite you for the movie, Ben, seeing it's your most

favorite movie ever, but you must be exhausted." Ox laughed and placed his hands on Benjamina's shoulders.

"Please tell me you are not going to make Kate watch that dreadful movie." Benjamina reached back, grabbing hold of Ox's hand.

"Dreadful?" Kate slid her feet out from under Bayou and pushed the chair back. She made her way around the table with her dessert plate.

"*Grumpy Old Men*, a true classic." Ox grinned.

Kate paused and reached over, smacking Ox's arm on the way to the sink. "I love that movie!"

"You two go watch your movie, and I'll get the dishes." Maggie rose from her chair. "Benjamina, would you mind helping?"

"I can't let you do that, Maggie. You and Ben are guests." Ox scrambled after to clear off the rest of the dishes.

Maggie set the plates on the counter and placed both hands on Ox's shoulders. "I have been coming here for years, and I will continue to for as long as I can. But if I tell you to do something, then you do it, Ox, or I will take my future business elsewhere."

Ox backed away, his hands up in surrender. "You better hurry, Kate, or Maggie will take you down next."

"Maggie, you are such a delight." Benjamina slid her chair out. "Go on, Ox, watch your childish movie. Maggie and I will clean up. I'm dying to slip into my cozies and start reading this new book I bought at the airport gift shop."

Kate placed her hand on Ox's back and pushed him in the direction of the living room. She continued pushing forward, mindful of the step down. Yet, since Kate had her eyes fixed on her feet, she missed that Ox had stopped and smacked into him – face first.

"Sorry." Kate rubbed her nose.

Every time she and Ox touched, it caused shivers to travel through her whole body. Kate's heart pumped so loudly that she swore Ox could hear it beating.

Ox loaded the movie into the DVD player as Kate snuggled into what was becoming her spot on the sofa. Ox joined Kate on the couch as a mass of yellow fur leapt up between them.

"Wow." Kate chuckled. "He made it up without making it seem like he climbed Mt. Everest."

Without warning Bayou spun around on the couch. His body slammed into Kate and Ox with the spin. He froze, his front paws spread wide.

"Calm down, Bayou," Ox warned.

"What's gotten into him?"

Bayou spun in a circle and jumped off the couch. He braced himself, his front legs spread out, his back end up, tail wagging rapidly.

"Don't you do it." Ox held his hand up to Bayou. "Don't." Through the stern voice, Ox tried to hide the onset of laughter.

"What is he going to do?" Kate whispered to Ox, without taking her eyes off Bayou.

Before Ox could answer, Bayou sprang up and bounced onto the couch between them. He spun and jumped back onto the carpet only to spin around again before leaping up on the couch. Once the spinning and jumping ended, Bayou did his yoga stretch and rested on the floor.

"What was that?" Kate's eyes were still wide, staring at Bayou.

"Zoomies." Ox reached out and placed his hand on Kate's wrist as their laughter faded.

Kate eased her body in Ox's direction. He and Kate were close enough that she could smell the fragrance of mint and evergreen. The end table lights were dim, and the fireplace's glow illuminated the sapphire of Ox's eyes. They took a deep breath together, aware of the moment. Kate leaned forward. *Kiss me! Kiss me!* Ox leaned forward.

"Hey, guys," Matt announced. "I guess there is no television in my room. You have a zero technology inn for sure."

Right behind Matt entered Maggie. Ox and Kate leaned away from each other. His hand slid from her wrist. Kate wanted desperately to grab hold of Ox's hand and place it back where it belonged.

"What are we watching?" Matt found a spot on the other side of Kate.

"*Grumpy Old Men*." Ox's words were rigid.

"Never seen it," Matt said.

Bayou stood from his spot and placed his chin on Kate's knees letting out a whimper.

"Sorry." Kate petted his head and then took it in her hands. "There's no room for you."

Bayou sighed, reclining back into his sloppy Labrador sit, eyeing Matt. Then, with a single clumsy forward movement, Bayou leapt onto Kate's lap, all one hundred plus pounds of him.

"Bayou!" Kate shrieked.

"Are you okay?" Ox covered his mouth to hide both shock and laughter.

"Let's just say I'm glad I'm not a man."

The living room filled with laughter. Snow fell outside the windows as the light from the television danced around the room. Kate dared not try to move Bayou as he rested his head and chest on her, and his back end on Ox.

"I never would have guessed this movie was a favorite of yours," Ox whispered, leaning toward Kate.

"I know." She smirked.

Chapter Twenty-Five

Kate eased into bed. Without Bayou, it seemed lonely and cold. Gazing at the roses on the dresser, her thoughts drifted to Benjamina and Ox. Picking up her cell phone, Kate swiped to her contacts and hit SEND. *Please go through, please.* It rang.

"Ali, is this a good time?"

"I'm just getting up for the day."

With the phone still in her hand, Kate rolled over onto her stomach. Her legs were bent at her knees, feet up in the air and locked at the ankles. If the cell had been a landline, she would felt like she'd gone back in time to when she called her high school friends before homework.

"Time difference, shoot. Sorry, it slipped my mind."

"What is so bad that you had to call me?"

Kate could hear the sound of something pouring in the background. "Now that you have your coffee, can I begin?"

Ali swallowed. "Yes."

"Ox's ex-girlfriend is here, and she is beautiful." Kate stood and went to the mirror.

"So are you, Kate. You are a beautiful woman."

Kate grabbed at her cheek and patted her curls. Her finger pushed at a sliver of a line across her forehead. "I think I'm getting a wrinkle."

"We all are, honey."

She peered out the window as snow fluttered down without plans to stop. Then Kate went to the vase nearby.

"Why is his ex-girlfriend there?" Ali inquired.

"He said two guests were coming and he called her Ben. I thought Ben was a he. But he is a she. She loves to fly and appears much less clumsy than me."

"Everyone is less clumsy than you. Ev-ery-one."

Kate rolled her eyes.

"But you said ex, so what's the problem?"

Standing on her tiptoes, Kate smelled the roses. "The problem is that he made it clear he doesn't want a relationship, yet apparently he has before."

"Kate, when did they date?"

"A while ago, college age."

Kate held the phone away from her ear as the sound of Ali's shrieking laughter filtered through the phone.

"It could not have been that special if there is no actual time frame."

"It's not like it was in middle school. College was not that long ago." Kate flopped on the bed, observing the textured swirls on the ceiling.

"How many men have you dated? More than me."

Kate giggled. "Yes, but none of them are here now or suddenly opposed to a relationship."

"You don't know that."

Kate sighed and rolled over.

"Hey, Sherlock, maybe you should find out why they broke up," Ali stated.

"Your sarcasm is not necessary."

"My sarcasm is always necessary, Kate."

They both giggled.

Kate covered herself up with the extra blanket at the end of the bed. "How did your interview go?"

"It went perfectly." Ali sighed. "Kate, I love it here. I don't even want to go back for my stuff."

"That's exactly how I feel about having to go back to Phoenix." Kate sprang upright in bed. "I'm going to miss it here so much. It's not just about Ox. My soul feels like whipped cream cheese, light and airy."

"Have you been taking photographs?"

"Yes, and I believe I have some great ones. I can't tell on the camera's tiny viewing screen though."

Ali took a long sip of coffee. "Did you not bring your laptop?"

"No, I forgot it."

"Does Ox not have one?"

"He is not a fan of technology. He has a landline! His entire inn runs off the books, actual books. Not to mention, he pays for everything in cash."

Ali laughed. "I bet you don't even care. Come to think of it, I haven't seen any updated posts on social media."

"Ali, I don't even miss it. I kind of like it." Kate giggled.

"Remind me why we're best friends again?"

"Ha-ha. So tell me what you're going to do about moving? I can't believe I'm even asking this. Look at us, Ali. I feel like we're breaking up."

"We're making ourselves happy. Don't you dare guilt trip me, Kate."

"I'm not. And no one is offering me jobs and setting me up in a high-rise apartment."

"You would hate my apartment."

Kate nodded her head, although Ali could not see it. "True."

"Plus, the whole Ox thing."

"I have to respect his wishes. Something is wrong, and he won't tell me exactly what. I think he might be sick." Kate sank back against the headboard. Her breathing was heavy and tight as she placed a hand on her chest. She closed her eyes and breathed deeply through her nose. "I've seen him with a stiff shuffle and a few off balance moments as though he might fall. He also dropped a cup the other day."

"Do you think that's why he doesn't want a relationship?"

Kate gasped. "How did I not see that?" Kate massaged her forehead with her fingers. "But what is going on with him?"

"Kate?"

Kate leaned sideways, drawing her legs to her chest and tugging the blankets up to her chin. "Yeah?"

"Make the move back home to Washington for you. Everything else will figure itself out. I promise. And for the record, you sound happy, Kate. Like you did years ago."

Kate squeezed her fist around the blanket. "Thank you."

"Now I have a million things to get done. My day is just starting."

"Bye, Ali."

"Bye, Kate, talk to you later."

Pushing END on her phone, Kate set it on the nightstand.

Ox flopped onto his bed as though he was fourteen years old again. The grin on his face was frozen. He could not believe Kate loved one of his favorite movies. Today turned out to be a great day, not only for his health, but also his heart. It felt cheesy to think about, but he could not ignore the feeling awakening inside. A knock at the door got Bayou's attention and he went to investigate by sniffing under it.

Ox rolled out of bed and opened the door.

"Ben." Ox's smile flat-lined.

"Expecting someone else?" Benjamina smirked as she stepped inside Ox's room without an invitation.

"Why would you assume that?" Ox followed Benjamina toward the sofa while Bayou flopped onto the floor by the window.

"Because I know you, Ox. I also know you are hiding

something." Benjamina sat sideways on the sofa and draped her arm over the back, facing Ox.

Ox sat on the arm of the sofa, his feet on the cushions. His elbows pressed on his knees. "How have you been?"

"Don't change the subject." Benjamina wagged her finger at him. "Remember why we broke up?"

"Yes, because you always have to be right."Benjamina smacked the front of Ox's leg with her hand and let out a fake laugh.

"Rubbish, because we are better off as friends. We were simply too opposite when it came down to what we wanted in life. You want family, and I want to travel and not be tied down."

"I want to travel, but I want to do it with family." Ox glanced at Bayou.

"And traveling with family and dogs and everything else that it involves." Benjamina stuck out her tongue and leaned her head back, pretending to sleep. "Just saying it makes me want to nap."

Ox arched his eyebrow.

"Now, when will you and Kate be getting married?" Benjamina grinned broadly enough to give the Joker a run for his money.

Ox's shoulders slumped. "No relationships for me. Ever."

"Oxnard Swanson, don't get cross with me. You better tell me what's going on." Benjamina crossed her legs.

Ox locked his fingers together, using his thumbs to rub his temples. "I have multiple sclerosis."

Benjamina gasped and covered her mouth. Her body falling forward into her lap. She pushed herself to her knees and wrapped her arms around Ox. Tears filled Benjamina's eyes and she wiped them as fast as she could. "Ox, no, oh no."

Ox returned the hug, squeezing Benjamina and engulfing her in his arms. Bayou got to his feet and sat below the sofa arm.

Ox reached out and rubbed Bayou's head, letting him know everything was all right.

Benjamina lowered herself back down. "When did you get diagnosed? Why didn't you tell me?"

"I don't like to talk about it." Ox ran his hand through his hair.

"Regardless of everything, we are friends, and you should have said something."

Ox rubbed his hand over the scruff on his chin and sighed. "I don't like to talk about how much something I can't control is taking over my life."

"Is this is why you don't want a relationship?" Benjamina slapped her palm on her leg. "Ox, you can't let this stop you from living your life."

"It is stopping me," Ox raised his voice.

"Rubbish, Ox, simply rubbish." Benjamina sprang up. "You're like a goody two-shoes kid who grounds himself when he does something wrong before his parents even get a chance." Her hands were planted firmly on her hips.

"I'm not dragging a woman down to be a part of a life that is uncertain day by day, especially not someone like Kate."

Benjamina rubbed her tongue over her front teeth and returned to the edge of the sofa. "I see the way you two are around each other. I could probably see it from a plane if you had skylights."

Ox chuckled. Benjamina squeezed Ox's socked foot. "It's true, so what are you going to do?"

Ox turned his head toward Benjamina. "Nothing, I will not bring Kate or anyone else into my life. Today is a good day, but I can't speak beyond that."

"Does she know? Did you give her any say?"

"No, she is a guest, an unplanned guest." Ox went to get the glass of water off his nightstand and took a long sip. "Nothing more."

"Sounds like a twist of fate." Benjamina stood, an eyebrow raised.

"Doesn't matter what you call it, it's not going to happen. Once she heads back home, I can push any thoughts and feelings aside."

"I see your stubbornness has not changed a bit." Benjamina pulled Ox in for another hug, which he accepted without hesitation. "I'm glad I got to stop in and see you, even with this dreadful news of yours. I won't mention anything to Kate, but I will give you my two cents."

Ox stepped back from the hug. "Of course you will."

"Don't let your diagnosis mess up your life in ways that it doesn't have control over. I know about MS as you remember."

"Your dad." Ox's head hung, nearly touching his chest.

"He continues to live a wonderful life, not a perfect life, but better than any of us thought. And there are so many new studies and drugs."

Ox's head shook no. "The neurologist tried one on me, but it didn't seem to help. There is a second drug, but I told him I wanted to wait to try it."

Benjamina grabbed Ox's hand with both of hers. "Don't give up hope."

Ox closed his eyes as if to wish away his disease.

Benjamina grabbed Ox's chin and squeezed it between her fingers. "Stop it. You are being the opposite of the Ox I knew and the Ox I love. Everyone handles this diagnosis differently, so stop acting like you are dying and live your life." Benjamina wiggled Ox's chin as she kept hold. "Okay?"

Ox nodded and Benjamina dropped her hand and kissed Ox's cheek. "Goodnight, you stubborn ox."

"Goodnight, Ben."

Chapter Twenty-Six

"I don't understand." Matt rolled his gray-blue work shirt up at the sleeves. Clearly he didn't dress down much. "How can they close a ski resort because of too much snow?"

"An avalanche threat will cause it to close." Ox placed warm-from-the-oven French toast onto a cream-colored serving platter and brought it to the table.

Matt and Kate dove forward with their forks trying to snag the first piece. A sideways smile shone across Kate's face in victory.

Benjamina entered the kitchen. "Lovely morning, I slept gloriously."

Maggie sat at the end of the table, leaving an open chair next to Kate. After pouring maple syrup over the French toast, Kate scooped up some fresh scrambled eggs from a bowl.

"What else is there to do in this one horse town?" Matt eyed the coffee carafe as though it were a spaceship. "The coffee place you spoke of, Ox, it has actual coffee?"

"This is far more than a single horse town. The McCallisters own at least six. And, yes, the coffee place has the short, tall, soy-nutter-flutter filled coffees." Ox pulled out the chair next to Kate, a full mug in hand.

"I just love black coffee." Benjamina reached for the carafe. *Of course she does.*

"Kate, you should join me. You look like the espresso type." Matt winked.

"Actually, I prefer black coffee." Kate held up her coffee

mug. "Although, on occasion I enjoy those store-bought coffee creamers. The fall flavors get me every time."

Kate caught Ox giving a wicked smile to his mug.

"Sounds like you would enjoy a latte." Matt grinned.

"I doubt you will be able to make it out to the coffee place this morning, Matt." Ox pointed toward the kitchen window. "If they closed Mt. Baker for an avalanche, it would be ill-advised to be out driving."

Outside, an endless sea of white surrounded the inn. The wind had caused the snow to stick to the sides of everything it hadn't already covered from falling straight down.

"I'm not a child and, therefore, not grounded." Matt stabbed his fork into the French toast. "There must be something to do around here. It's not as though it never snows here. The roads should be plowed within the hour I'd assume. And, Ox, no more of those nineties movies. Anything but that." Matt laughed, but stopped when he realized he was the only one.

"I'm all for more nineties movies, Ox." Kate mentioned between bites. A twisted smile of glee spread over Ox's cheeks.

After Bayou finished his breakfast, he made his way around the table getting his morning greetings. When he reached Matt, Bayou quickly learned there would be zero attention from him and kept on moving before settling between Ox and Kate.

"What about the trail, Ox?" Maggie piped up at the other end of the table.

"What trail?" Matt asked, before Ox could even answer.

Ox put his coffee mug down and concentrated on taking a few bites of eggs before answering.

"It's off the backyard, goes on for about three miles." Ox slid the French toast platter toward Benjamina. "With it snowing as heavy as it is, I don't think that's the best option. It's confusing enough without all the extra snow."

"It is a beautiful trail," Kate mentioned.

"So you've been?" Matt set his fork down and wrapped his fingers together.

"Yes, Bayou and I went. It's beautiful, but Ox is right, it can be rather tricky to find your way. Plus the snow is much deeper than when we went."

"I've skied in worse conditions. I can handle myself." Matt itched at a spot in his hair, trying to avoid messing up his gel-styled part. "Kate, join me please."

Ox, Benjamina, and Maggie shifted their eyes toward Kate, as though her decision would announce the next President of the United States. A part of her wanted to go, another part of her wanted to stay. She had already planned to be cold today anyway with skiing. This would not be too terribly different.

"Ox, are you sure we can't go skiing?" Kate picked up her mug. "You know everyone in town, you have connections."

"Sorry, Kate, I don't have a key to get the ski lifts working. They might open again before you leave though. I wish you had mentioned it sooner. We could have gone when it was nicer."

"With everything else going on, it slipped my mind." Kate returned her focus to her breakfast.

Benjamina eyed everyone at the table. "Ox, what's the difference between an inn and a bed and breakfast?"

Ox sipped his coffee, lowered the mug back to the table, and leaned back against his chair. "It's easy to distinguish. An inn has more rooms and serves three meals a day. As the name suggests, a bed and breakfast only offers breakfast."

Matt stood, his chair sliding back with such force it teetered as though it might fall over.

"Kate, come on, join me," Matt encouraged.

"Okay, Matt, I'll tag along." The words left Kate's mouth, and she covered it with her hand from shock. Her stomach suddenly felt unsettled as though knowing she had upset Ox in some way.

"Great." Matt grinned as though he had won Kate's heart.

"Benjamina, do you want to go with?" Maggie offered.

Matt froze at the bottom of the stairs.

"No, thank you. I have a conference call in," Benjamina paused to check her watch, "ten minutes."

Matt beamed and turned back to the stairs, taking two at a time. "We're leaving in ten minutes, Kate."

They all heard the sound of his door closing at the end of the hall.

"Kate, I don't know how I feel about you going on this … city man's adventure." Ox spoke to his eggs, refusing eye contact. "It's still snowing hard."

"Excuse me?" Kate attempted to make eye contact with his hidden eyes.

"I know you went before, but the snow wasn't falling like it is now and the trail is already hard to see."

"Why are you okay with letting Matt go?" Maggie wiped her mouth with a napkin.

"Do you think I could tell that man what to do? If he sits around here all day, he will complain. If he goes to town, he will end up getting stuck or having an accident. I can't stop guests from doing what they want, especially big-headed fools like Matt."

Ox shoved a heaping bite of French toast into his mouth.

"Send Bayou out with him," Maggie suggested.

Ox finished chewing. "The snow is too deep for him. Bayou is in shape, but he couldn't make it the distance of the trail and back on his own in this weather. I doubt Matt would know what to do if Bayou needed help."

Kate stood, scooting her chair out as though in slow motion, alerting Bayou to move. "We will be fine. I have a great memory."

She avoided making eye contact with Ox and took her dishes to the kitchen sink. Kate was more than capable of going for a short hike in the snow.

"I'm not from Phoenix. Remember, Ox? I can handle the outdoors." Then Kate headed upstairs to ready herself with Bayou at her heels.

"I'm sure they'll be able to handle themselves," Benjamina said over her mug. Ox shook his head, pushing at the food on his plate with his fork, unable to finish eating.

Chapter Twenty-Seven

The snow gathered in deep drifts up against the trees as Matt and Kate made their way on the path. While the beauty of it was amazing, it also had warmth and a stillness. The stillness allowed her thoughts to venture for answers. Yet, Benjamina's face kept appearing in her mind. From Kate's point of view, Ox and Ben were a great match, and she wondered if he might be willing to drop the no relationship clause and get back together.

She rubbed her gloved hand over the compass hidden inside her pocket. Ox snuck it into Kate's palm on her way out.

"We don't need that compass," Matt stated, as though he could hear her glove gliding back and forth over it. "I saw him give it to you. I have never in my life been lost, and some snow is not going to suddenly cause me to now."

"This is my first time in snowshoes." Kate wobbled and leaned, gathering her balance. "Could you wait up for me?"

Matt turned and stopped. "Sorry."

Ox had several pairs of snowshoes for use, but still held his face firm with disapproval as he strapped Kate's on.

"I'm short, and your one step is about two steps for me. Do you know where you're going? The snow is much deeper than before."

"Yes, the trees ahead appear to part left and then right. We are just staying with the trail."

As soon as Kate caught up, Matt continued on.

"We've been walking for maybe an hour and I don't

remember this view." Kate paused observing the pines. "Matt this doesn't look familiar at all." She slid the compass from her pocket, careful not to drop it into the snow.

"Don't you dare use that compass," Matt warned. "Trust me. It doesn't come across as familiar because it's covered in snow."

"I was out here in the snow." Kate reluctantly tucked the compass back into her pocket.

"You had that fur ball with you, so you probably were not paying much attention. Plus, I think having a dog when you run a business is not a good practice. People can be allergic to them."

"Bayou is a therapy dog in training," Kate announced. "He is trying to help me with my anxiety while flying. He brings me comfort and even makes me laugh."

"Sounds like the type of man you need, not a dog. Besides, it's all in your head, the fear. I could have you flying around the world without a care," Matt gloated. "Like I said earlier, it's not my favorite, but I manage just fine."

They walked in silence for what seemed like forever. Matt led the way as Kate lingered behind lost in her thoughts. After a while, Matt stopped, allowing Kate to catch up again.

He placed his hands on her arms, pulling her forward at the elbows. "Has Ox even told you how beautiful you are?"

"Matt, that's rather forward of you to ask. I came out here because I needed to clear my head or at least try. I wish we could have gone skiing."

What Kate didn't mention was that by "we" she didn't mean Matt at all. She would much rather be out skiing with Ox right now than here on the trail with Matt. But, she thought his head would deflate and float away, getting snagged in a tree like an escaped balloon if she mentioned it.

Matt's face leaned toward Kate's, and before she knew it, she could smell cinnamon on his breathe. She drew her head back. "What are you doing?"

"I'm going to kiss you. The setting is perfect." Matt closed his eyes, leaning in further.

"No." Kate raised her hand up, covering her mouth.

Matt's lips touched her glove. Matt's eyes popped open, his eyebrows up in shock. The bridge of his nose wrinkled where it met his forehead. Matt's expression meant he didn't have a history of being stopped.

"You have a boyfriend?" Matt asked.

Kate shook her head no. "I'm not looking for a relationship."

The words sent her back to Ox and his exact same comment. The comment that caused Kate's chest to tighten and her mind to question what might be wrong. Had Ox told her no for the same reason she told Matt? Did Ox not like her beyond her looks? But there were at least three times when she and Ox had almost kissed. And it felt the complete opposite of the spark-less almost-kiss she and Matt nearly had.

"Matt, I'm here on vacation. I'm leaving soon; you're leaving soon. Let's not complicate it." Kate sighed. She didn't want to hurt his ego.

"You don't think you can fall in love on vacation? Because I'm sure that finding love doesn't stick to a work schedule." Matt rubbed his gloved hands together.

The moisture from the snow had dampened the styling of his hair. Matt's black wool sweater peeked out from under his charcoal peacoat. The tips of his ears already pink from the temperature.

"Of course, you can fall in love on vacation, Matt." She placed her gloves over his. "But not with me."

Matt's lips formed a pout, and he lowered his head. A second later, he returned his eyes to Kate. They were a lighter shade of brown against all the white. His face showed fine lines, she had not noticed until now. While Kate clearly found him attractive, it didn't go any further than that.

In the past, she would never have put her hand between hers and incoming lips. Being here the last few days, Kate had opened back up and been honest with herself. Not that it mattered. Ox had made his feelings clear several times over.

"Kate?" Matt asked. "You zoned out for a minute."

"Sorry." She returned her focus to the problem at hand.

The snow continued to fall in oversized flakes. Their tracks completely disappeared behind them.

"Matt, which way were we going?" Kate felt frightened by the disorienting snow. Everywhere she turned, the firs and pines appeared as the mirror of each other.

"This way." Matt pointed, confidence in his voice.

He started stepping, and Kate did her best to keep pace with him.

"Matt, the trail was not this long when I went with Bayou. We should have reached the end and turned around some time ago." Kate removed the compass from her pocket. "Inn of the Woods is south of where we started and this is," Kate held up the compass to prove her point, "pointing west, not north."

"Paths are not straight, Kate," Matt warned. He stepped forward, continuing west.

Kate did not want to risk being alone, so she leapt along, quickly stepping in Matt's tracks. "I don't think we should keep going."

"Kate, trust me. I am in tune with nature." Matt's arms raised as laughter filled the snow-covered wilderness. "The snow and I are one."

"Matt, just stop talking." Kate paused.

Matt continued on, as though deaf to Kate's warnings. The newest falling snowflakes joined, forming quarter-size balls of glistening white. The path narrowed more and pines closed in as the distance between them and the inn, without doubt, continued to grow. Kate became lost in her thoughts yet again, focusing on her steps as they trudged forward.

"I don't think this is part of the trail. We took a wrong turn." Kate rotated at her hips, glancing behind her. She turned around; everything was white. Matt was no longer in her line of sight.

"Matt? Matt!"

Flipping her scarf up to her nose, she inhaled the lingering smell of leftover lavender oil. She shut her eyes thinking of Ox. She thought of his face, his eyes, the warmth of his voice when he spoke. Kate's thoughts flashed to Matt and every other guy from her past. They all spoke at her, not to her. How had years of college and continuous Saturday date nights not taught her the mistakes in life to avoid? Kate shook her head. How long would it take to learn who she was and who she needed to be? She breathed in the scarf again.

"Kate! Kate!"

The sound of her name broke through the thoughts. She pivoted in her spot. "Matt?"

Kate swiveled her head to the left and then right, nothing but white. She pivoted her snowshoes in a complete circle, nothing but white.

"Matt!" she jerked the compass out of her pocket again. All she could think of was Ox, and Bayou. Inn of the Woods was south. Kate turned south and started marching.

"Matt!"

"Kate!" Matt called again, this time closer than before.

"Matt, I'm heading south, back to the inn. Can you find me?"

"Stop moving, and just keep talking!" Matt called out.

"I think you're to my right," Kate yelled. "Keep coming straight, I'm facing the direction of your voice now and watching for you."

"Don't stop talking!"

Odd to hear a man say that. Despite her fear, Kate had to laugh.

Searching her mind for what to say, all she found was Ox and her undecided future. She went out on a limb, hoping that with all the anxiety Matt would not remember any of this later. But she needed to get it out. She wanted to. She had to.

"I think I'm falling in love with Ox, but he doesn't want a relationship. I'm not happy living in Phoenix. I'm not happy in life. I took this trip to step back and examine my life, and it has opened my eyes. Have you ever had that before? Where once you left your comfort zone, you realized so many things? Have you ever taken a leap in life?"

Matt's outline came into view through the evergreens.

"I see you!" Matt jogged forward as best he could in snowshoes and embraced Kate like an old college friend.

"I promise not to tell Ox about what you said, if you don't mention that I'm not as one with the wild as I stated," Matt said, over her shoulder, remaining in the hug.

"Promise." Kate smiled.

Ox paced in front of the living room window. "I never should have let her go."

"You don't own her. You could not stop her." Maggie's knitting needles tapped together. "You warned her, it's all you could do."

Bayou sat at the window ledge, his chin resting upon it. With each pace Ox made, Bayou followed with a whimper.

Ox pointed at Bayou. "See? Even he is worried."

"Because you are worried." Maggie paused and glanced out the window. "Oh, dear, it's snowing again!"

"Maggie, they've been gone far too long for that trail. I

can't let something happen to Kate."

"Don't you think you already are by not telling her the truth?" Maggie rested her knitting needles on her lap.

Ox paused, his hands shoved into his jean pockets. "She doesn't need the truth. Between you and Benjamina, I've gotten enough pointers for a lifetime."

"Don't get short with me, Oxnard. You know I'm right. I'm just waiting for you to figure it out." Maggie sighed. "I'm glad to hear that nothing is lingering with you and Benjamina."

Ox faced Maggie. "Did you think that Benjamina and I were …"

Maggie spoke up before Ox could finish. "I had made a few assumptions, but this morning over breakfast it was vividly clear that while Benjamina and you have a past, you don't have a future."

Ox crossed his arms. "Thanks, I think."

"You remind me of Stan, such a bull at times." Maggie picked up her needles. "I waved the white flag, and finally, he realized I was standing right there. Kate's been waving it too, if you'd bother to stop being so stubborn."

"She is far from waving anything." Ox returned to pacing and checking his watch. "That's it! I can't do this. I'm going to find her."

"Them! She and Matt; both are your guests."

Ox shook his head and stomped out of the living room. Bayou dashed behind him.

Chapter Twenty-Eight

Kate held the compass like a baby bird in her gloved hands.

"I'm all about experiencing life. I had the opportunity to travel for business to Mongolia, which flipped on a light switch of adventure inside of me." Matt held his cell phone out as though he needed to find the right light for a selfie. "There has to be a signal someplace. Anyway, I had been living in muggy Florida, of all places. I spent every night at a club, talking business, trying to get my foot in the door. Yet, I left Mongolia with a business offer to move to New York, and I said yes without a second thought. Arriving in New York with my entire life in three suitcases, I felt — and don't ever repeat this — like crying until my mom came to pick me up. After I stopped being a baby, I realized that New York is amazing."

"But you live in Tucson." Kate's eyes jetted to the side.

"Yes, but I kept an apartment in New York for when I'm done in Tucson."

Matt paused and stared deeply at her. "Close your eyes, Kate."

"Matt, we have to find our way out of here before it gets dark and we freeze to death." Kate studied the compass. "We have to keep going south." She turned and pointed.

"Kate, give me one minute first. Close your eyes."

"Fine." Kate squeezed her eyes shut. Pressing them together tightly enough that stars started to sparkle in the darkness.

"Picture your home in Phoenix," Matt's voice appeared.

"What do you see around you that's important?"

Kate pictured her soft rugs under bare feet, the photo frames with memories of family and friends, and the plush cream chair with a gray and green blanket her parents brought back from Ireland draped over the side. In the mornings, she took her coffee there, watching television or reading a book. The view out the window flickered from bottle cacti to snow-covered evergreens.

She squeezed her eyes closed even tighter.

"What do you see, Kate?" Matt whispered. "What is important? How do you feel, Kate?"

"It's flickering to things that are here in Washington."

"Open your eyes, Kate." Matt touched her arm.

"What does that mean, Matt?"

The snow, which had let up a few minutes before, returned in full force.

"I realized what made me happy was the energy of work. Coming up with new solutions and solving issues was my passion. Going to clubs to mingle for business gave me heartburn," Matt laughed. "I needed the buzz of New York City, the high-rise buildings, the business suits. It's what worked for me. It does not work for everyone, trust me. I'm moving back to New York this summer once I finish up with the merger in Tucson."

"Then why come out here for a ski vacation when there are plenty around New York?" Kate brushed the snow from the top of the compass.

Matt shifted his weight in the snowshoes. "I set a goal a few years ago to ski in every state and country possible. This place, if this snowstorm ever lets up, will be number twenty-seven."

Snowflakes brushed on Kate's eyelashes. "Matt, we have to head back, now."

Kate stepped south, Matt following behind. The thickness of the snow fought their snowshoes with each step. With the sun hidden and the wind picking up, it grew more frigid. Worry crept into Kate's stomach, knotting it up like a cinnamon twist donut. It would not matter if she figured out her life if she froze to death.

"How far do you think we are from the inn?" Matt's voice filled the silence of the woods.

"I have no idea," Kate predicted. "We went out pretty far before it sank in that we were lost."

"Don't remind me of the obvious," Matt scowled.

Their snowshoes fell into the same rhythm as they plowed south through the powder. It became harder than ever to make out any sort of path in front of them. Kate twisted her head and paused. "Matt, I'm really worried, please stay close."

With each onward step, Kate's legs grew weaker, her fingers more numb, and her nose colder. Her breath was cold as she pictured the inn as though a mirage in front of her. She could see a nice mug of hot chocolate and a slice of green tomato pie on a plate and Bayou snuggled at her feet and the fireplace crackling. Thoughts of Ox and his ever-beautiful sapphire eyes and his striking smile filled her mind. For a second, maybe even five seconds, Kate envisioned sharing a kiss with Ox, the kiss that they had come oh-so close to sharing a few times now. Kate could almost feel the warmth of what his lips on her freezing cold mouth might be like.

"Kate! Kate!"

She didn't hear her name until it was too late. Kate lifted her head just as her snowshoes went to either side of the tree trunk. Her nose smacked into the bark. She held herself upright with great difficulty, arms swimming to maintain balance, but it didn't help. Kate drifted backwards, arms out, landing with a plop like a snow angel.

"Matt!" Kate whined, holding her nose.

She lifted her gloved hand up into view. No blood shone on the glove's knit. The snow shifted around Kate's head as Matt knelt down, his knees at her side.

"Are you all right?" Matt took his hand and placed it on

Kate's forehead. "I thought for sure you broke your nose. But, I don't see any blood."

Kate reached for her nose again. It hurt when she touched it. Lifting her head up, she pushed her body into a sitting position.

She examined her lower body and snowshoes. Since they were made of metal, it would take a lot to damage them, but she could have ripped her shoe out of the holder. Thankfully, everything remained intact. A headache began to form as Kate rubbed her temples.

"Let me help you. Are you all right to stand?" Matt held on to Kate under her arm.

"Yes, I think so." Kate bent her knees.

Matt wrapped his arm around her and lifted Kate's weight up as she pushed off with her legs. Once standing, Matt slowly took his hand off Kate's back. "Sure you're all right? You're not dizzy?"

Kate turned her head to the left, and then right, up and down. "No dizziness. Just a sore nose and headache."

Matt smiled. "Perfect. Let's get moving."

"Oh no!" Kate's eyes searched in panic, her hands patting her pockets. "The compass! I dropped it when I hit the tree."

Kate locked eyes with Matt. Her eyes were wide with worry, and tears glossed over them as fear sank in.

"Stay calm, Kate," Matt warned. "Ox knows this area; he knows when we left and where we were headed. He will come and find us, but we can make it out ourselves." Matt's gloved hands squeezed Kate's gloved hands.

"All right." Kate smiled, and then wiped her fallen tears away before they froze. Her spirit shaken, when they parted hands, Kate noticed her bones trembling. The icy air seeped through the layers of her clothing. "Matt, it's so cold."

"Kate, let's focus. It's just like in the corporate office, when the CEOs and higher ups come in for a meeting, and we have to prove our project is the best. This is not any different."

Kate shook her head yes and took a deep breath of chilly air. "Okay, so I was walking this way when the tree and I became friends." Kate pointed. "Let's keep going this way."

Matt wrapped his arm around Kate's as they stepped toward what they hoped was south and toward the inn.

Chapter Twenty-Nine

The sound of Bayou's barking brought tears back to Kate's eyes. Her legs were weaker than ever. With each step she struggled to keep upright. Bayou did a circle around Kate and then Matt, before returning to Kate. Falling to her knees, she wrapped Bayou into a hug.

"I missed you too, buddy." Kate buried her face into his fur.

"Glad to see you, Ox!" Matt called out.

Kate peered up from above Bayou's back. Ox's figure broke through the snow, and then he bolted to her. Yet Kate could not stand on her own, her strength gone. Ox slid to his knees in the snow.

"Kate!" Ox was now eye-level with her.

She reached out for him even though Bayou remained standing in front of her. Ox drew his arms around Kate, and she welcomed the heat from his body. His chest pressed against her nose, and she pushed away.

"Ouch." She clutched her nose.

"What happened?" Ox held Kate at arm's length.

"I-I was distracted."

"She ran into a tree," Matt added.

Ox glared up at Matt as though he had interrupted the final play of the World Series.

"You ran into a tree?" Ox's eyes narrowed.

"I lost your compass. I'm sorry, Ox." Kate hung her head.

Ox slid a finger under Kate's chin and lifted her head back up. "I don't care about the compass. Let's get you out of the snow."

Kate tried to stand, but her legs were too weak. "How far is the inn? I don't know how much more I can walk."

"Less than half a mile." Ox wrapped his arms around Kate and lifted her out of the snow. "Can you make it?"

Kate took a step forward, but barely. "Yes, I can't go fast though."

"I'll support you." Ox wrapped his arm around her waist, and together they moved forward. After a few minutes, Ox's right leg weakened, and his gait went unbalanced. Kate felt Ox shift to his right, his legs wobbling as much as hers.

"Ox, are you all right?"

Ox waved off her question.

Matt and Bayou made their way through the snow, following Ox and Kate. "Let Bayou lead the way, Matt. We will be home in no time. Matt, would you mind assisting me with Kate?"

Matt appeared at her left side, without question, and wrapped his arm under Kate's.

"Thank you for coming to get us." Kate's voice was soft.

"I'm sure you would have found your way back. But Bayou was whining at the window. He insisted."

"Was he pounding at the window like he does my door? He's like a grumpy old man." Kate's laughter was frail.

"Sheer determination." Ox's lips turned up.

"I have to admit, I'm rather overjoyed to see you and that yellow mass of fur," Matt stated. "You might have the most old school inn ever, but at least you don't forget about your guests. If I'd stayed at a hotel, no employee would have thought twice about coming search for me."

Kate shifted her weight more toward Matt, unsure what was going on with Ox. Clearly, something was not right.

"Ox."

"Whatever it is, Kate, it can wait," Ox whispered.

Without the strength to argue, she dropped it. All of her thoughts could be mistakes. Maybe she hallucinated this all. It would be best to get back to the inn, thaw out, and eat before she made any major decisions.

The inn came into sight, and Kate smiled once again. Maggie and Benjamina waved frantically from the living room window. Reaching the front of the inn, the door swung open. Maggie greeted them with open arms, followed by hugs from Benjamina.

The heat from inside escaped, causing Kate's face to tingle as it thawed. Matt, not one for hugs, gladly accepted Maggie and Benjamina's embrace, if only for a second of warmth. Benjamina took Matt's spot, wrapping her arm around Kate and assisted Ox.

Ox paused once inside, leaning against the door frame.

"Ox, go rest. I'll help Maggie with Kate." Benjamina and Maggie assisted a shivering Kate to the couch.

The fireplace crackled and popped. Maggie removed Kate's boots, jacket, and gloves. Kate shivered as Benjamina piled two quilts on top of her.

"Bayou, come lie down with Kate and keep her warm." As if understanding exactly what Maggie instructed, Bayou sauntered to the couch. He made his way up, laying his body across Kate's. She used what little energy she had left to stroke the fur on his head, even if she could not feel it with her swollen, pink fingers.

Maggie left the living room but quickly returned with a steaming mug. "Hold the handle for now. If you try and warm your hands around the heat of the mug, it will burn. Your hands are too cold."

Maggie bent forward, lining up the handle for Kate to grab.

"Thank you," Kate replied, her voice scratchy.

"Rest," Benjamina instructed. "You must be simply famished! I will make you anything Ox has in the kitchen."

Kate frowned; she could only think about fast food. Freezing to death can do that. Every single drive-thru window floated through Kate's thawing mind.

"Whatever you want to make is more than fine. My mind is full of fast food because I honestly thought I would never make it out alive." Kate's voice quivered as her thoughts went back to the woods.

Benjamina sat next to Kate on the couch. "Go on now, tell me what you are wanting and if I can attempt to make it, I will."

"I really want a mushroom burger with cheese and fries." Kate leaned her head back as though she asked for a diamond tiara.

"I will do my best. Now rest. Bayou, don't let Kate get up." Benjamina left the living room as Matt entered.

"Much better view of the snowstorm from inside." Matt warmed his hands near the fire. He seemed to be faring better than Kate.

"Doing better?" Kate turned her head, still resting on the couch pillows. "I think I'm thawing, finally. Is Ox all right?"

"Don't worry about Ox. You had us all worried." Maggie took her regular spot in the armchair, fingers looped into her knitting. "I thought you two should never have gone."

"We didn't die. I think we did fine," Matt declared.

Maggie shook her head at Matt's attitude and continued to focus on counting stitches. Kate placed her mug on the end table. She closed her eyes, and the sounds of the inn were amplified around her. With Bayou's heartbeat and the rhythm of his breathing steady in her lap, Kate drifted to sleep.

Benjamina's hand on Kate's shoulder gently woke her. "Dinner is ready, think you can make it to the table?"

"I got lost in the woods, I didn't fall off a cliff," Kate stated.

Once Bayou had climbed down, Kate lifted the blankets off. Benjamina reached out her hand. Kate pushed off the couch with her free hand. Weakness hit her once she was upright and she was thankful for Benjamina's hand. Together they made their way to the kitchen table. Matt, Ox, and Maggie were already seated.

On the table were homemade chips and what appeared to be mushroom burgers. Kate smiled at Benjamina. She had been kind and nothing but warm toward Kate since she arrived, even when Kate had given Benjamina the cold shoulder.

"You made what I asked for?" Kate lowered herself onto the dining room chair.

"Lucky you, Ox had everything I needed. Hope you like it."

Ox held his burger up. "This looks amazing, Ben."

He waited to take a bite until Kate took one. Sinking her teeth into the burger, Kate was suddenly ravenous. The juices exploded with flavor.

"Benjamina, it's perfect. Thank you." Kate covered her full mouth as she spoke. "You're such a great chef."

"I'm delighted you like it." Benjamina beamed.

"I second that." Ox wiped his mouth. "You get a room discount."

Kate did not so much as glance up from her plate until the last crumb had been devoured.

"Best burger ever." Kate leaned back in her chair.

"I would agree." Matt took his last bite.

"I'm requesting this be on the menu next year when I visit. So Benjamina better be here to make it."

"If my schedule allows, it'd be my pleasure." Benjamina smiled warmly.

Kate tried to ignore the wave of jealousy that crashed into her. Even Maggie was warming up to Ox's ex-girlfriend.

"I still need to check Washington off my ski list, so I'll be back as well." Matt shoved the remaining chip into his mouth. "I find the whole rustic-no-internet thing rather odd, but it allows me to take a much needed break. Next time, there needs to be a way to ski."

"Can't control the weather," Ox remarked.

Maggie raised her wine glass. "To the weather, for allowing us all to gather. And for the safe return of Kate and Matt."

They lifted their glasses together, leaning in as they clanged.

"While you two were out trying to die, I remembered this place by the airport. It's not a ski hill, but we could go sledding." Ox stood, gripping a cane in his hand. Kate hadn't seen it hiding under the table. He went about and cleared the dinner plates with his free hand. "If Kate wants to go that is."

She hoped he had not hurt himself helping her out of the snow. Although she could not imagine how that could have happened or how he could've gotten a cane so quickly. It took a good deal of her remaining strength to not go to him. She wanted to tell him that whatever it was, she didn't care. Her heart struck with the fact that his relationship comments might have to do with the cane, even if she did not fully understand why.

Returning from her thoughts, she said, "Sledding sounds horrible, but ask me again in the morning when I'm not exhausted."

"My flight doesn't leave for forty-eight hours." Matt swigged the last of his wine. "Sledding would be better than nothing. Do you think the roads will be clear enough to drive on tomorrow?"

Ox peered toward the kitchen window, snow continued to flutter down.

"Earlier, the weather report on the local news said it's stopping tonight at some point," Maggie informed them. "So the flights should be fine tomorrow, and the roads should be clear if you all want to do some sledding."

Kate stood up from the table, feeling a bit stronger now with food in her stomach. Bayou stuck to her side as she pushed the chair in.

"Kate." Matt sprang from his chair. "Let me help you. Are you going upstairs?"

Kate nodded. The sound of a plate dropping into the sink startled everyone, including Bayou who let out a bark. Ox stood over the sink staring at Kate and Matt.

"I can help her up there, Matt." Ox took large strides toward Kate with his cane.

"I can do it." Matt grabbed onto Kate's arm.

What is happening here? Kate had been more than clear to Matt earlier.

"No, you're a guest. I'll help her upstairs." Ox stood on the other side of Kate.

Maggie and Benjamina remained seated at the table. They had a front row seat to the squabble over who would help Kate up a flight of steps.

"Ox, honestly, I'll help Kate." Matt held firm to Kate's left arm. "You seem just as tired as we do."

"Go relax, Matt. I can take her." Ox wrapped his arm around Kate's waist.

"Guys," Kate raised her voice, "Bayou is going to take me upstairs."

Matt and Ox glanced at each other and then down at Bayou who wagged his tail.

"Come on, Bayou," Kate said.

Ox and Matt reluctantly removed their hands from Kate. Kate grabbed the handrail and eased herself up each step, Bayou waiting and taking each step two paws at a time. The sound of Maggie muffling a laugh could be heard from the table. Ox and

Matt eyed each other before Matt chased up the stairs after Kate.

"Hey," Matt whispered.

Bayou blocked Matt from Kate.

"What's wrong with you?" Kate growled.

"See?" Matt pointed down toward the stairs. "He likes you."

Kate blushed.

"I don't blame him."

Kate rolled her eyes.

Chapter Thirty

A knock on Kate's door caused her heart to skip a beat and alerted Bayou, who was now awake on the bed. "Come in." Kate did not want to get up.

Maggie appeared at the door. Kate was surprised to see her instead of Matt or Ox, but she welcomed her presence more than either of the men. Kate waved for Maggie to enter.

"Are you feeling better?" Maggie sat at the edge of the bed.

"I'm tired, but alive and thawed." Kate snuggled up under her blanket, leaning back onto the stack of pillows surrounding her. At the corner of the bed, Bayou curled up near her feet.

"When are you going to tell Ox how you feel?" Maggie shifted on the bed.

Maggie's straightforwardness came off sharp, hitting like a weedwacker. She was like a gardener of words without any bushes left to beat around. Kate sighed as though she wanted nothing to do with answering the question. Maggie crossed her arms.

"It doesn't matter how I feel. Ox has already made it clear. Why waste my breath? I'm leaving in a few days, but I want to stay. I have no pull to go home, even if Ox wants nothing to do with me. I want to move back here, to quit my job and start over."

"Then do that," Maggie asserted. "Move back here, regardless of Ox." Power and pose illuminated Maggie's face. Kate wished she had half the gumption Maggie presented.

"While I want to, it's not as easy as snapping my fingers."

"Don't make it complicated, Kate." Maggie patted Kate's leg hidden under the blanket.

"I'm trying not to. Yet a part of me cannot handle the boundaries of Ox's feelings. It might be clouding my judgment some. If I move back and never see Ox again, will that root in the depths of my heart? Even if several months passed, I don't know if I could move past my feelings for him."

Maggie nodded her head. "I understand, and I think you're a strong capable woman."

Kate half smiled. "When I'm in Phoenix, my life is in motion, like a train on the tracks. It's like each day is the same journey, with the same path and same destination. Things are going forward without a different track in sight. I move around day by day, muddling through, but don't live day by day. When I'm here, I'm off the track. I'm excited for my future here. It doesn't feel stagnant."

"That's how I felt when I moved to Oregon. It was home the second I arrived. I can feel it when I'm there, and I miss it, with or without Stan."

"Homesick." Kate realized it as it slid from her lips.

Maggie placed her hand on her chest, a tear formed and she let it fall.

"How do you live without your husband?" Kate pulled her knees in, much to Bayou's dislike, and hugged them.

"Same way I did before we met, with the faith that I am not alone. Faith and hope is all around me. We can choose to be happy, even if we're missing a piece of our self."

Kate moved onto her knees, leaned forward, and hugged Maggie. Bayou lifted his head and then lowered it down again after seeing what all the fuss was about.

"Do you feel homesick, Kate?"

"Not here, but when I think about being in Phoenix, that's exactly what I've been feeling. I have had this odd sensation lingering inside of me that I couldn't put my finger on. It took stepping out of it, coming here, to realize what was happening. When you fear flying, you don't leave home much. There is never a chance to step back far enough. Maggie, I want to talk to Ox, but I worry he will give the same excuse as before."

"In case you forgot, about five minutes ago he and Matt were arguing over who should walk you upstairs."

"They were just being immature boys. Plus, Ox has a business to run. If I get hurt on his watch, that would be bad for him."

"You didn't see what I saw after you and Matt were gone." Maggie stood up, ran her hand over Kate's hair, like her mom always did when she was a child. "Kate, talk to Ox."

Maggie exited the room, shutting the door in near silence. Kate wiggled back down into bed, exhausted from the day. She covered herself to her chin. The lamp's glow spread across the room, warming the corners. The room, the bed, Bayou snoring felt more and more like home.

Kate shot forward in bed, her thoughts switched to worry, her chest tightened thinking about Phoenix. She would not be able to avoid getting back on a plane. The thought of flying caused her heart rate to spike. Bayou lifted his head, as if sensing Kate's fear. He crawled across the bed, nearly pushing Kate to lie back down. He rested his head on the front of her shoulder.

"Thanks, Bayou." Kate stroked his fur. "What will I do if I can't fly with you?"

Bayou let out a long sigh, his brown eyes heavy with sleep. Kate watched the moon's glow illuminate the snow falling outside the bedroom window. There were countless signs telling Kate she needed to come home to Washington for good. But she had to return to Phoenix and end the chapter there first, Ox or no Ox. She smiled and hugged Bayou's head. He woke, barely opening his eyes as though it happened often. Kate's mind flashed back to seeing Ox barreling through the snow toward her, embracing and comforting her.

A whisper of a knock rapped at Kate's door, soft enough Bayou didn't stir.

"Come in," Kate instructed, wondering who it could be. She glanced over at the clock on the nightstand. It was not even seven p.m.

Matt entered and Kate's disappointment showed with a frown.

"I didn't mean to bug you." Matt recoiled seeing her face.

"No, Matt, sorry. I just … it's not important, come in."

Kate sat up in bed, Bayou repositioned himself on a pillow and went back to sleep. Matt remained standing in the center of the room, his hands in his pockets, rocking back and forth.

"Matt? What's wrong?"

"I like you." Matt studied the rug, avoiding eye contact.

Kate's mind jumped back in time to second grade, when Lyle Lee Lawson stated that he liked Kate more than chocolate and frogs in front of the entire class. Unfortunately, Kate's feelings about Lyle were right up there with her grandma's goulash.

"You're a simple woman, Kate. You brighten a room with a small spark. You don't overdo who you are."

Kate's eyes softened. "Matt …"

"Let me finish," Matt interrupted.

Holding up her hands in defense, she settled back onto the pillows. Matt pivoted and paced two more times before he stopped and faced Kate.

"You are everything I don't want."

Kate tilted her head, her face scrunched. Matt knelt on the floor, his elbows on her bed.

"But you are everything I need. A woman that is not about status, but love and family. I need better balance in my life."

Kate leaned forward. *Am I dreaming?* She could not believe this was actually happening. Kate squeezed her eyes closed and rubbed them just in case.

"I need you, because you are like chicken noodle soup."

"Matt." Kate reached for his hand. "Stop, please. Did you forget about my confession in the woods? I'm not the girl for you. I'm falling for Ox. Plus, I have no desire to live in New York. I'm not one for starched shirts and waiting around in a penthouse for someone who is staying late at the office."

"But, Kate, you would keep my world from continuing down a workaholic path."

"I'm honored that you see those qualities in me, Matt, but I'm-I'm falling in love with Ox."

Matt stood, and Kate's fingers slipped from his hand.

"There is a woman that is perfect for you. I know you will find her; give it time."

Matt glanced down and then back up at Kate. His eyes looked defeated. "I'm twenty-seven, Kate, twenty-seven." Kate sighed a laugh and scooted over to the edge of the bed.

"Calm down, I'm twenty-six. Not everyone finds their forever love at twenty-five, thirty or even thirty-five." Kate reached her hand out and touched Matt's arm. "Believe me, Matt. I promise you will."

"I'm grasping at straws, I know. I see the way you look at Ox. And I see the way he looks at you."

"If you see that, why are you here now?" Kate questioned. "Why are you trying to date me?"

"Because I always want what I can't have." Matt's body slumped. He kissed Kate on her cheek and left the room.

Kate twisted to her side, lying down. Staring at the light streaming in from under her door, she wished Ox would appear at her door and knock. She snuggled under the warmth of the blankets when a knock came to her door. Her eyes grew with excitement. *Please be Ox.*

"It's Ox."

Kate straightened herself up in bed and breathed into her hand, checking her breath. *Not too bad.* "Come in."

The door opened and Ox entered with a stack of library books under his arm. "I thought you might like to go through my library stack to see if there's anything you want to read, other than these old books on the shelves here."

Kate glanced at the classics resting on the dresser. "Thank you, Ox."

"I'll just leave them here." Ox placed them on the dresser and pivoted back toward the door with his cane.

"Is everything okay, Ox? I hope I didn't hurt you today … the cane."

Ox paused and turned his upper body toward Kate. "Yes, I'm glad you're okay. Matt too."

"Sorry you had to come and find us."

"I'm glad I could."

They stared at each other, only the sound of Bayou snoring filled the room.

"I'll let you rest. I guess I get the bed to myself again tonight." Ox pointed at Bayou.

"I can kick him out if you want."

"No." Ox waved his hand. "He likes you, let him be. Night, Kate."

"Goodnight, Ox."

Ox exited the room, as Kate gathered her strength and rose from the bed. She went to the closed door, placing her hand on the wood. She didn't know Ox stood right on the other side, their hands in the same spot.

Kate sighed and moved to the stack of library books. Several of them she had read and enjoyed, but one she had not heard of before, *The Daily Coyote* by Shreve Stockton. Removing it from the stack, she took it to bed and cracked the spine.

Chapter Thirty-One

Bayou scratched at Kate's door, causing her to stir. Her head popped up from around the mass of pillows.

"What no rapid knocking?" Kate flung her feet over the edge of the bed. "You probably need to potty."

She cracked the door open enough for Bayou to slide out.

"Morning, Kate." Ox's voice came from the other side of the door. Kate froze. She had yet to check herself in the mirror, let alone brush her teeth or hair. She stepped behind the door. "Good morning, Ox."

Kate could see Ox's shadow in the hall peeking into her room. He must have been standing directly on the other side of the door now. She faced the door, her toes wiggled in her socks.

"I think we can go sledding today as planned. Are you feeling better?"

Kate traced the outline of the wood grain with her pointer finger. "Sounds great, and yes I feel fine. I'll get ready." Kate ran her other hand over her neck.

"I'll make breakfast."

Kate lifted her head as though she could see through to Ox on the other side.

"Kate?" Ox whispered, his voice closer than before.

"Yes, Ox?"

"Can we talk before breakfast?" Ox's voice rattled with contemplation.

Kate's heart raced instantly. If she had not just rolled out of bed she would fling open the door. "Thanks for letting Bayou stay with me last night."

"I'm beginning to think he likes you more than me these days." Ox let out a chuckle. "May I come in so we can talk?"

Kate's eyes widened. "Oh, now?"

"Yes, that's why I'm standing here."

"Give me one second." Kate pushed the door closed. Rushing to the mirror, she examined her face. Wiping the sleep from her eyes, she tamed the wild curls. Kate rubbed on some gloss and popped a mint from her purse.

"Come in." She stepped aside allowing Ox to enter her room.

Today, Ox appeared without the cane. He had a strong stride as he approached the bed and sat. Kate shut the door and sat next to him. Silence remained for seconds upon seconds.

Ox let out a sigh, his shoulders sinking with the exhale. "Kate, I have multiple sclerosis."

Blood rushed to Ox's face causing it to flush.

Kate reached her hand out and took Ox's, wrapping the softness around his hand. She rubbed her thumb over his thumb. They sat in silence. Kate didn't offer up an "I'm sorry" or question him about it. She just continued to rub her soft fingers over his.

Kate's mind was like a hall of mirrors in a clown house. Confusion, fear, loss, and worry at appeared in every angle of her heart. She didn't know what a diagnosis of multiple sclerosis meant. She dared not ask Ox; she didn't want him to know she had no idea what the diagnosis entailed. When Ali told Kate her mom had cancer, she knew just what to say and what not to because she understood that diagnosis.

"Thank you for telling me, Ox. I appreciate it." Kate held tight to Ox's hand, unsure of what to do now.

"Technically, I started off with a diagnosis of CIS. It's known as clinically isolated syndrome. It's a fancy way of saying that I have a nervous system disease where my body hates to send messages to my brain. They didn't know if it was multiple sclerosis at the time. Then my neurologist gave me the official diagnosis of relapse-remitting MS."

"So that's why you have the cane?"

"Yes, at times my legs are weak or stiff. Sometimes my fingers tingle and go numb, causing me to drop things. It can affect everything in my body from head to toe. It can even affect my ability to taste, smell, speak, walk, and even care for myself. I can also become incredibly fatigued and need naps."

Kate nodded in a poor attempt to let Ox know she understood.

Ox stood and rubbed his hands together, unsure of where to put them. "I'll see you downstairs. We'll leave for sledding right after breakfast."

"Okay." Kate stood, wrapping her arms around Ox in an embrace.

"I'm going to start making breakfast." Ox pulled away.

"Okay." Kate nodded. "Ox?"

Ox turned and faced Kate, but his eyes darted down to his shoes.

"Does the kind of MS you have mean that you will get better?"

"It means I will have good and bad days. It means I could stay like this, or if I have a bad relapse, it could get worse."

A lump formed in Kate's throat. She became light-headed and sat on the side of the bed. "Medicine? Is there medicine for it?"

"There are two on the market right now. I tried one."

"And the other?"

"Not yet." Ox made his way to the bedroom door. "Come down for breakfast, Kate. It should be ready in about twenty minutes." He paused, and glanced back at Kate whose head hung down. She appeared to be staring on her knees. Ox pressed his hand around the doorknob and turned it, stepping into the hall.

Kate's head raised at the sound of the door closing, tears glistened in her eyes. She wished she had never asked Ox what was wrong. Wrapping her arms around her stomach, she fell sideways on the bed, her head hitting the pillows.

Burying her head deep into the pile, her faith clearly shaken. She sat back up and pulled several bits of yellow fur from her lip. "That dog is everywhere even when he isn't around," she murmured.

Kate took a deep breath, craving a chat with her dad. He would know how to give her a sense of reason and hope. Instead, she found her cell and called the next best thing.

"Ali."

"I thought the cell phone signal was horrible there, how are you calling me? This is way over my limit of actually talking to anyone, even you. Text me."

"Ali, Ox has something called MS."

"That doesn't sound good."

"You haven't heard of it either? I don't have a clue what MS means. I feel so guilty. I need your help." Kate held her cell out, checking the signal in the upper right. "My cell has the data signal of a carrot for the internet."

"If this Ox is so old school, maybe he has an encyclopedia?"

Kate groaned. "I won't find current information in some antique book. Can't you send me a screenshot in a text message?"

"Hold on, I just walked into my hotel room."

Kate sat nervously on the bed; her left fingers tapping her legs, the right fingers tapped the back of her cell phone.

"There are three types: relapsing-remitting MS, primary progressive MS, and secondary progressive MS."

"The first one. He has the first one. Give it to me in layman's terms." Kate heard Ali mumbling as she read aloud to herself from the internet. "Says that if he relapses, he may not be able to bounce back. Symptoms of MS range from dizziness and weakness to depression, incontinence, and cognitive issues. Kate, do you want the good news?"

"There's good news, after all that?"

"Patients can stay in this pattern for ten to twenty years before the disease worsens. It says everyone is different and that physical therapy and medication might help."

"So there is hope." Kate rubbed her forehead.

"Is he on the medication?"

"He said he took one, and I got the feeling it didn't work. He also mentioned there was a second one."

"Kate?"

"Yes." Kate gazed out the window. The sunlight was just making itself known.

"Does this change the way you feel about Ox?"

Without a thought, Kate spoke. "No, not for a second."

"Make sure Ox knows that."

Kate nodded and wiped away a falling tear.

"Did you tell her?" Benjamina exited her room as Ox passed down the hall.

Ox stopped and shoved his hands into his pockets. "If I did the right thing, why do I feel so defeated?"

Benjamina took Ox's arm, his hand sliding from his pocket. "Did she say something to make you feel that way?"

Ox's eyes squinted and he shook his head. "No, the opposite actually."

Benjamina pressed her lips together. "Not a 'sorry' or 'that's horrible?'"

Ox let out a chuckle. "She actually thanked me." He crossed his arms. "I thought she would feel sorry for me, but she seemed pleased I told her."

Benjamina hugged Ox, then pulled back and rubbed

the sides of his arms. "It might take a bit of time to process the information. It's not good or bad. Give her time."

"Time to process?" Ox shook his head. "No, it does not change anything. I will not bring anyone, especially someone like Kate into a sinking relationship."

Benjamina grinned. "'Especially someone like Kate.' Listen to yourself. I won't tell you what you already know, but I will tell you, you deserve someone. We all do. We all deserve the best life possible."

"Then what do you have to say about yourself?"

"When I'm ready, I will find what I need. But don't forget, I'm happy with my life. Can you say the same about yours?"

Ox kissed Benjamina on the cheek. "Do you need me to drop you at the airport?"

"My rental car is still in the driveway. I can take that in." Benjamina checked her cell phone. "Speaking of, I need to go. As usual, I'm late. Tell Kate I said goodbye. I'd say it myself, but I'm sure she is still processing your news and getting ready for breakfast."

Ox gathered Benjamina's luggage as they headed downstairs.

Chapter Thirty-Two

"Remember, I'm not sledding. I just needed to get out of the inn." Maggie smirked. "And, nothing could please me more than watching adults tackle a child's sport."

"Maggie, don't rain on our sled parade because you can't hang with the cool kids." Ox glanced at her.

The truck filled with laughter as they headed to their destination. Staring out the truck's window, Kate reflected on Benjamina's visit. She wished she had had a chance to say goodbye to her and to apologize for initially giving her the cold shoulder.

Once they arrived, Matt helped Maggie out, while Ox assisted Bayou. Ox had been kind enough to bring a folding chair for Maggie so she didn't have to stand the entire time.

The hill was nothing more than a slope. It went about a quarter of a mile from where they stood to the top. Multiple bundles of hemlocks sprinkled the area. Matt untied the three black rubber tubes from the bed of the truck. He handed one to Kate, and Ox took the last one.

"Here you go, Maggie." Ox unfolded Maggie's chair and set it next to the rear tire.

"Ox, I'm seventy, not ninety," Maggie snipped, flopping into the chair.

"Sorry, Maggie, I didn't mean it to sound like that."

"You're letting them get away."

Matt started his trek up the hill, with Kate on his heels. Bayou lagged behind sliding his chin against the snow and rolling around. Noticing Ox trying to catch up, Kate paused, waiting for him.

Ox rewrapped his hand around the tube.

"Everything all right?" Kate reached her hand out to touch his arm.

"Loose grip."

"Do you want me to carry it for you?"

"No, I'm fine," Ox snapped.

Kate retracted, shocked by the tone of his voice. Her heartbeat sped up in excess of what the hill demanded. Sure Ox felt the need to be prideful, but his tone was unnecessary.

"You know, Ox ..." Kate started. "Never mind."

She spotted Matt standing at the top, taking in the view.

"I didn't mean to snap at you, I'm sorry," Ox said.

Her eyes were furious as she stared at Ox. Everything came into razor-sharp focus.

"Kate, please." Ox noticed the fury, "I need you to understand."

She peered up the hill and then back at Ox. "This is supposed to be a fun adventure, not a fight."

Kate pivoted in the direction of the hill, then back down toward Ox, then back again. Bayou acted like a grand game of chase was about to take place. "Your name suits you, because you are stubborn and bull-headed."

"Kate," Ox pleaded.

She placed her free hand on her hip, and then realized she might look like a two-year-old about to have a tantrum. Quickly, Kate dropped it to her side.

"Ox, I don't give a flute's toot that you are not always able to do everything you think you should be able to do because of your MS. I care about the fact that you don't see how much I'm starting to fall in love with you in such a short amount of time. It's heartbreaking to see you think MS means you can't find love, be in love, or live life. If anyone should live life, it's you, Ox. You!"

Kate swung around and marched up the hill. Powder flew into the air as Ox stomped after her; step by step his strides grew longer than hers, until he caught up.

"Kate, please." Ox reached out for the back of her arm and missed, swiping the air.

She reached the top of the hill. "You ready, Matt?"

Before Matt could reply, Kate had set her inner tube on the snow and plopped down onto it. With one frantic push, Kate started her decent.

"Wait up!" Matt pushed off next, sliding mere seconds behind.

Ox took a shortcut and jolted sideways on the hill just before Kate came whizzing by. He tossed his tube onto the snow and belly flopped onto it. Bayou followed, running to catch up, his barks echoing off the hard packed snow. With a final leap of excitement, Bayou landed on top of Ox as they raced past Matt. Kate continued to speed down the hill, but Ox was catching up. He knew this hill well, and nothing had changed, including the unseen dip in the snow ahead.

"Kate!" Ox yelled. "Steer to the right! Kate!"

Kate could either not hear Ox, or she didn't care to.

"To the right, Kate!"

She didn't know why Ox kept yelling at her. The space in front was wide open. Suddenly, the tube dipped and then bounced back up. Kate landed and rolled, the snow covering her. Matt and Ox turned their tubes to the right, both sliding to a halt.

"Kate!" Ox yelled. Bayou leapt off, and Ox stood, dashing toward Kate, who remained lying in the snow. Matt stumbled behind, kneeling next to Ox.

"Oh, ouch," Kate moaned, as Ox brushed her hair from her face along with the snow.

"What hurts? Can you sit up?" Ox asked.

"I'm fine." Kate pushed herself up with her hands. "Oh, no, no, no." Kate fell back into the snow. My left ankle, it hurts."

Matt scooted around and reached for Kate's leg. Bayou laid his head in Kate's snow-covered lap.

"Don't move her ankle, Matt," Ox warned. "Do you think it's broken?"

"I don't know what broken feels like."

Ox placed his hand on her knee.

"You mean to tell me, with all the tripping and clumsy moves you make, you have never broken anything?"

Kate raised her eyebrow. "Yes, Ox, I have never broken anything … yet."

Ox started to laugh, Matt joined in, as did Kate. She lay back into the snow, laughing so hard she had to hold her stomach.

When the laughter faded, Maggie loomed over Kate. "Are you okay? I could see the height you got off that dip."

"I think she might have sprained it," Ox said. "We need to get her to the urgent care in town."

Matt stood on Kate's right, Ox on her left, and together they lifted Kate out of the snow.

Kate envisioned that only Ox was carrying her to the truck. Realizing that her desire to keep Ox all to herself meant she could not stay mad at him for long.

Ox and Matt made their way to the truck, with Maggie and Bayou close behind.

"I'm sorry, Kate," Ox whispered. "If I hadn't snapped at you, you wouldn't have rushed off down the hill."

Kate stared straight forward, refusing to respond or make eye contact. She didn't want to hear the same thing yet again. Ox's ability to be stubborn benefitted no one, and she couldn't change a stubborn man's mind. No matter how much she wanted to.

Chapter Thirty-Three

"I'm glad it's only a sprain." Kate hobbled on her crutches to the living room couch.

"That's a good thing." Matt followed behind and stood in front of the window. "Appears as though the weather will not be causing any further interruptions. I can try and catch my flight home tomorrow."

Outside the sun pushed through the cotton ball-like clouds. Ox entered with a bowl of homemade mac and cheese. Steam wafted from it as Kate took it in both hands like a mug of hot chocolate. "Thank you, it smells and looks delicious."

"Matt, there is some left on the stove if you want any." Ox pointed toward the kitchen.

"Thanks, I'll grab some."

"Do you need anything else?" Ox hovered over Kate.

"No, but where is your bowl? Not hungry?" Kate asked. "Do you want to talk now?"

"Later, I'm going to go lie down." Ox shuffled out of the living room, Bayou trotting behind him.

Taken aback by his instant dash from the room, Kate twisted on the couch to watch Ox walk away. She noticed his stiff gait, but if she had not been watching for it, she never would have been the wiser. A wave of wanting to go after him came over her. She felt the need to comfort him, to remind him that she didn't care, and that she would not run off.

Taking a bite of mac and cheese, she let out a sigh. The

art of flavors in something as simple as noodles and cheese melted in her mouth. Matt entered the living room, a bowl in hand. He stood at the window, shoveling bite after bite into his mouth. "Way better than the box kind."

"Can you even tell gobbling it up like that?

Matt chuckled and turned to Kate. "What's going on with Ox? I tried to talk to him the other night. He is a man of few words."

Kate lowered her head, as though trying to hide it in the bowl. "Nothing is going on." She did not have the right to tell others about Ox's diagnosis. "I think he's just tired."

Matt shook his head as if he understood and scooped the rest of the mac and cheese from the bowl. "I'm going to get packed. My flight leaves early in the morning. I can't wait to have access to the internet again. A break is nice, but I'm over it now."

Matt's comment made Kate realize she was not even sure where she left her cell phone. And she smiled at the fact that she didn't miss it. Instead, she missed Bayou's snoring and Ox's presence, and even the light tapping of Maggie's knitting needles.

Footsteps came to the edge of the living room. "Do you need anything?"

"No, Maggie, I'm fine, thank you."

She entered the room, sitting on the couch next to Kate, and faced her. "Ox having a bad day?"

Kate nodded her head. "I think so; he went to lie down."

"He has been stubborn since the first time Stan and I met him." Maggie placed her hands on her knees, rubbing them.

"Sore?" Kate asked.

"Nothing compared to what you went through. I guess the body becomes less capable each day as we age. While Ox might be stubborn, I can see that he lessens it to some degree around you."

"That's Ox being less stubborn?" Kate laughed.

"Hard to believe, but yes. Stan and I found out about Ox's diagnosis on our last visit. I won't go into details, those are not mine to share. He never meant to tell us, but there was an incident, and Ox wasn't able to hide it from us. The fact that he even told you means his emotions are mixed. Which could only mean one thing to me."

Kate's eyes widened. "What is that?"

"He is falling for you, Kate." Maggie rose slowly, her hands on her knees. "I see he shared his stack of library books with you."

Kate glanced at *The Daily Coyote* resting on the end table. "We do seem to have similar taste in non-fiction. I'm halfway through it and loving it."

Maggie nodded her head as she left Kate alone to ponder her noisy thoughts in the silence of the living room.

Chapter Thirty-Four

Leaning on her crutches, Kate knocked on Ox's bedroom door. His steps were so soft that when he opened the door, it startled her.

"Sorry to bother you, but I don't think I can get upstairs to my room."

Ox covered his face with his hands. "I'm sorry, Kate, that slipped my mind."

Kate remained at the door, but caught herself peeking around Ox to see his room of black and gray decor, books stacked in corners and overflowing from bookcases. Bayou squeezed past Ox, nosing the door, causing it to swing wide open.

"Are you feeling better?" Kate asked, now having a full view of the room.

The walls were white, but artwork added pops of color.

"I am, thank you. Please come in and sit down." Ox moved out of the way.

Taken aback by his forwardness allowing her into his room, Kate crept in. Once all the way in the room, Kate could see the artwork was actually photography. On one wall held a series of photos depicting a red barn during each of the four seasons. The other wall held a large print of swampland with trees growing out of the water.

"Is that a picture of the bayou?" Kate pointed and limped closer to it.

"Yes, it's near where I found Bayou in Louisiana. I visited a local photographer's gallery and got lost in the images. I'm sure your photography is just as magical."

Kate half smiled, but didn't respond.

Ox had a black leather couch, which faced a panoramic view from the window. A mess of navy blue sheets and blankets covered his bed. Two classic seventies-style wood end tables flanked the bed with photos of a younger Bayou.

"Sit." Ox directed his palm to the couch.

Without hesitation, Kate limped over and attempted to lower herself down. She had one crutch in the air, the other stuck under her armpit. She leaned sideways trying to dislodge it. As it finally freed itself, it went crashing to the floor. It would take some practice to get used to using the crutches and sitting. Kate looked up to see Ox covering his mouth.

"Don't laugh." Kate smirked.

"You're the only one I know who could injure herself while already injured."

Ox sat next to Kate, but within less than three seconds, Bayou jumped up, spreading them apart. The view out of Ox's bedroom window mirrored the breathtaking scenery from the living room. The sun, low between the evergreens, cast slivers of gold around the walls.

"Kate." Ox's voice a weak whisper. "Days like today scare me."

A lump formed in her throat, and she reminded herself not to get emotional. Her father always said it was her personality to fall hard and fast and to love deeply. Her mother always said it was a fault.

"Do you see why being in a relationship of any kind means I can't be … a man?"

Kate turned to Ox, not just her head, but her entire body. Pain stabbed her heart, and she put her hand on it, as if to calm the wound. Opening her mouth to say something, she struggled with how to start. Ox kept staring toward the world beyond his window.

She reached over Bayou's sleeping mound of fur and placed her hand gently on Ox's arm. "A man? I was not aware of any specific definition describing a man. And I see you're thinking for someone else by making the decisions based on what you think someone else thinks, instead of asking."

"But I'm right." Ox lowered his head and placed his hand over Kate's.

"No, you're wrong. The only one who bears the burden of your diagnosis is you."

"I couldn't carry you all by myself to the truck. What if Matt hadn't been there? What happens when you need me to climb a ladder or what if you hurt your foot again?"

Ox faced Kate, struggling to keep eye contact.

Kate squeezed his hand. "What if I gain weight? Or weighed more right now? You wouldn't be able to carry me regardless."

The edge of Ox's mouth twisted.

"So, it's a mute point. But, I can see why you worry about having to care for me. I'm a walking nightmare of injuries."

A smile, although small, warmed Ox's face. Kate rubbed his arm. "I think that chivalry is a great thing, but it comes in so many forms. The most impressive form is not about lifting me from disaster or reaching things in high places."

Bayou lifted his head up as though she said the word "treat," and lowered it back down with a sigh.

"Ox, you impress me with your kindness, your gorgeous eyes, your love of books, the way you care about my fear of flying. I love how you rescued Bayou, how people are drawn to stay at your beautiful inn. I enjoy your many talents, your encouragement of my photography, and the way you make me laugh. When I think about who I want to spend my forever with, I don't think about who can chop the most wood for the fire, but who cares enough to know that I need a fire."

"My MS could stay the same or get worse. I have no way of knowing. It's unknown how long I can keep running the inn or flying my plane."

"Good thing I don't care about any of those things." Kate placed her other hand on top of Ox's. "I have this thing called a job. They have those pretty much everywhere."

Ox's cheeks blushed with a smile. "Are you saying you are moving back home for sure?"

"I hope you're okay with that."

"Of course." Ox beamed.

"I have one condition."

Ox pivoted his upper body closer toward Kate, Bayou back asleep in between. "Name it."

"You give us a chance."

Ox turned back toward the windows. The sun's light was completely gone; shadows stretched around his room.

"Kate …"

"Ox, it's your decision. What do you want? Do you want a life of just you and Bayou, and the guests coming through your inn? Or do you want something more?"

Kate moved to pick up her crutches which rested next to the couch. Ox reached for her arm, she paused. He took his other hand and placed it on the side of Kate's cheek. She closed her eyes. *Kiss me.* This thumb rested just below her ear. *Kiss me!* Then as though lightning struck, he pulled away. Kate's eyes opened.

She shook her head, pushed herself off the couch, and snatched her crutches. Continuing to shake her head, she made her way toward the bedroom door.

"Kate, wait. Kate."

She hobbled forward, not waiting, not stopping. Then she felt Ox grip her arm. Kate sprang back at the force, bumping her back on Ox's chest. As Ox spun her around, the crutches crashed to the floor. Wrapping his arms around Kate, and using all the strength he could gather, Ox lifted her off the ground. Then, he kissed her with everything he had held back since he first glanced up and saw her over the pages of his book.

Kate was grateful Ox had swept her up. She would have lost whatever strength remained in her legs from his kiss. As their lips parted, Kate's feet dangled above the floor.

"Are you going to let me go?" Kate swung her non-sprained foot.

Ox shook his head and kissed her again.

"I meant put me down."

"Oh, down." Ox laughed.

He lowered Kate and handed her the crutches. She stood like a statue, unsure what to do next. "I can't believe my vacation is almost over. I hope I can get on the plane."

"Have you ever not been able to?" Ox held back his urge to put his arms around Kate again.

"Yes, two times I gathered up the nerve, bought tickets, only to watch the plane takeoff without me."

They made their way out the door and down the hall. "And where did you miss out on going to?" Ox asked.

"Virginia and Louisiana."

Ox's eyes lit up. "Louisiana is beautiful, you missed out for sure. Maybe I can take you there?"

"There is a reason why Kate never made it to Louisiana." Maggie appeared in front of Ox and Kate startling them. "You're supposed to go together." Maggie turned and disappeared up the stairs.

With smirks on their faces, Ox and Kate turned to each other, but remained silent.

Chapter Thirty-Five

Kate sprawled out on Ox's bed, while he was upstairs in her room. The sheets smelled of wintergreen. She offered to sleep on one of the couches, but Ox had insisted she take his bed. Bayou appeared to be okay with the switch as he snored on without a care. Kate's mind stretched like the moon's shadow on the ceiling. Even though they shared a kiss and discussed his diagnosis, they never spoke of Ox changing his views on a relationship.

Every time Kate drifted off to sleep, thoughts of the upcoming flight popped into her head. She had visions of turbulence and oxygen masks dropping from above her seat. The view out of the plane's window showed the metal cowling ripped from around the engine. Next, Kate envisioned fire spreading through the plane as she desperately attempted to crawl to the exit door. She bolted straight up in bed, her heart beating fast and strong, as if it might burst through her chest. Bayou instantly sprang up and placed the upper half of his body over Kate's lap.

Kate began petting Bayou, but her body would not stop trembling. In an effort to calm her breathing, she took deep breaths, but every time Kate breathed in, she coughed.

"You are okay," Kate continued to whisper. Yet, nothing she did worked; she held her head in her hand, unable to stop shaking.

Bayou swung his paw at Kate as though he was trying to get her attention. Feeling a wave of nausea come over her, she ignored Bayou's pleas.

Bayou leapt off the bed. He stretched his body upwards in a half hop, smacking his paw on the door's lever handle. The door unlatched and cracked open. Bayou nosed the door open further, pushing his way through. Kate could hear the sound of his nails tapping the floor as he scampered up the stairs.

The anxiety had grown too much for Kate to handle and she started to cry. She covered her face, the tears wetting her palms. A rap at the frame of the door startled Kate as Bayou shook the bed jumping on it.

Kate continued to cry, as Ox entered the room. He sat at the edge of the bed, Kate sitting with her knees to her chest, hugging them and sobbing.

"What's wrong?" Ox touched her knee.

"I can't get on the plane," Kate mumbled. "I can't do it, Ox."

She thought of the last time she was up in his plane and how they stayed out longer than planned, putting her in an utter panic. Scooting further onto the bed, he pulled Kate toward him, careful not to squish her sprained ankle.

Between the crying and the shaking, Kate's body trembled in Ox's firm grasp. Bayou crawled behind Kate, lying down, pressing up against her back.

Wiping her tears, she pushed herself out of Ox's arms. "I'm sorry, I'm acting like a baby."

"You're not at all, Kate. I wish there was something I could do to make it easier for you to fly back to Phoenix. I wish you loved flying as much as I do."

"I wish I didn't have to go," Kate pulled her shirt sleeve over her hand and wiped her nose. "I have to get back to work, put my notice in, and find a job. I have a month's worth of house stuff to get ready to sell. At least I don't have to fly back when I'm ready, since I'll drive here with my car. And I still have to ask my parents if I can move in with them while I get everything set up.

But I can't even bring myself to get on the plane to set everything in motion. Ugh, I'm a mess."

"One worry at a time." Ox rubbed Kate's knee. "Remember, don't look too far forward."

Kate pivoted her upper body and wrapped it around Bayou. "I wish you could come with me."

"That's it!" Ox clapped his hands, startling Kate and Bayou.

"What is?" Kate pivoted back up.

"I'll take you home, with Bayou!" Ox nearly screamed out in joy. "We'll have to make a few stops along the way; my plane will need to refuel," Ox started writing in the air with his pointer finger, "about twice, if I'm doing the math correctly."

"You can take me home, as in, in your plane with Bayou?" Kate asked eagerly.

"Yes." Ox plopped back onto the bed, his face beaming. "If you get scared, we can just land the plane. And Bayou will be there to help with your anxiety." Ox rubbed his hands together at the thought of his great plan.

"Ox, I can't ask you to do that. I'm not even sure if I can do it."

"You can with Bayou. I believe in you, and I know you can overcome this."

Her heart rate slowed and the trembling subsided. Just his words were calming her already. Reaching for Ox's arm, she attempted to swallow the marble of fear remaining in her throat. Kneeling on the bed, she hugged Ox. "Thank you. Thank you," she whispered into his ear.

Chapter Thirty-Six

"I need to go to my parent's home." Kate reported the next morning over Ox's homemade cinnamon rolls.

"Are they back early?" Ox pulled out a chair at the kitchen table.

The inn remained as quiet as when Kate first arrived now that Matt and Benjamina had left.

"No, but I need to …" Kate paused, shook her head and took a second bit of the gooey roll. "Never mind, it seems silly now that I have said it aloud."

"Kate," Maggie rested her elbows on the table. "Don't turn into one of those."

"One of what?" Kate asked between bites.

Kate recognized her own words. Ox took a long of coffee. Bayou finished crunching his kibble. Last night had been a roller coaster of fear, surprises, and joy. She couldn't help but wonder if the kiss was a onetime thing, an accident during a moment of weakness. She needed one more thing to make sure she was on the right path with her decisions. Outside of Ox, she needed to figure out the truth of her soul. To be honest with herself as vitally important for her future.

"I need to sit on the porch swing." Kate snatched her coffee mug and tried to hide the embarrassment of sounding like a head-case.

"Nothing wrong with that," Ox mentioned. "I'll take you right after breakfast, if you'd like." He used his thumb and forefinger to rub his eyes. His face grimaced.

"Are you all right?" Kate leaned toward Ox.

"My eyes are hurting today, but I'll be okay."

Kate lowered her mug. "Thank you, but maybe you should rest."

"Take my rental car, the roads should be safe again," Maggie said. "I'll give you the keys."

"Thanks, Maggie," Ox and Kate said in unison.

"Do you think you can drive with your sprain?" Ox blinked hard.

"Yes, it's not a stick shift. I don't need both feet."

Ox scooted his chair out and attempted to rise without luck. Bayou stood up and moved closer to Ox as if aware of his struggle.

"Ox, can I bring you your cane?" Kate stood, grabbing hold of her crutches.

"I said I was fine!" Ox snapped. Bayou's ears folded tight and back. Ox pushed himself up to stand once more. He clenched his fist around the table.

Kate hobbled toward Ox, her crutches clacking.

"How do you plan to help me, Kate?" Ox's face hardened, his lips tight and straight.

Glimpsing down at her wrapped left ankle, she tightened her grip around the crutches. Ox pushed past her, his gait stiff, wide and slow. Bayou followed next to Ox as he made it to the edge of the hall. He used the wall to support himself the rest of the way. The slam of Ox's door echoed through the inn. Silence filled the kitchen as if an avalanche had rolled through.

"I'll get the keys." Maggie stood from the table and headed up the stairs.

The tires of Maggie's rental car crunched over the rocks as Kate parked the car close to the front porch.

Kate exited the driver's side and hobbled to the backseat door, opened it and removed her crutches. As she made her way up the porch steps, she took in a deep breath.

She lowered herself onto the porch swing and allowed her crutches to rest against the house. Kate pulled her phone from her jacket pocket and placed it on her lap. Rocking herself with her right foot, she closed her eyes. The front porch held a history of many moments where she and her family contemplated life. Kate spent many days and nights swinging as she cried over a break-up or studied for a test. It became her only escape when she was grounded and couldn't go play with friends. Most often, she came to the porch swing to ponder her future decisions. Which is exactly why she needed to be here now.

Kate's mind tried to focus, but returned to the irritation on Ox's face and the sound of rage and pain in his words. She could not change Ox's diagnosis, but she hoped she could change his attitude. Yet, it seemed hopeless.

Sighing deeply she rested her head on the back of the swing. Kate needed to focus her thoughts on her life. Something nagged in the back of her mind. Beyond the want and need to move was the unsettling thought about her job situation. Kate feared that landing another engineering job here would only cause another loop of unhappiness. How else can *I make a living? And what about Ox?*

Kate picked up her cell, scrolled through her contacts, and hit SEND.

"Hi, Kate, everything okey-dokey?" her mom asked.

"Yes, Mom. Can you put Dad on?"

"You know how much he doesn't like using the phone."

Kate rolled her eyes. "I know, Mom, but tell him it's important."

"Gene, something is wrong with Kate," her mom raised her voice away from the phone.

"Mom! Just give Dad the phone."

Kate shook her head and nibbled on the tip of her gloved finger.

"Katie, sweetheart, what's wrong?" her dad asked.

For as long as Kate could remember her dad had called her Katie, never Kate, and no matter who came into her life her dad remained the only one to ever to do so.

"Nothing is wrong, Dad." Kate rubbed her free hand on her pants, the roughness of her jeans against her glove. "I need some advice."

"You're on the porch swing thinking." Her dad's voice the same softness as when she was five years-old, sitting on his lap as he read to her. When she grew tired of the books, he would make up stories with wild horses and princesses.

"Dad, I like a man, and I hate living in Phoenix, and I want to move home."

Silence spread through the line. Kate's dad never replied quickly, he pondered everything in life before speaking.

"I think it would be great to have you back home."

Kate smiled, just like him to use a positive statement to get around it. "Do you think I should, or am I going through some life determining crisis?"

"Do you think you are?"

"Dad, I'm serious."

"Katie, your mom and I would love to have you back near us, but do it for you, not because of a man."

"I want to for both, but I don't know if I want to get an engineering job or find something else. Something creative and with meaning."

"Your photographs are beautiful, and your cooking is delightful."

"Can I make a living doing that, Dad?"

"I don't know, and you won't know unless you try. Now,

Katie, who is this man?"

Kate blushed. She remembered the first time her dad had asked her about a boy and she blushed just the same as she had back then. "He is this great, stubborn man. He is a pilot and runs Inn of the Woods, and he has a lovable dog named Bayou. But, Dad, there's one thing. He has multiple sclerosis."

"Oh, yes, we have heard of Inn of the Woods. Now tell me, Katie, how does his diagnosis affect you?"

She rubbed her lips together. "It doesn't, but he thinks it does. He has a lot going for him, but he could lose it all because of the diagnosis."

"Regardless, can you be his blessing?"

The words hit Kate's heart like an explosion. "Oh, Dad, how do you always make everything so clear? Thank you. I love you, Dad."

"Love you too, Katie."

Ox punched his pillow. If not for Maggie's being there, he would let out a long scream. A knock on the door momentarily broke him from his anger.

"Maggie, I don't want to talk."

The door cracked open. "And I don't care."

Maggie entered and rubbed Bayou's head as she sat on the edge of the bed.

"How dare you snap at Kate like you did? Regardless of what is going on between you two, she is still a guest. Your parents are not here to remind you to stop being such a pain in the bottom, so I will."

"Maggie." Ox shifted on the bed.

"No." Maggie held her hand up. "Listen to me, Oxnard. You will lose this inn and all your dreams if you don't live your life beyond the MS diagnosis. Stop focusing on the shortcomings. Focus on now."

Ox folded his arms. His eyes remained on Maggie.

"MS does not have a set date or a set outcome, everyone is different, even your neurologist told you that. The best thing you can do is make yourself happy. And push past your thoughts of negativity."

Maggie rubbed her palms over her legs. "About ten years ago, Stan had a stroke."

"I never knew that," Ox mentioned.

"You and he are like two peas in a stubborn pod. He went through several months of physical and occupational therapy and fought me off every time I tried to help. He recovered fully, and we moved on. Yet it took him hitting his lowest point to realize that he needed help. It took time for Stan to learn that allowing me to care for him didn't mean weakness but love. Everything I did was because of love. I didn't know if he would get better, no one did."

"A stroke is not MS." Ox folded his arms the other way.

"Correct, but love is love." Maggie gave Bayou one final pet before leaving Ox with this thought.

Ox remained with his arms crossed. He knew he needed support.

The words of her dad etched deep into Kate's mind as she parked Maggie's rental car back in its spot. Sunshine softened the colors around her, showing off the inn's maple wood color. Kate stared at it and all the beauty within the hemlocks and red cedars. She breathed in the crisp cold air, her breath casting small cloud puffs with each exhale.

Kate's bright smile fell when Bayou didn't greet her as she entered the front door. The hall was dark and Ox's bedroom door was shut. "Maggie?" Kate called as her crutches clapped on the wood floor.

She found Maggie knitting in the living room arm chair.

"How did everything go?" Maggie asked.

"Fine. Is Ox still hiding out in his room?"

"I'm afraid so." Maggie didn't look up from her needles.

Kate glanced at the miniature grandfather clock on the other side of the fireplace. It read one-thirty p.m. She didn't realize she had been gone so long. The scamper of paws down the hall caused Kate to turn her head.

Bayou approached Kate, his tail wagged and he hopped his body, lifting his front paws just off the floor. Kate lowered her face, supporting her weight on the crutches so Bayou could sniff her lips, ears, and eyes, and give her a few kisses.

"Has Ox prepared for dinner yet?" Kate stood and turned back toward Maggie.

"No."

"Good, I had an idea, but," Kate held up one crutch, "I need your help."

"Of course."

"Can we run to the grocery store? I'm all right to drive, but pushing a cart or carrying a basket is kind of out of the question."

"If your plan involves snapping Ox out of being stubborn or at least coming out of his room then I'm in." Maggie placed her needles into her sewing bag and stood.

Kate grinned. "I hope so."

"Oh, grab your camera. We'll need to make another stop first."

Chapter Thirty-Seven

Maggie instructed Kate to take them to the local library. It took a few turns in the memory bank, but Kate soon remembered its location.

"While you were out, I made a phone call to a friend in Portland, a long time friend who might be able to help you out." Maggie unclipped her seat belt as Kate put the car in park.

"Help me out?" Kate climbed from the car and balanced on her good foot while Maggie grabbed the crutches. Maggie carried the camera bag as they made their way to the library's entrance. Hemlocks and Japanese maples surrounded both sides of the white washed home with a cedar roof. Nothing appeared to have changed since Kate's late visit.

Kate hobbled along the brick path leading from the four-car parking lot to the library's front patio. The home had been converted to a library long before her birth. Maggie pushed down on the classic black doorknob unlatching it. The pine floors creaked all the same and the smell of oak bookcases filled the poorly lit entrance.

"Little Kate Wilson?" a rusty voice came from behind a mahogany desk.

Maggie shut the door as Kate pivoted on her crutches toward the desk.

"Mrs. Alder?"

Mrs. Alder still resembled Mrs. Claus. Her crimson dress swished as she came from around the desk. Mrs. Alder's hands were waving in joy. She grabbed Kate and wrapped her in a hug.

"You're still cute as a button!" Mrs. Alder kissed Kate's cheek, her rosy lipstick leaving a mark.

"Thank you." Kate beamed. "This is Maggie, a guest at the Inn of the Woods, where I am also staying."

"Oxnard's inn, and oh yes, your parents are in Hawaii." Mrs. Alder reached out her hand and shook Maggie's. "I'm Mrs. Adler."

"Maggie."

"To what do I owe the pleasure of this visit?"

"I'm not sure." Kate chuckled.

"We need access to the internet," Maggie stated.

"Yes, of course. Now usually you need a valid library card, but I'm guessing yours has expired, Kate?"

Kate staggered behind Maggie and Mrs. Alder. "I'll need to get a new card."

Mrs. Alder spun around, her dress filling the space in between. "My word, are you moving back home?" She reached her hand out and placed it on Kate's arm.

"Yes, not today, but once I get things squared away back in Phoenix." Kate frowned as the feeling of failure flowed through her. "I'll be moving in with my parents."

"Don't you frown about that, missy. There's nothing wrong with a little rearranging and getting your feet pointed in the right direction." Mrs. Alder led the way to the single computer station, and dragged over an extra chair from the nearby study table.

"Oxnard has such a lovely inn." Mrs. Alder slid her hands into the pockets on the sides of her dress.

"Yes, the library books, of course they are from here. I'm borrowing one from his stack."

"Yes, honey, every month Mr. Alder and I bring him the latest books, and he makes us a scrumptious meal. He offers to come pick them up here, but Mr. Alder loves the view off the living room. Mr. Alder also loves Oxnard's blueberry pie for desert. Say, I heard he won the pie contest this year at Winter Wonder Day. It's about time!" Mrs. Alder laughed. "But," she lowered her voice as though she were sharing a secret. "I heard it was some crazy thing with green tomatoes in it, and that a woman ..." Mrs. Alder's mouth formed the letter O as she drew her hand over it. "Kate, it was you! Oxnard and you made that crazy pie."

"Yes, Mrs. Alder, we did."

"For next month's book delivery, I will be requesting to try some of it. I can't fib; it's been on my mind ever since I heard the rumor." Mrs. Alder grinned and rubbed her lips together as she envisioned eating something sweet. "I'll let you two be. Kate, we will catch up shortly."

Mrs. Alder swished away, the floor creaking in time with her steps. Maggie had already taken the main seat at the computer.

"What are we doing here and why did I need my camera?" Kate lowered herself onto the extra chair, resting her crutches against the desk.

"Odd that Mrs. Alder didn't ask you about the crutches. But, seeing as though your clumsiness is never ending, she probably didn't see anything unusual about it."

Kate grumbled. "Gee, thanks, Maggie. Now what is going on?"

"While you were out, I scrolled through your camera."

Kate raised an eyebrow and crossed her arms.

"You have several amazing captures and the friend I mentioned, runs a greeting card company out of Portland. He also has a gallery where he sells prints. Last time we spoke, he was on the hunt for a new photographer. So I gave him a ring while you were at your parents' place."

"Maggie, thank you, but I don't know if anything I have would be good enough."

"Hush, now you pick the ten you think are the best, and we will email them to him."

Kate wrapped her arm around Maggie in a sideways hug. "Now, it might be nothing, but maybe it's a start in a new direction for you."

"It means a lot, thank you, Maggie." Kate grinned as a sparkle of hope filled her eyes.

Chapter Thirty-Eight

"What's with all the noise out here?" Ox exited his bedroom door.

As he bent forward, his nose caught a whiff of garlic from the kitchen. "Are you burning my kitchen down?" Ox straightened his shoulders and raised his head before taking another step forward with his cane.

As he moved closer to the kitchen, the smell of rosemary and onions filled the air. The aroma made his stomach growl like a bear, and his mouth watered. Ox could not remember the last time he smelled something so fragrant. Bayou shuffled behind Ox, appearing still half-asleep from his nap.

"Kate?" Ox entered the edge of the kitchen.

Fixing her eyes on Ox, her heart nearly doubled in size with happiness to see him up and about.

"Please take a seat, dinner should be ready in about ten minutes." Kate used a wooden spoon to stir the simmering ingredients in the large navy Dutch oven.

"What are you making?" Ox balanced his weight on the cane. When he made it over to the kitchen table, he reached for the top, needing the added support.

Seeing Ox's weakness, Kate swiftly put the spoon down, pivoting toward him. Caught up in Ox's eyes, Kate completely forgot about her ankle and her crutches. Within two steps, Kate's eyes flashed wide as she reached for the nearby countertop. But it was too late, her arms shot forward as she attempted to break her fall.

Maggie caught the action from the corner of her eye. She reached down to Bayou's bed, spinning it in Kate's direction. As Kate's knees were a foot from hitting the floor, the dog bed slid directly under her. Kate landed with a softened blow as a spray of yellow fur danced into the air from below.

At once Ox and Maggie gasped as Kate rolled over, laughter erupting from her mouth. She clutched her chest as tears streamed across her cheeks from laughing so hard. Bayou trotted over to investigate why Kate was laying in his bed.

"Maggie just saved me." Kate petted Bayou's chest as he hovered over her sniffing her tears.

"Are you okay, Kate?" Ox supported himself with the table.

Kate sat up and Maggie offered her a hand. "Yes, barely, thank you."

"That's something we won't forget for a while." Maggie covered her mouth as she snickered.

With her crutches under her arms, Kate hobbled to the table. Balancing on them, she pulled out a chair for Ox.

Ox glanced at the chair and then at Kate. "Thank you."

Kate nodded as they gazed into each other's eyes. Ox never noticed Kate's eyes sparkled with hints of hazel and gold. They were not aware of how long their gaze lasted as they subconsciously matched their breaths. The clock chimed, breaking their trance. Ox lowered himself onto the chair and Kate hobbled back over to the stove.

"I appreciate the help, Kate, but you didn't have to cook. I could have." Ox entwined his fingers together, his mouth watering yet again from the aroma.

"Say thank you, Ox." Maggie set the table and poured the Merlot.

"Thank you, Ox." He smirked.

At the stove, Kate giggled and turned her head toward

Ox who winked. She quickly pivoted her head back in the direction of the stove to hide her blushing cheeks.

"Dinner is ready. Maggie, could I get a hand please?"

Spooning helpings into the bowls, Maggie then took them to the table. Next, Kate handed Maggie the basket of cranberry rolls. Then, Kate made her way to Bayou's dinner bowl and added two scoops of food.

"Thank you, Kate." Ox smiled.

She hobbled over, set her crutches against the table, and sat down. Maggie followed.

"Tonight, I have made a rosemary and white bean soup with homemade cranberry rolls and orange marmalade." Kate unfolded a napkin and placed it in her lap.

"It all looks amazing, Kate, and Maggie."

Maggie broke her roll open. "No credit for me, all I did was carry the shopping basket. This was one hundred percent Kate."

"Turns out even with a twisted ankle one can balance well enough to cook." Kate grinned. "I hope you both like it."

Ox tore open his roll and spread the marmalade across the warm inside. His eyes flickered with delight. "Kate, this is amazing."

Blushing she stared at her soup. "Thank you."

"No, thank you."

"The soup is perfect too." Maggie slurped up another bite.

"I'm glad you both like it. I'm not the best with recipes. I do well whipping things up that I feel might go well together." Kate took a sip of Merlot.

"Cooking makes you happy, I can see it." Maggie wiped her mouth with her napkin.

"How did it go at your parents' house?" Ox devoured the roll and reached for another.

"Well, I spoke with my dad on the phone, even if it's not his favorite thing. He helped me see things clearly. I did drive around a bit afterward. I drove past my old high school and the park where I used to pick wild flowers in the spring."

"Did you take any photos?" Ox blew on his soup.

"I did." Kate smiled.

"Kate, you must enter them in the photo contest in *Photography Life* you mentioned. I'm sure you have many to pick from," Ox encouraged.

"Actually, I sent a few off already to Maggie's friend in Portland." Kate took a bite of the roll.

Looking up from his soup, Ox's eyebrows arched in question.

"Maggie has a friend who owns a greeting card company and gallery. He was kind enough to allow me to submit a few to him for consideration."

"That is amazing, Kate!" Ox's mouth widened with a smile.

"I don't know anything yet. But ..."

Maggie's finger waved in the air. "No 'but,' Kate. He said he would get back to me in a week or so. I have a good feeling after seeing your shots larger on the computer monitor."

"It would be nice. However, I don't think it will be enough for me to make a living."

"I'm sure it would be enough to make half a living," Maggie remarked.

"So," Ox cleared his throat. "You're moving back here for sure? I mean as long as you are still allowing me to fly you home?"

"Yes, nothing has changed, I'm still moving back home. I checked with my dad today, and he sounded elated about my plan."

"Then why do you still look unsure?" Maggie asked.

"Because, job-wise, I still don't know what I will do once I'm back here. I don't want to live with my parents forever."

"Do you think you want to land another engineering job?" Ox sipped his Merlot.

"That's the problem. I don't. I want to create, and while there are opportunities to create within the engineering field, it's not exactly the creativity venue I want. My passion is expressing myself creatively through baking and photography." Leaning back in the chair, her body slouched.

"I'm sure it will all work out, Kate," Maggie chimed, a smile of hope spread across her face.

"It will. I believe it will." Kate wanted desperately to believe. She wanted to believe in herself.

Bayou finished his meal and lay at Kate's feet. She held the moment in her heart, the scents, the people, the sounds of the fireplace and gentle music stretching in from the living room. In that very moment an idea came to her, but she dare not let it slide from her lips.

Chapter Thirty-Nine

During dessert, the phone rang in the inn's hall office. Maggie jumped to her feet, the chair sliding out behind her legs. "I'll get it!"

Ox and Kate watched with surprise as they observed Maggie nearly jog to the office. They looked at each other and giggled. While they couldn't hear everything Maggie said, they tried. They sat in silence, leaning back against their chairs and tilting their ears in the direction of the office. *I'm being ridiculous! It cannot be her friend yet. He wouldn't be calling the inn phone anyway.* Kate returned to her soup and slurped several bites into her mouth.

"Did you see Mrs. Alder at the library?" Ox asked.

"Yes, she said she drops off your books and in exchange you cook for her and Mr. Alder."

"I enjoy our monthly get-togethers. We chat about the newest books, and I get to put in a request for some less popular titles."

"Do they know?" Kate winced, immediately regretting the question. "I'm sorry, Ox, it's none of my business."

"They don't know. Few do, and that's how I want it for now. I know there will be a time when I can't hide it anymore, but I don't want the town feeling sorry for me."

Kate nodded in agreement, as she would want it the same way.

"So, I had this idea—" Kate mumbled. She had the patience of Bayou waiting for a treat.

"Kate! Kate!" Maggie rushed into the kitchen.

With the commotion, Bayou leapt up from his spot at Kate's feet.

"He loved your photos! He had not planned to view them until later in the week, but after a quick glance, he said they 'captured him.' He didn't even need to take a second to think before calling about them. Ox, I hope you don't mind, I gave him the inn phone's number, just in case."

Ox waved her off and smiled.

"That's great!" Kate beamed. "So which one did he like?"

"All of them! And he wants you to send more! He wants to do a whole line of cards and a gallery showing just of your photos!"

Ox stood, grabbing his cane as Maggie pulled out Kate's chair and yanked her up into a hug. Ox made his way around the table and joined in the embrace. Bayou bounced on his front legs attempting to get himself high enough up to join in.

Once the excitement calmed, Maggie cleared the table and insisted Ox and Kate rest on the couch. In the kitchen, Bayou kept Maggie company, hoping to assist with cleaning the plates.

Ox reached his hand out and placed it overtop of Kate's hand. "I'm beyond happy for you, Kate."

The light from the lamps cast the room in a soft creamy glow as she turned to Ox. *Does he want to kiss me as much as I want him to?*

"Kate, I wanted to ask you something."

"Yes, Ox?"

"But you were going to tell me something at dinner. You said you had an idea. You go first."

"No, Ox, you go first."

They smiled, warm and slow. Ox reached for Kate's other hand, and his thumb ran over her smooth skin. He studied her hand, tracing the lines of her palm with this finger.

"First, I decided I will speak with my neurologist about trying the other medication."

Kate squeezed Ox's hand. "That's great!"

"And I want you to help me with the inn." Ox focused on their hands.

"You do? Ox, are you asking for my help?"

Ox's head barely gave a nod as he started to worry about Kate's response.

She wrapped her finger around Ox's thumb. "Because that's what I wanted to suggest to you—my idea. I'd be honored to help you with the inn. I want to be your blessing."

Ox's eyes fixed on Kate's. "You are my blessing. From the first second our eyes met, you were."

Ox leaned toward Kate's lips. "Great minds."

Kate leaned forward. "Great minds."

With one breath, their lips joined.

Maggie peeked around the corner into the living room, then turned to Bayou and knelt down. "You sensed this would work out all along, didn't you?" Bayou's head tilted and Maggie beamed.

Epilogue
One Year Later

Springtime in Louisiana at the Jungle Gardens of Avery Island left most without words. Kate was no exception. The purple wisteria and azaleas bloomed around the marshland as Bayou, with a black bowtie waited next to Ox in his tuxedo. Kate smiled, linking her arm with her dad's. They made their way to the edge of the small stone footbridge, overlooking an algae filled swamp. Birds chirped, filling the air with soft music. Palm trees and oak trees held draping moss that whispered in the breeze.

Kate's dress, a pure white chiffon, with a delicate strap top hugged her frame tightly, while the white tulle circled to her ankles. For an added splash of color, she wore blue suede peek-a-boo heels.

The last year had been an adventure for Kate. It took two days to fly back home in Ox's plane, but she made it. She packed up her house and gave notice at her job. After moving in with her parents, she landed a part-time engineering management position within weeks. Ox and Kate spent time adventuring, either by land or by short plane trip. She assisted Ox around the inn, cooking most of the breakfasts and dinners. Her photos at the gallery and her photo greeting cards were an instant hit, which soon allowed her to quit her part-time job.

A few family members had flown out to witness the wedding of Ox and Kate, including her parents, Josie and Gene. Of course, Ali had flown in from Shanghai and had assisted Kate with her hair and makeup. A few other friends made the journey, including Maggie and Richard, Ox's neighbor who unexpectedly lost his wife in the spring. Matt and Benjamina sent gifts.

Kate smiled warmly at Ox, taking him back to when they first met in an empty airport on a snowy January day. Bayou lightened the mood by using his back leg in an effort to scratch off the bowtie around his neck.

Ox continued to run Inn of the Woods, but switched his main focus to helping fearful fliers with Bayou's therapy assistance. In the last year, Bayou had helped over forty people face their fears. Not everyone was a success story, but most were, and that pleased Ox.

Kate held tightly to Ox's left hand, his right hand on his cane, as the pastor read from the Bible. Tomorrow, as long as Ox was having a good day, they would begin their honeymoon in Virginia. Every day had a loose plan, but that didn't bother Kate. She soaked up the happiness with Ox and Bayou, making each day count.

Ox wiped a tear from Kate's eye before he slid the ring on her finger. She followed suit with Ox's wedding band, only to have Bayou let out a bark, causing laughter to fill the park.

"I now pronounce you husband and wife," the pastor declared. "You may kiss the bride, unless Bayou wants to first." With that, Bayou barked again.

Ox pulled Kate in around her waist and kissed her until she was nearly in need of a breath. He and Kate turned and faced the guests, their arms locked as they strolled off the bridge and onto the mossy grass.

The use of the cane continued to come and go depending on the length of the relapse. Yet, his MS symptoms had not worsened thanks to the newest medication trial. Kate remained by his side, and Ox worked on leaning on her for care and support when needed. In return, on good days Ox showered Kate with everything from romantic picnics to sweeping her off her feet, literally. The new medication had provided some relief and thus Ox remained optimistic.

Maggie rushed after them, and handed Ox and Kate a tissue wrapped square with a large red ribbon on it.

"Open it now, don't wait," she instructed.

Without hesitation, Kate tore the gift open. Inside the paper was a rough oak picture frame. Kate gasped and brought the frame to her chest, before pulling it away and taking the photo in. She had never seen it before, and it warmed her heart instantly. Ox held the edge of the frame, angling it in the light so he could see what had touched Kate so much.

"Maggie, I never knew you took this," Ox stated.

Maggie smiled. "I saw it, the way you were together. It's why I ran and snatched up Kate's camera. I had to capture the moment. I knew you two would have a happily ever after."

"How did I not see this when we went through my camera at the library?" Kate questioned.

"Remember when I sent you to go catch up some more with Mrs. Alder?"

The side of Kate's lip rose. "Yes."

"I figured out how to send a picture to my email and then I deleted it from your camera before you returned. I'm not that senile."

They laughed. The framed photo held a picture which had been taken on the afternoon Ox and Kate were out back, making snow angels and having a snowball fight. Apparently, Maggie had taken the photo from the living room. The picture showed Kate and Ox laughing as they lay in their outlines of snow angels. Bayou in the middle sprawled out on the snow.

"I think I'm going to go find a spot to enjoy this view and some champagne." Maggie peered around searching for the perfect spot.

"How about over there?" Ox pointed at the picnic table

occupied by Richard and Ali.

"Is that your sweet neighbor who lost his wife?" Maggie whispered as though he could hear her.

"I'm sure he could use the company." Ox grinned.

"Oxnard." Maggie wagged her finger at him; a pondering smile reached the corners of her cheeks.

As Maggie made her way to chat with Richard, Ox kissed Kate on the head, and then bent down petting Bayou. The three of them taking in the beauty of Louisiana around them.

"Husband," Kate stated.

"Wife," Ox replied.

"I have a gift for you." Kate waved her parents over. Gene held a thin, but massive box. Ox glanced at Kate. "It's been beyond challenging to keep this from you for so long. But, I knew I had to wait for the right moment."

Ox took the thin box from his father-in-law and placed it on the nearby picnic table. He removed the wrapping paper to reveal a framed photo. "Is our wedding theme photos?" Ox laughed, pulling back the rest of the wrapping paper.

Beyond the wrapping was a photo of Bayou, sloppy sitting on the bench seat in the back of Ox's plane. Around him, a view of evergreen tree tops and streaks of blue sky.

"When I was going through the photos I saw this. It turned out great and I could not think of a better time than now to give it to you." Kate rubbed Ox's back.

His eyes filled with tears. "It's perfect." He shifted his body weight on his cane and wrapped Kate in a hug with all the strength he had.

"So are you." Kate kissed her husband.

"I think it's time to cut the pie." Gene interrupted their kiss.

Ox and Kate beamed as they made their way, together to

the table. On it, a green tomato pie, with a bride and groom rested in the middle.

The End

Kate and Ox's Official Green Tomato Pie Recipe

Preheat oven to 350°F

Pie crust (homemade or store bought)

5 decent medium size ripe (not overly ripe) green tomatoes sliced in wedges

1 tablespoon lemon juice

1 teaspoon ground cinnamon

$\frac{1}{2}$ teaspoon nutmeg

$\frac{1}{4}$ teaspoon cloves

$\frac{1}{2}$ teaspoon salt

1 cup white sugar

1/2 cup brown sugar

2/3 cup flour

Mix all the ingredients and add with a slotted spoon (to drain a good portion of the liquid out) to the homemade or store bought pie crust. Lattice the top or completely over with another pie crust and cut slits for air to release.

Bake for about 30-45 minutes, until bubbling, as ovens vary.

About the Author

Savannah Hendricks was born in California, raised in Washington, and now resides in Arizona. She is a medical social worker during the week and a devoted writer on the weekend. Savannah is still trying to decide which she loves more, tea or wine. You can find everything, and then some at her blog: TheSeaShellsofLife.wordpress.com

CPSIA information can be obtained
at www.ICGtesting.com
Printed in the USA
FFHW021921230419
51953716-57358FF